The Duchess Pursues Her Pleasure

THE SOCIETY OF WANTON WIDOWS
BOOK 1

BY KIRSTEN S. BLACKETER

© Copyright 2026 by Kirsten S. Blacketer
Text by Kirsten S. Blacketer
Cover by Kim Killion Designs

Dragonblade Publishing, Inc. is an imprint of Kathryn Le Veque Novels, Inc.
P.O. Box 23
Moreno Valley, CA 92556
ceo@dragonbladepublishing.com

Produced in the United States of America

First Edition March 2026
Trade Paperback Edition

Reproduction of any kind except where it pertains to short quotes in relation to advertising or promotion is strictly prohibited.

All Rights Reserved.

The characters and events portrayed in this book are fictitious. Any similarity to real persons, living or dead, is purely coincidental and not intended by the author.

AI Statement: No AI or ghostwriting was used in the creation of this story, or any story, published by Dragonblade Publishing. All text, structure, content, ideas, and concept are 100% human generated solely by the author whose name appears on the cover. It is prohibited to use this material, or any copyrighted material, for AI engine training.

ARE YOU SIGNED UP FOR DRAGONBLADE'S BLOG?

You'll get the latest news and information on exclusive giveaways, exclusive excerpts, coming releases, sales, free books, cover reveals and more.

Check out our complete list of authors, too!

No spam, no junk. That's a promise!

Sign Up Here
www.dragonbladepublishing.com

Dearest Reader;

Thank you for your support of a small press. At Dragonblade Publishing, we strive to bring you the highest quality Historical Romance from some of the best authors in the business. Without your support, there is no 'us', so we sincerely hope you adore these stories and find some new favorite authors along the way.

Happy Reading!

CEO, Dragonblade Publishing

Chapter One

London, October 1894

DEATH REEKED OF spilled port, tobacco, and a lifetime of regret. Unfortunately, the truth was far less poetic. Cassandra Sterling, the Duchess of Tolland, sat in her late husband's study drowning her misery in a third glass of port and staring into the flickering flames.

"To you, James." She saluted the vacant room with her nearly empty glass. "May you rot in hell."

Only three hours earlier, she'd attended a lavish dinner held in memory of her deceased husband. Everyone in attendance had sung his praises, yet she'd burned with seething hatred for the man they so elegantly touted as a visionary and a saint. He had been a brute, a cad, a worthless bastard who'd loved whores and money more than his own wife. Her arm throbbed where the bruises lay beneath her black widow's weeds. The fabric chafed her skin and the high neckline threatened to choke her. A long-dormant scream lodged in her throat, suffocating her. She tore open the fastening and gasped, filling her lungs with musty air.

Cassandra nearly threw her glass into the hearth at the memory of their final confrontation. But that would have been a waste of perfectly good liquor. Instead, she swallowed the remaining liquid and then tossed the empty vessel into the fire. A smile complemented the hum of satisfaction coursing through her at the sound of shattering glass against iron and stone. It was almost worth destroying every piece of glassware in the enormous house to purge the rampant fury racing through her veins. She eyed the decanter with malicious glee but decided against it.

The servants would know. But they already knew every horrid detail of her nearly three-decade marriage to an absolute tyrant. Their miserable union was no secret to them. Would they... *Could* they blame her for wanting to burn it all to the ground?

It would take little effort to destroy everything. She had dismissed the servants for the night, wanting nothing more than silence. James had been dead for less than three days, and she'd endured endless waves of heartfelt condolences and sympathy. It would have been enough to drive her to madness if James hadn't done so already *before* his death.

One spark, and she could burn it all to ashes. But could she bear to burn with it?

"Your Grace." A deep, cultured voice broke her morose thoughts. "Are you well? I thought I heard a crash."

With a start, Cassandra turned to find her late husband's valet standing in the doorway. "Evans, what in the devil are you doing here? I dismissed you all for the evening."

His presence sent a delicious shiver of awareness through her as he stepped into the room. With a tall stature and broad shoulders, he filled out the simple black suit perfectly. The sharp angles of his face blended both boyish charm and seductive grace while maintaining a professional demeanor. Her gaze skimmed the top of his dark head, finding not a hair out of place before traveling over the rest of his immaculate attire. A lord's regal bearing in the body of a servant. A damned temptation.

"You did, madam, but you should not be alone. Not tonight." Evans came alongside her, his hands clasped behind him.

"I thank you for your concern, but I am quite content on my own." She reached for the decanter and another glass.

His lips pressed into a thin line and concern echoed deep in his hazel eyes as she poured herself another glass of port.

"For heaven's sake, Evans. Out with it." She took another drink.

"You should not be drinking alone, madam." His lips tightened before he added, "It is not becoming for a woman of your stature."

Cassandra choked on the liquid but quickly recovered her composure. She glared at him.

"It is unbecoming for a servant to speak to his mistress in such a condescending tone." She set the glass aside.

A rush of dizziness threatened to topple her. She gripped the chair with one hand to catch herself. A pleasant warmth radiated through her where Evans's hands rested upon her waist, steadying her. His touch burned through the thin silk of her gown, igniting a need she had suppressed for years. She jerked out of his grasp, knowing if she lingered, she might make a fool of herself.

He stepped away, clasping his hands behind his back and awaiting instruction.

"I can do whatever I wish." She waved her hand. "I will not have a *servant* lecturing me." Cassandra sniffed, uncomfortably aware of his silent judgment. "If I wish to indulge in a nightcap, then so be it."

Evans glanced at the half-empty decanter of port.

It had been full when she'd entered the study several hours ago. Had she really drunk that much?

Her thoughts clouded, crowded by horrible memories enhanced by the port, and she frowned. Perhaps she *had* indulged in one too many. She swayed as she took a step toward the door, to put distance between her and reckless temptation.

Evans's watchful gaze followed her.

When her husband had hired Evans as his gentleman's gentleman five years ago, she'd had reservations. The young man of twenty-five had had no recommendations and no history. Her husband had *won* his services in a game of cards from another gentleman with little restraint and no common sense. Nevertheless, Evans had shown talent and forethought, his services had kept James content, and so he'd become a steadfast member of the household as a valet. A position she no longer had any use for as a dowager, even though she could find a hundred uses for the man outside of his expected duties.

She licked her lips, ignoring the hum of attraction pulling her toward him. Her hand tightened on the doorframe. "You are dismissed, Evans."

He inclined his head in recognition of her words as a clear dismissal but took no action to leave.

"I have no use for a valet any longer," Cassandra clarified, her voice tight. "If you need a recommendation, I shall be happy to provide one for your impeccable service."

Hurt flashed in his eyes before it vanished with a blink. "I beg your pardon."

"I have no need for a valet. Your services are no longer required." Cassandra stood her ground, confident it was the right decision. Having such a distraction in her home would only prove disastrous. She was close to breaking and desperation made fools of even the strongest women.

"I have other skills, madam." He inclined his head, regarding her carefully. "I can manage an estate. I can cook. Perhaps a gardener or a stablehand."

"I have no need for an estate manager or another cook." Her courage slipped. He truly was a man full of surprising talents and secrets. But his insistence that he remain in her employ left her baffled.

"Have I done something to displease you that you would banish me so quickly from the household?" His full lips parted, as if caught on a breath waiting for her response.

For five years, Cassandra had avoided the handsome valet. She was keenly aware of his presence and quickly established a routine in which to circumvent him. With her husband's death, he had no one to serve but her. The knowledge left her both desperate and overheated.

He was handsome, talented, and young. Evans was closer to her son's age than her own, a reminder that sobered her instantly. At six and forty, and now a widow, Cassandra had certain expectations placed upon her shoulders. A dalliance with her late husband's valet was most assuredly not permitted...or acceptable.

"You have not displeased me." She smoothed her hands over her dressing gown. "You served my husband faithfully, but I have decided to reduce the number of staff I employ and move to a smaller home. My son will take over his father's household, but he has a valet of his own. My allowance going forward will diminish substantially. It is simply a matter of economics."

"Then allow me to take on the position as butler."

His charming smile made her heart flutter. Oh, he was dangerous, this one. Charming and clever, he missed nothing. Was it possible he'd overheard her conversation with her son earlier and his plea for her to remain in the house until he found a bride?

None of that, she scolded the offending organ. "And what makes you think Orson will give up his post?"

"Orson is nearly eighty and has expressed his desire to retire to Wales and live out his remaining days there." Evans held her gaze steadily. "It would be merciful of you to grant him these remaining years to pursue his own passions. I am sure the duke would agree that I would fill the role admirably."

"I suppose you have a valid argument." Cassandra pointedly ignored his choice of words and the turmoil they created within her. She fought for any excuse not to keep Evans on staff, including her unhealthy and quite vivid daydreams about the younger man. Even if she remained in this house, as her son had suggested, she could not bear to see him every day. She could find no fault in his performance or any undue behavior on his end. "But why do you wish to remain with me? I could find you a more suitable post elsewhere."

"I do not wish to serve another house."

"You were loyal to my husband." Cassandra's heart twisted.

Not me, her mind added in secret.

"I am loyal to all in this family." His gaze bored into hers. "I was his servant as I am *yours*."

The words echoed like a drum in her head painting a vivid image in her mind. *I am yours*. The impropriety garnered by those simple words left her breathless and flummoxed.

"I have served you as faithfully as I did your husband."

Cassandra licked her lips, cursing the port and his persistence for making her head swim. "What do you mean?"

Evans stepped closer, and she braced her hand against the wall for support. The scent of cloves and clean cedar surrounded her as he drew near yet still maintained a reasonable gap between them. He shook his head and dropped his gaze. A heavy sigh filled the space between them, and for a moment, she thought he would reach out and touch her. Stroke his finger along her jaw, cradle her chin in his hand, force her to meet his gaze as he closed the distance and—

She pushed the thoughts away. How could she imagine such a thing so soon after her husband's death? Did she even *want* Evans to touch her or was it the years of loneliness and neglect that had left her desperate and trembling with need?

Cassandra held her breath, unable to bear his proximity without indulging in the fantasy that had plagued her since he'd walked over the threshold. Her husband had neglected her for years, abstaining from all forms of affection or kindness except to put on a show for society. He'd abandoned her bed after their son had been born, choosing the companionship of whores and mistresses over his own wife. Her body burned for a simple caress or a tender kiss. It was starved and fearful, and yet it *craved* that physical connection. Her husband had given her none of that.

She leaned toward Evans, even though she turned her face away, unable to meet his eyes. Shame choked her, stealing her confidence. Fear tore through her at the prospect of his rejection…or reprisal. Curse James for instilling such dread in her. Cassandra closed her eyes and inhaled deeply to ground herself.

The scent retreated. Her eyes flew open and a deep breath filled her lungs. The cloistering panic subsided even as disappointment flooded her when he took a step back.

"It no longer matters." His smile offered a small measure of comfort as he placed distance between them. "If you wish for me to leave you and this household, then I will obey without question." At her silence, he bowed, shattering the intimacy of the moment. "Forgive me, madam."

Evans skirted around her to exit the study.

Cassandra grasped his arm, pulling him to a halt. His lips parted as his gaze met hers. "Evans." Her voice cracked. "Promise me one thing."

"Anything you desire, madam." Heat flickered like a matchhead in his expression before shifting to one of cool composure.

"If you remain here, you will never mention my marriage in any capacity to me—to *anyone* ever again." Cassandra tightened her grip on his arm. "James is dead. While I cannot stop others from their words of sympathy and endless condolences on my loss, I can ask that you refrain from doing the same."

"Madam." He shifted his gaze from her hand resting on his arm to her face.

"My husband is dead, and my marriage is over." Cassandra's grip slowly loosened until her fingertips barely brushed his sleeve. "I have no desire to be reminded of it daily." Her voice wavered as a realization came over her like a gentle rain, washing the film from her mind and leaving her stunned.

As a supposedly grieving widow, she would find a whole new world of opportunity before her.

"As you wish, madam." Evans's response broke her from the reverie.

"This new post will come with vastly different expectations." Cassandra removed her hand from his arm. "Are you willing to take on the challenge?"

"For you, I would take on the Lord of Devil's Acre himself."

"Quite a bold statement," Cassandra quipped, amused at his

choice of metaphor involving one of the most infamous crime lords in London. "Would you have challenged my husband in my defense?"

"Without question." The vehemence of his statement stole her response. She blinked twice before he continued. "Is there anything else you require this evening, madam?"

Cassandra admired his ability to shift the ebb and flow of a conversation to divert tension or instill it. A truly masterful gift when wielded in a social setting. She filed that little tidbit away for later musings.

"No, that will be all, Evans." She smiled, a true smile, the first one in ages. "Thank you."

"Good evening, madam." He bowed and left her in the still silence of the study.

In a matter of moments, everything had changed. No longer was she under the yoke of a tyrant, but free to make her own decisions—to live her own life. With her son grown and now duke, Cassandra could explore her passions and desires—her dreams.

If only she knew what they were.

REUBEN EVANS COUNTED himself fortunate to still be alive.

Since the first moment he'd walked into the opulent house on 25 Grosvenor Street, he'd known beyond a shadow of a doubt that this house—this family—would be his demise. And he'd embraced it. This was his purpose, and he would not stray from it.

Yet he had not anticipated the captivating allure of the Duchess of Tolland. *Curse her.*

As he climbed the quiet staircase toward his chamber, Reuben analyzed the evening's events in his mind. The house had been a flurry of activity with the funeral and the constant parade of guests paying their respects. Not that the man deserved it.

In life, the duke had been an insufferable bastard, although no one would have known it. He'd hidden it well from his peers, but the servants knew. His *wife* had lived in fear, as she'd suffered the brunt of his madness.

Reuben's hand gripped the railing tighter. When he'd caught sight of them through the crack in the door, his heart had ceased beating. In all his years, he had seen men brutalize women, but never to the extent he had witnessed that night. There would still be bruises on her fair skin, of that, he was certain. She deserved better.

And now... she was free.

Well, as free as a wealthy, titled widow could be.

He inhaled deeply and continued the trek up the stairs. At the top of the landing, he turned down the narrow hallway and unlocked his room. There was no one in this house he could trust, and he guarded his personal chambers with a protective passion.

Nothing of value lay within it. No hidden coin or incriminating documents. Not one item of pilfered silver or jewels. One could ransack the entire room, ripping up floorboards and shredding the mattress, and they would find absolutely nothing to invite temptation.

Once inside his chambers, he closed the door, locked it, and leaned against the wood. The simple bed frame, wardrobe, and dresser with washbasin were a luxury compared to what he'd been forced to endure in the past. He took pride in maintaining a clean room and ensuring the linens were freshened often. But more importantly, this small chamber was his and his alone. It was the solitary place he could allow himself to breathe.

He pulled at the silk knot around his neck, tugging the fabric loose. Meticulously, he removed one garment at a time, hanging them on the small stand in the corner to wait for use the next day without fear of wrinkle or crease.

Reuben prided himself on his appearance. If there was one

thing Simon had taught him, it was to remain clean and tidy. No one would spare him a second glance if he looked as though he belonged.

Then the reality of his situation settled on top of his head, weighing him down like a cart of bricks. How in the devil's name was he supposed to remain in the dowager duchess's service?

Granted, his argument had been sound. Orson needed to retire before he met his end in the entryway answering callers. It had not been his intent to pursue the position of butler. After all, he had been trained as a valet. How hard could it possibly be to take on this new role? It wasn't as if he had not encountered obstacles in the past and had to renegotiate his path.

Truth was, Reuben could not leave this house. Not yet. Not until he uncovered the truth to a mystery that had plagued him for years. He knew her decision to leave had been a bluff as he had overheard the duke speaking to his mother earlier entreating her to remain in his home. The duke much preferred his bachelor lodgings to this over-stuffed mansion. The situation could not be more perfect. He had been placed here for a reason, and until that solution revealed itself, he would remain. But there was a problem. A lovely, complicated problem wearing widow's weeds and drinking port alone in the study.

He retrieved a small flask of gin from the back of his wardrobe and poured a dram in the glass on the table beside his bed. Reuben exchanged the bottle for the glass and lifted it to his lips. Instead of sipping it, he poured the liquor down his throat, letting it burn a path straight to his gut.

Fuck. He sat on the edge of the bed and hung his head. What the hell was he supposed to do?

Without the duke's presence casting a fearful shadow over the household, the demeanor of every servant, every guest would shift. He couldn't help but wonder if hers would as well, or if she would close herself off as she had in the past, isolating in fear of reprisal.

A small smile tugged at his mouth. Somehow, he didn't think

that would be the case. The lady was too vivacious, her spirit suppressed for too long under her husband's rigid rule and volatile temperament. She would blossom, of that, he was sure.

But could he trust himself to remain impassive, unbiased, and unaffected?

He poured himself another drink, this time savoring the burn as it settled in his stomach and warmed him from the inside out.

Reuben had pushed a boundary with her tonight. Testing the waters. Teasing her with his words and subtle inferences. Had she noticed?

A soft knock echoed through the chamber. He pulled on his shirt before answering the door.

Don, the young man who worked in the stables, stood outside his door, spinning his cap in his hand.

"Yes?"

"Sorry to bother you, sir, but your man is outside waiting. Do you have a message for him?" He glanced over his shoulder, likely uncertain of the validity of such a meeting.

"Ah, yes. One moment." Reuben crossed the room, pulled a small, folded paper from his coat pocket, and returned to the lad's side. "Give him this. Tell him I'll meet with Simon next week." He placed the missive in the lad's hand as well as a shilling. "Keep it between us, yes?"

"Always, sir."

"Good lad. Off you go." Reuben watched as the young man skittered down the hall and disappeared down the servants' staircase. He shook his head. Smart lad. Took initiative and direction, kept his mouth shut. If he didn't know any better, he'd have thought Simon had had a hand in his employment as well. But who knew how far his reach really extended.

After closing the door once more, Reuben locked it and placed his shirt back on the rack.

Part of him had hoped it was his mistress.

Saints, wouldn't that put him in a right state of conflict? Mixing business with pleasure. A nobody like him tangling with one of the most prominent women in society. It was like one of those comedies he had seen on the stage. A comedy of errors.

The dowager duchess would never come to him in search of something so scandalous. Hell, did she even *have* desires after living with such a beast for so long?

Reuben cursed the old fool. If he hadn't already been dead, Reuben would have killed him out of pure penance for what he'd done to his wife.

Lying on the bed, Reuben closed his eyes and pictured her. *Cassandra*. He could never call her that in the light of day, but he relished the sound of her name on his tongue in the quiet of his own chambers.

"Cassandra," he murmured. "You torment me, Your Grace."

His hand drifted over his chest and down his abdomen. He hissed in a breath, wishing it were her hand, not his, exploring the bare expanse of his skin. When he slid his hand beneath the waistband of his trousers, he groaned.

Images of her flashed through his mind. Her standing in the study, wearing her silken robe with unbound hair. The sparkle of amber liquid in her glass as she took a sip to fortify her courage.

"Come here, Evans." Her husky voice filled his head, and his body tightened in response.

"Your Grace," Evans murmured, dropping to his knees. His attention fixed on her lovely face as he gazed up at her. "Let me taste you."

His imagination jumped into action as his cock hardened beneath his touch. If only she were here, her hand on him instead of his own. Her panting breaths filling the quiet air instead of his. He opened his trousers and took his cock in his hand. With long, languid strokes, he sought his release, chasing it with the fervor of a man possessed.

Her dark eyes sparkled in the firelight when he imagined her reaction to his attentions. His fingers sliding beneath the fabric of her robe, his mouth leaving a trail of kisses along her thighs. Alternating with each press of his lips, not leaving any part of her exposed flesh without his adoration.

When he finally placed his mouth on her hot center, she cried out his name, threading her fingers through his hair. He explored her with his tongue, tasting her, devouring her. Every lap of his tongue brought a moan from her lips, a cry from the depths of her soul. He wanted all of it, craved it as a man starved.

Reuben stroked his cock faster, gripping harder as he moved, edging himself closer to release. His imagination overwhelmed him, driving him toward the pinnacle of pleasure and insanity. He wanted *her*, not this piss-poor substitution. She plagued him. Haunted him. Tormented him.

He would do anything for her. Lie. Cheat. Steal. Murder. She could command his very life, and he would surrender it to her willingly.

With a heavy groan, Reuben coated his hand with his seed, savoring the pulsing awareness of his body's reaction to the mere thought of Cassandra. Heaven help him if he ever acted on his desires. He just might perish.

Quickly wiping up the mess he had made, Reuben returned his countenance to a grounded place of reason. There would be nothing between him and the duchess. There could never be. No matter how much he wanted it. Even if she arrived at his door clad in only an enticing smile, he would reject her.

He had to. For both their sakes.

Reuben had a job to do. If his past ever came to light, if she ever knew the truth, then he would lose her forever. So, it was better that he never had her to begin with.

One day, they would part ways. He loathed the thought, but it was a sad reality of his existence. They were of two different classes. Nothing could change that. The expectations on both of them were vastly different. Even if it were possible, it would be a never-ending challenge.

She deserved better than a servant like him. An orphan taken in and trained in the company of criminals and thieves. His time in this house was slowly ticking away, and he needed to focus on his mission.

Her Grace was safe now. He had made sure of that.

But Reuben was still in dangerous waters, and if he weren't careful, he would drown. And there would be no one to save him.

Once he turned out the light, Reuben lay in the dark, staring at the paint peeling on the ceiling, illuminated by a faint sliver of moonlight drifting through the window.

"Keep your wits about you and focus." He inhaled a deep breath then let his eyes drift closed. "Once this is done, you're gone."

But the words didn't help. They flittered into the wind, unheeded.

Instead, visions of the illustrious widow filled his mind and danced in his head until sleep finally claimed him. Cassandra followed him into his dreams, the only place where he could indulge in his desires and not feel the wrath of reality breathing down his neck.

Chapter Two

London, 1896

THE FIRST NIGHT out of mourning, Cassandra did the unthinkable.

After donning her finest blue, silk gown and matching sapphire jewels, she ventured forth to the Lyceum Theatre to indulge in a performance of *Cymbeline*. Tucked inside the carriage on her way to the performance, she realized this would cause quite a scandal, even though she had followed the requisite two years of mourning her late husband in solitude.

It went against her inner nature to close herself off from society in such a way, after being such an active participant with her position as duchess. Alas, upon her husband's death, the title of duke had gone to her son, Phillip, and in order to ensure a quiet transition, she'd kept to herself, adhering to the standards laid by the queen. Although she remained in the house at the request of her son, who seemed determined to keep from finding a wife by traveling constantly and keeping his bachelor's lodgings. Who was she to argue, as this house reminded her of her strength.

No matter how much she loathed the idea of being isolated in a false state of bereavement, Cassandra had used her time wisely, studying many of the books in the library and biding her period of mourning with the grace and aplomb expected of a dowager duchess.

Cassandra tugged on the hem of her gloves, shifting restlessly in the carriage. It had been too long for many things. Self-denial was not something she enjoyed. She longed to go out to the markets and shops, attend the theater, and appear at social events. But her wait was finally at an end.

Just this morning, no fewer than three invitations arrived. Evans had brought them to her on a silver tray as she'd sat in the study where she spent most of her afternoons.

A flutter of restlessness shook her at the thought of the handsome butler. For years, he had been her husband's loyal valet, and upon the former duke's death, had transitioned into the position of the butler long held by Orson, who, bless his soul, had passed not long after his retirement.

Her face warmed at the memory of her confrontation with Evans two years ago. He had caught her in a dark place after her husband's funeral, half-drunk on port and desperation. She harbored no love for the deceased, and his absence had come as a relief. The bruises he'd left on her skin the night he'd died had remained for nearly a fortnight after she'd buried him.

Evans had provided a moment of reflection in that shadowed reprieve. His concern for her well-being had left her bolstered with a newfound confidence. Knowing that he would not abandon her in her hour of grief had given her a glimpse of hope. There was life after death. Now that her husband was gone, she could finally live. But dare she be as bold as to pursue her own desires?

The driver stopped the coach outside the theater. She waited for the footman to open the door and escort her down the step, careful not to trip on the hem of her gown.

Cassandra inhaled sharply at the sight of the crowd milling outside the theater. Perhaps it had been hasty to venture out on such a busy evening to such a well-attended affair. She squared her shoulders and lifted her chin.

Into the fire... She fueled her own courage with the words.

"Your Grace." The first woman dropped into a curtsy at her appearance.

Cassandra acknowledged her with a smile and a nod. "Miss Baxter, a pleasure to see you again."

The crowd, like the Red Sea, parted at her approach. Every eye fell upon her as she walked up the stairs toward the entrance. The conversations dimmed with every step as society took her measure.

Not that it mattered to her. She had endured their stares and gossip for years. The whispers of this evening would surely make the rounds for the next few days. For good or bad, the invitations would quickly arrive in droves. Cassandra felt a twinge of remorse in abandoning her quiet days in the study.

But those days had given her knowledge and confidence. Now, she would do as *she* wished, and not what was commanded of her.

Inside the lobby, a servant took her cloak, and she paused to survey the milling attendees around her. They watched her with sly glances, almost afraid to acknowledge her presence. Had she been that formidable and intimidating in the past?

Cassandra had anticipated the whispers and surprise, but not the small group of three women coming in her direction. The Widows of Mayfair.

Everyone knew of the Widows of Mayfair. Each had married a titled gentleman and settled into wedded bliss before losing their husbands. Cassandra envied them, if only for their ability to say that they had experienced love in their marriages. Although she could never say such a thing aloud, even in private confidence.

"Your Grace." Hyacinth Corby, the Dowager Viscountess Corby, and her companions curtsied while wearing matching smiles. "What a pleasure to see you here."

"Lady Corby." Cassandra inclined her head demurely to the other two ladies she recognized immediately as Victoria Smythe, the Dowager Marchioness of Winstead, and Eleanor Maldon, the

Dowager Countess of Amesbury. "Lady Winstead. Lady Amesbury." She greeted each in turn, taking a brief moment to assess the women. They all seemed to be of a similar age, although Cassandra had already been married by the time they'd entered society. It made sense why they congregated together.

"Such a delight," Lady Winstead interjected. "Seeing you back in society."

"It is rejuvenating to be among my peers once again." Cassandra chose her responses carefully. No one knew the truth of her marriage. No one but Evans and her servants, apparently. She pushed them from her thoughts. "I could not miss an opportunity to see *Cymbeline*."

"I have heard such wonderful things about this performance." Lady Amesbury flicked open her fan. Her pinkened cheeks reflected the rising temperature of the lobby despite the winter chill on the other side of the doors.

"Would you care to join us?" Lady Corby asked, her wide, blue eyes hopeful. "I have a private box, and there is room for one more."

Cassandra considered her own lonely box for a long moment before responding. "I would love to."

"Wonderful." Lady Corby clapped her hands together. "Shall we?"

Leading the way, Cassandra took careful note of the patrons she passed along the way. There were many familiar faces, most of whom she had not seen since her husband's death two years ago. It was her own fault, honestly. She chose to follow the queen's guidance and cloister herself away during the last two years, taking time only to visit her son's country estate in Coventry for the summers.

She had contemplated retreating to Scotland to take up residence in the hunting lodge her husband had kept in the Highlands. In such a remote location, there would be none to question her decisions regarding etiquette and fashion while in mourning. But at her son's request, she'd remained in London, leaving the house only when absolutely required to do so.

Cassandra nodded to the servant who drew aside the curtain for her to enter the box. Inside, she skirted to the far seat angled toward the left of the stage. From here, she could not only watch the performance, but the audience as well. Unfortunately, there was no way to block their view of her. Aware of their attention on her, she sat, forcing her gaze to study the program with the performance details.

"I have been anxiously awaiting this play." Lady Corby took the seat beside Cassandra. "I adore Shakespeare."

"As do I." Cassandra folded the program and glanced at her companion. "Lady Corby," she said, lowering her voice between them, "I do not wish to intrude on your evening, but I appreciate the opportunity to join your entourage. Thank you."

"The honor is mine." Lady Corby fanned herself. "I apologize for not calling on you. My children, bless them, have taken complete control of my time, it seems."

Cassandra's heart warmed at the statement. "I was not much in the spirit for visitors, but I do appreciate your kind words."

"The duke has taken to his position with ease." Lady Corby's comment pierced her heart for a moment before she realized the dowager viscountess meant her *son* and not her *husband*. Although she had been managing more of his responsibilities than he had been on the few occasions a month he came to the estate to give his blessing. At some point, he must start taking his duties more seriously.

"Yes, he has." Cassandra motioned for a drink from the servant standing near the curtained entryway. He delivered it promptly, saving her from having to expand upon her response.

"Such a handsome young man, and quite popular with the debutantes this year." Lady Corby chuckled. "The duke has his pick of the young misses for his bride."

"I dare say he does." Cassandra sipped her drink. "And how does your eldest fare? Has he found a bride yet?"

"Not yet." Lady Corby sighed with a wave of her hand. "Four

children, two married, leaving just the eldest and youngest."

"I am sure they will make splendid matches," Cassandra assured her.

"My dearest hope is that they find love above all else."

Cassandra regarded her silently, noting the way her eyes softened and she blinked rapidly, as though hiding tears. "Yours was a love match, was it not, Lady Corby?"

"Oh, yes." She dabbed her kerchief at the corners of her eyes and brightened. "We were quite madly in love. I miss him dearly even after all these years."

"I admire your steadfast devotion to your late husband. You were truly blessed in your union." Cassandra ignored the way her heart ached with jealousy. Lady Corby had at least tasted love—passion. Cassandra knew nothing of it. Her union with James had left her desolate and cold.

"Thank you, madam." She smiled again, radiant.

Although they had both been in society together and mingled at events, Cassandra had never taken the time to know any of her peers. She followed through with the motions, but there had never been any true connection or friendship. Mainly because she feared the truth of her marriage becoming gossip among the ton. Some of the women could be downright vicious. This small interaction allowed her a glimpse into Lady Corby's personality, and Cassandra realized she quite enjoyed her company. Perhaps there was hope for her to expand her social engagements, after all.

The lights flickered, signaling the play was about to begin. The four women settled into their positions, waiting with excited comments and murmured expectations.

During the play, Cassandra lost herself in the story on stage. She reveled in the performance, noting the way the actors captured the characters with such vibrancy and passion. When Cymbeline learned his daughter had secretly married his ward, a man of low birth, Cassandra sighed. Could love ever be uncomplicated?

Cassandra's thoughts drifted to another man. A man not of her station. A man she admired for his loyalty and thoughtfulness. A man whom she could never have. Even after her son married and his wife stepped into her role, being the dowager duchess still left Cassandra in a vulnerable position for scandal.

She shook Evans from her thoughts. Why was she even considering such a thing? Evans was her servant. Aside from that night following the funeral, he'd shown no indication of desire toward her. No flirtation. There was *nothing* between them, and there never would be.

After the play, Lady Corby drew Cassandra aside. "I would be honored if you would join us for tea tomorrow afternoon, madam." She gestured to the other two ladies. "Unless you already have plans."

Cassandra's heart warmed at the thoughtful gesture. "I would be delighted accept your gracious invitation."

"Wonderful." Lady Corby placed a card in her hand. "Here is the address. I look forward to seeing you there."

"You are very kind." Cassandra made her goodbyes and took her leave, slipping out the door before she encountered any other members of the ton.

The carriage waited patiently at the edge of the curb. She climbed into the seat and shivered before pulling a blanket across her lap. The nights were growing colder.

Her eyes drifted closed as the carriage lurched into motion. As much as she had enjoyed her evening out and the unexpected new acquaintances, Cassandra longed for the comfort of her chair by the fire, the novel she'd started the night before, and a glass of port.

Mrs. Mercer, the housekeeper, and Evans would surely be waiting for her when she arrived.

She decidedly ignored the way her heartbeat quickened at the thought of seeing the handsome butler. Perhaps she was coming down with something, for surely, it was not natural to have her heart race with no cause or exertion.

Turning her mind from Evans and his charming presence, she focused instead on the invitations awaiting her on the silver tray. In the morning, she would make a point to respond to each of them, and then join Lady Corby, Lady Amesbury, and Lady Winstead for tea.

Finally, the dark skies overhead were starting to look less ominous. Life after death, indeed.

WITH A SOFT curse, Reuben replaced the leatherbound tome on the shelf in the study. Where in the devil could it be? He leaned against the edge of the desk and stroked his jaw.

This was the only logical location. Since the former duke's death, Reuben had spent every moment of his leisure time searching the house from the attic to the wine cellar. Nothing out of the ordinary. Nothing incriminating. The only room he had left to search was *her* bedchamber, but why would the duke have hidden anything there? No, it had to be the study. This was the only room the duke had deliberately kept to himself. Even his wife had not been allowed admittance.

His frustrated groan filled the quiet space. Reuben could not think of her. Not now. Not when he was so close to uncovering the very thing he had spent years searching for. It was here. It had to be.

During the two years she'd lived in mourning, she'd spent the majority of her time in this room. Why this room specifically, he could not fathom, aside from the fact that he'd banished her from it while he'd been alive. This had been her late husband's private sanctuary when he hadn't been out whoring and gambling. He'd forbidden anyone from entering his study, even her. *Especially* her.

When Reuben had encountered her in the study the night of her husband's funeral, he'd been stunned by her presence. His intent that night had been far from pure. Even now, his desires muddled together, creating a wicked chaos in his mind, pulling him in opposite directions.

Reuben's gaze drifted over the floor-to-ceiling bookshelves laden with heavy books ranging from popular fiction to well-worn two-hundred-year-old bindings. When he spied the wingback chair beside the fireplace, he suppressed a grin at the memory of her seated there every day for months on end. She devoured every book with dedication, making notes and leaving small slips of paper between the pages to mark a particular passage. It was endearing, truly, but it also left him with little opportunity to search the room.

When she'd absconded to the country for the summer, he'd remained in London. It was unusual for the butler to travel with the family, yet part of him did not wish to leave her unattended. He'd taken the opportunity to search the study in her absence and found nothing unusual, and yet it had to be the only logical hiding place within the house.

The clock on the mantel chimed the hour. *Damn.* She would return soon and he was still no closer to finding where the bastard had hidden it. Reuben raked his fingers through his hair in frustration before smoothing the strands into place again.

With Her Grace back in society, Reuben would have more opportunities to search the study. All he required was patience and resolution. It grew increasingly difficult to harness the desire that came bubbling to the surface when he saw her. Especially this evening.

She had glided down the staircase wearing the most striking blue gown, diamonds and sapphires glittering from her ears and around her delicate neck. He'd longed to press his lips to the hollow of her throat where that brilliant jewel lay, to feel the pulse of her heartbeat beneath his lips, and hear the catch in her breath as he tasted her skin.

It had taken every fiber of restraint to keep from reaching for her. Instead, he had offered his assistance in placing the fur-edged cloak around her shoulders and stepped away. The teasing scent of lilac and citrus had mingled with the heat of her skin, enticing him, inviting him to partake. But he'd abstained, taking up his post by the door as she'd exited the house.

Reuben shook his head in a vain attempt to break free from the spell she wove around him. It was nonsensical, the way he responded to her. The way he protected her. He scoffed and turned back to the mantel. Carefully, he surveyed the wall, searching for seams and gaps. Something he may have missed. Something out of place.

The ticking of the clock echoed through the room, reminding him of her impending return. He glanced at it again. Ten minutes after eleven. *Damn*. She would arrive home any moment.

Reuben narrowed his gaze on the ornamental clock. Was that—surely not. He crossed the room and examined the oak clock with its intricate carvings and gilded face. The pendulum inside the wooden case ticked back and forth, counting the passing minutes.

He ran his fingers over the face and the sides in hope of finding some kind of hidden compartment. His fingernail snagged on a frayed edge. Reuben's breath caught. *Finally*.

"What are you doing, Evans?" Her achingly melodic voice echoed behind him.

He swore beneath his breath and quickly readjusted the clock before turning to face her.

"Your Grace." He bowed. "I was merely inspecting the clock. The time was incorrect and I feared it may be broken."

The duchess strode into the room, silk skirts shuffling around her like a jewel-colored cloud. "You were not at the door when I arrived home. I feared some horror had befallen you."

"Forgive me, madam. It will not happen again."

"Evans," she tutted as she crossed the room, stopping beside the leather wing back chair. "You have been a stalwart and loyal servant. I believe I can forgive you for this one lapse."

"You are too kind." He inclined his head in respect. "Is there anything I can get for you? Some port, perhaps?"

"That sounds delightful, Evans." She gracefully sat in the leather chair.

Grateful to have something to do with his hands, Reuben busied himself with pouring a glass of port from the crystal decanter once he'd summoned a chambermaid to build a fire. When he presented the glass to Cassandra, she took it with an ungloved hand, her fingertips brushing his.

He suppressed any reaction, but deep inside, his body ignited like tinder beneath the touch of a flame. Reuben cleared his throat and drew back.

"Is there any other way I can be of assistance?"

Her dark eyes sparkled in the dim gaslight. "Join me."

"I am unsure that is proper."

"It was not a request, Evans." She gestured to the chair opposite her. "Sit."

Reuben sat, his trousers bunching uncomfortably thanks to his body's uninvited reaction to her touch. His gaze remained fixed on the glass in her hand until she spoke.

"How old are you, Evans?" she asked, regarding him intently as she lifted her glass to her painted ruby lips.

"Two and thirty, madam."

"So young." Her smile betrayed nothing but sincerity. "So handsome and capable."

His face warmed at her compliment. How was he supposed to take her words? Was she merely stating an observation or was this a subtle flirtation? He straightened and returned her smile, unable to form a response.

"Why are you here, Evans?" Her smile faded and uncertainty laced her question.

Reuben's anger at the duke grew as he saw her fold in on herself, hiding the loneliness and pain her husband had placed there. She knew nothing of her own worth, of her potential. The duke ensured her spirit was shackled to his twisted demands, his unrelenting torment. Over her period of mourning, he'd seen her slowly blossom, testing the waters of her newfound freedom, but she still clung to the past, to what was familiar and safe. Dare he draw out the passion he knew lay beneath her uncertainty, even though he knew it would only end in disaster?

"May I speak freely, madam?"

A smile tugged at the corner of her mouth. "I would be disappointed if you were not completely honest with me, Evans."

"I remain for solely one reason." He held her gaze, ensuring he captured her reaction in its full glory. "You."

Her lips parted and a soft gasp filled the space between them. The crystal glass trembled in her hand, but she did not waver, remaining focused on him.

"A bold confession." She took a sip of port. "What makes you think I require your presence?"

Reuben inhaled deeply, taking in the scent of her and the earthy smoke of the fire in the hearth. "You do not require it, but you *enjoy* it."

"That is no reason to remain in my son's employment."

Reuben's hand closed around the crystal glass in her grip, his fingers lingering against hers, a gentle brush of skin against skin. The touch was innocent in a way, but as he drew it from her grasp, she took a sharp intake of breath and her lashes fluttered softly. He affected her in the same way she affected him. There was no denying it.

When he withdrew his hand, he stood, returning to the decanter and pouring another dram of the tawny liquid. She watched his every move, eyes darkening like a midnight forest. He lifted the cup in salute and downed the contents.

A solitary brow rose as she regarded him. Silence pulsed around them, thick like the morning fog. For a moment, Reuben thought he had crossed a line, pushed farther than was necessary, but she said nothing. No word of chastisement or warning.

Instead, the dowager duchess rose to her feet and met him directly before the crackling fire, like an altar in the background. He held his ground, unwilling to move for fear of breaking the tension burning between them. This was not the closest they had ever been, and yet his confession lingered in the air, thrumming like a beating heart and creating an intimacy that left his knees unsteady and his head spinning.

She intoxicated him with her presence. She had for years. This only added more fuel to the already-raging inferno.

"Perhaps we should renegotiate the terms of your employment, Evans." She traced her finger along his jaw, making it tense. He held his ground. "If you desire to remain in this home."

"I am sure we can come to some *arrangement*, madam." Need raged through his veins, and desperation nearly moved him to action. He wanted to kiss her, to lay claim to her mouth, her body, her very soul. She deserved passion. Devotion. Love. But could he really provide that?

Reuben blinked, dragging himself from the edge of the cliff, and stepped back. "If you will pardon me, madam, I must attend to my duties." He bowed. "Unless you have further use of my services."

"Not this evening, Evans." Her Grace turned to stare into the fire, breaking the trance between them. "You are dismissed."

"Very well, madam." The wall of propriety slid back into place and Reuben seized the opportunity to leave the room with his pride still intact.

The moment he stepped into the hall, he should have felt immediate relief. But the sensation that accosted him was nothing short of a brutal assault on his conscience. His stomach twisted and guilt pierced the well-armored shell around his heart.

The dowager duchess knew nothing of the power she wielded over him, and he feared it may very well lead him to ruin before he could uncover the truth and the proof he needed to bring peace to his shattered soul. *Curse it all.*

Chapter Three

CASSANDRA FOUND HERSELF in quite a conundrum thanks to Evans.

After their encounter in the study last evening, Cassandra had indulged in a second glass of port before retiring to her chamber where she lay in bed, staring at the canopy above while wondering what in the devil had just happened. Had she been dreaming? Delusional? Perhaps the excitement of her excursion to the theater had left her in some delirious state and she had imagined the whole encounter.

Unfortunately, that was *not* the case, as Evans's attentive gaze lingered on her a moment longer than propriety dictated when she passed him in the hallway on her way to the dining room. All through her morning meal, she relived the previous evening's exchange over and over, searching for something—*anything* to convince her *not* to follow him down this dangerous path.

Fortunately, she did not see him for the duration of the morning. By early afternoon, she realized the futility of wandering around the house hoping she would see him and called for her maid. As Sidlow styled her hair in an elaborate coiffure, Cassandra stared at herself in the oversized mirror.

What did he see in her? She was eight and forty with a full-grown son. Evans and Phillip could have been brothers, they were so close in age. She snorted indelicately, startling Sidlow. Heavens, she was nearly old enough to be Evans's mother.

Closing her eyes, Cassandra pushed the thought from her mind. It mattered not. If her son were of an age where he could seduce any woman he pleased, then Evans could do the same. As could she, for that matter.

Oh, she had heard the whispers from gossipmongers among the peerage who delighted in revealing the untoward behaviors of the upper class. The queen might not have appreciated such activities, but it was human nature to indulge in such carnal delights. And even Cassandra had heard the tales of the absolute depravity some in her social circle chose to partake in. Why, just before James had passed, Lady Jacoby had told Cassandra of the actress who'd revealed her pierced nipples on stage accidentally during a performance. It had been outrageously erotic.

Cassandra shifted uncomfortably in her seat, which earned her a stern look from Sidlow, who nearly poked her with a hairpin. How could she possibly function with all of this knowledge in her mind and no way to sort it out in a way that helped her understand it? Being married was one thing, but understanding the truth behind sexuality was something else entirely.

Her husband had shared her bed on occasion. Sometimes he'd forced her to it. But there had never been any pleasure in the act for her. Her mother had not prepared her for her wedding night or the expectations placed upon women by their husbands. When she'd discovered the hidden delights of erotic literature and heard the sordid tales from the wagging tongues of her peers, only then had she truly realized what she had been missing.

"You look lovely, Your Grace." Sidlow stepped back to admire her handiwork.

"Thank you, Sidlow." Cassandra cast aside her wayward thoughts and focused instead on selecting a gown to wear to meet the other widows for tea. "Would you fetch the green muslin gown with the plaid overcoat?"

"Right away, madam." Sidlow bustled to the wardrobe and retrieved the garments. With the expected efficiency, the maid had her dressed in less than fifteen minutes. Sidlow curtsied and disappeared from the room.

Cassandra took one last look at herself in the mirror. Small creases lay at the corners of her eyes, but her skin glowed with a radiance to rival a young woman of eight and ten. She allowed herself a small smile. If only she could tell the young lady she had once been that not all hope was lost, she would. Turning from her reflection, she ventured into the hallway and down the stairs, nearly colliding with a servant in the foyer.

Not just any servant.

Evans bowed. "My apologies, Your Grace. I thought you had already departed."

"I was just about to take my leave." Her gaze drifted over him, drinking in his distinguished form and hoping to spy a hint of the flirtatious man she'd encountered the night before.

The silent footman aided her with her wool cloak and muff before opening the door.

"Enjoy your excursion, madam. The weather is quite lovely, if not a bit brisk." He bowed again.

"Thank you, Evans." She ventured from the house, ignoring the pang of guilt as the door closed behind her.

Damn and blast. She heaved a frustrated sigh. Why was this so complicated? Surely, if she had someone with whom to discuss this whole conundrum, she could settle her conscience once and for all.

By the time she'd reached Lady Corby's home, Cassandra craved distraction from the mixed feelings and conflicting thoughts racing through her mind. She needed this. To be among her peers. To rejoin society. Being alone for so long had left her in quite a state. Perhaps her decision to go into self-isolation during her mourning period had left her at a disadvantage. She had been away from society for too long, but today's outing would change the course of her life. She knew it.

The housekeeper led her to the sitting room, where the three widows waited for her arrival. The ladies stood upon her introduction.

"Your Grace, welcome to my home." Lady Corby bustled forward, blue eyes sparkling, smile warm and sincere. "Thank you so much for coming."

"Lady Corby." Cassandra acknowledged her and then turned to the other two ladies. "Lady Amesbury. Lady Winstead. A pleasure to see you both again."

"Come, sit. We have just rung for tea." Lady Amesbury gestured to the small settee beside her.

After a few moments of pleasantries and compliments, Cassandra slowly fell into a comfortable rhythm. Perhaps she had not forgotten how to socialize, after all.

"Thank you again, Lady Corby, for the invitation." Cassandra placed her tea down. "It is refreshing to be in your company after such a long absence from society."

"Of course." Lady Corby glanced at the other two ladies. "We were surprised by your decision to spend two years in isolation while you mourned the loss of your husband. Our condolences."

It took all of Cassandra's effort not to choke on a brash response. No one knew the truth of her marriage. They had kept up a good façade for years. For the sake of her husband's position, but also for her son. No one had needed to know; therefore, she'd held her tongue. But the bitter memories burned in her mind and soured her stomach.

"Thank you," she demurred. "Tell me..." Cassandra shifted the topic away from her horrid marriage. "How does a widow of means spend her days in society? I fear I am at a loss on what to do with myself now."

"Well," Lady Winstead began at a nod from the other two widows. "I am glad you asked. You see, we"—she motioned to the rest of the ladies—"have formed a small charity school for girls who are less fortunate."

"A school for young ladies, how lovely." Cassandra brightened at the direction of the conversation.

"As the founders and patronesses of the institution, we take pride in overseeing the school and raising funds for its success," Lady Amesbury added.

"That is a noble cause." Cassandra nodded. "I am certain it takes a lot of time and resources to keep a school functioning."

"It does," Lady Corby said. "We were hoping you might be interested in joining our ranks as a patroness of the Mayberry Academy for Young Ladies."

Cassandra blinked in surprise at the sincerity in their request but recovered quickly. "I would be honored."

A collective sigh of relief filled the air around her.

"Wonderful," Lady Winstead replied.

"Fantastic," Lady Corby added.

"You will make the perfect addition to our little organization," Lady Amesbury said with a bright smile. "And here we were worried you might find it silly."

"'Silly'?" Cassandra asked. "Why in the world would I find such an invitation silly?"

Lady Amesbury's cheeks pinkened. "I—Well, we—"

"To be honest, we were unsure you would be interested in such an endeavor." Lady Corby twisted her hands in her lap.

"Why would you think that?" Cassandra regarded each of them in turn, reading the embarrassment in their expressions, and realized that they had been intimidated. Too intimidated to approach her before the theater last evening.

Lady Corby spoke carefully, "You have always been that to which we aspire. So graceful, elegant—"

"Aloof," Lady Winstead supplied.

With a sigh, Lady Corby continued. "*Reserved* is the word I would have chosen, Victoria."

"Yes, reserved." Lady Winstead blushed. "That is precisely what I meant."

A deep regret settled over her. Had she truly been so isolated during her marriage that she would ignore such opportunities? It pained her to know that such possibilities existed and she had been so distracted by her own personal marital problems that she had not sought refuge in friendship and community. No longer.

"What we are trying, and failing, to convey is that we did not wish to inconvenience you with our proposal since you have other, more pressing matters to occupy your mind."

"Being a dowager duchess can be quite taxing." Cassandra smiled. "But I assure you, I am fully invested in learning as much as possible about your school for young ladies."

"We are delighted you feel that way." Lady Corby relaxed and retrieved her tea.

"And what of your little trio?" Cassandra asked, excited by the prospect of expanding her horizons in all areas of her life, not just philanthropy. "Would you be willing to add another to your ranks?"

Lady Corby's eyes widened, as did Lady Winstead's and Lady Amesbury's. "We would be honored to have you join our little band of widows, if that is your desire, but I must confess, it is nothing more than afternoon teas and the occasional outing."

"Oh, and our reading discussions," Lady Amesbury added.

Lady Winstead choked on her tea, while Lady Corby gazed toward the heavens, as if asking God to grant her serenity.

"You have reading discussions?" Joy suffused Cassandra. She could *finally* talk to someone about the things she read. The ideas and questions that plagued her.

Lady Corby took a sip of her tea and set it aside. "We select a book to read and then discuss it the following week."

"How delightful. I have spent much of my time these past two years cloistered in the study reading every book that catches my fancy."

"We read mostly fiction." Lady Winstead reached between the cushions of the settee and retrieved a book. "But I must warn you, it may be—*scandalous.*"

Lady Corby hid behind her hand and shook her head. Her face turned a deep crimson as she watched in horror.

Cassandra took the book from Lady Winstead. *"Fanny Hill—Memoirs of a Woman of Pleasure?"* Clearing her throat, she opened the book and skimmed the passages randomly.

"Have you read it?" Lady Amesbury asked, her voice tentative.

"I have." Cassandra closed the book and placed it on the table. "Have you all finished it?"

All three women nodded eagerly, relief softening their features.

"What a delightful selection." She gestured to the book. "Well, then, shall we discuss it?"

The three widows covered their open mouths and exchanged a look before nodding in unison again. The tension and embarrassment had dissipated when Cassandra had shown her interest in their choice of literature.

As they launched into an animated discussion about the novel, Cassandra found herself invigorated by the lively debate and exchange of ideas. This was not what she had expected when she'd set off for tea this afternoon, and yet it was precisely what her soul craved. A connection with likeminded women. A companionship, camaraderie.

While this was a welcome surprise, Cassandra wondered what other delightful revelations would unfurl during the course of her newfound friendship with these ladies. Finally, she felt at home among her peers. Comfortable, not because of her rank and status, but that they welcomed her regardless of it.

For the first time in her life, Cassandra discovered a newfound purpose and the promise of exciting things to come.

Whoever thought a woman's purpose died with her husband was a liar—and this small band of tenacious widows proved to be the exception to the established belief.

THE ENCOUNTER WITH Her Grace in the foyer had been a disaster. She'd looked radiant in a deep-green muslin gown. The color brought out the vivid color of her eyes. It had taken Reuben several heartbeats to find the proper words and not just stand and stare like a lovestruck fool.

Reuben had blundered it masterfully. Truth be told, he'd thought she had already left for her afternoon outing when he'd come across her. After avoiding her for most of the morning, he'd decided to take the chance to survey her chamber once she'd left the house. Instead, he'd stumbled right into her path.

Once he'd sent the Sidlow and Mrs. Mercer out of the house for the afternoon and ensured the rest of the staff was occupied with their daily tasks, Reuben took the opportunity to finally broach the one chamber he had avoided. Her Grace's private sanctuary. It was the only room he had not searched, if solely for the fact that he believed Her Grace had nothing to hide, and he had not wanted to violate the sanctity of her chambers—purely out of respect. But his patience wore thin.

The moment he'd stepped over the threshold, her signature scent wrapped around him, threatening to choke him with the memories it elicited—with the fantasies it conjured to his overstimulated mind. He shoved all of it aside, determined to make his time in her chamber quick and efficient, lest her maid return from the errand with which he'd entrusted to her.

Within fifteen minutes, he had searched the room twice over. Nothing. No letters. No personal items to betray her. The only items with any sign of attention or wear were the books stacked on the table beside the bed.

He picked one from the stack and flipped through the pages. *Jane Eyre*. He quickly discarded it back to the top of the pile, careful to place it exactly as it had been. Perhaps he should read one of these books. Then he would have something in common with her.

Shaking his head, Reuben turned back to the empty chamber. He had a mission to accomplish, damn it. Where in the devil had the old bastard hidden it?

This was madness. Nearly five years in the old duke's service and two in the new duke's, and he was still no closer to finding what he needed. He ran his hand over his face. Could it be possible she *knew*? No. Even with all the torment the former duke had put her through, she couldn't have known the extent of her husband's depravity. It would have ruined her. But if Reuben told her—asked for her help—would it make any difference? Or would it only drive a wedge between them and earn him a one-way ticket to the poorhouse?

In the distance, the distinct sound of a door closing reached him. Had she returned so soon?

Quickly, Reuben abandoned her chamber, ensuring there was no trace of his presence. He closed the door behind him and hurried down the staircase.

The tall, athletic figure of Phillip Sterling, the young Duke of Tolland, stood in the entryway as David, the young footman, removed his overcoat. He turned at the sound of Reuben's heels clicking on the wooden floor.

"Ah, Evans, there you are." The duke extended his arm bearing the coat and his top hat to the lad standing beside him. "Is my mother in?"

"Your Grace, what a pleasant surprise." Reuben nodded, firmly in character. "I am afraid you have just missed her. She stepped out for the afternoon."

"Do you know when she will return?" the duke asked, watching him carefully.

"I am afraid I do not have that information, sir."

"Perhaps I shall wait for her." He crossed to the study and opened the door. "Bring me something to eat, would you, Evans?"

It was not a request. Reuben bowed and ventured to the kitchen to scrounge up something simple to serve the duke. Mrs. Johnson, the cook, made a small tray of sandwiches and tea cakes, arranging them on the tray for him. He took it with a stiff smile, regretting his decision to send Mrs. Mercer and Sidlow out on an errand. During his time as valet to the old duke, Reuben had found the man's son, Lord Sterling, to be a spoiled, self-centered child. No matter he never had to work a day in his privileged life. Lord Sterling had expected everything to be handed to him. People had fawned over him when he'd been the Marquess of Sterling, but now that he was the Duke of Tolland, they positively fell over themselves to even make his acquaintance. Reuben scoffed. *Entitled ninnyhammer.*

The duke, he knew, harbored no love for him, either. He often found the young duke scowling at him with no provocation. But the moment his mother entered the room, the mood shifted and he brightened. Their relationship was far stronger than most, and the duke often took her side, even if it went against the standard. Her Grace's request that Reuben remain as butler in the household had been the only thing that had saved him. He knew should the duke give up his bachelor lodgings and endless travel to return to this house, Reuben would either need to change his personal opinion or search for a new post. Reuben prayed the apple fell far away from the tree in regards to the late duke.

With a deep breath and a prayer for strength, Reuben returned to the study, bearing the tray laden with fruit, sandwiches, and freshly baked cakes.

"Your Grace." Reuben set the tray on the desk where the duke sat thumbing through the household ledger. "Will that be all?"

The young duke glanced up, his brow furrowing. "Mother asked me to increase your pay, Evans." He selected a sandwich. "Any idea why that might be?"

"None, sir." Reuben stood his ground, biting his tongue so hard, it bled. The sharp sting of pain took the edge off his frustration.

The duke leaned back in his chair and ate the small sandwich in one bite, leaving Reuben to stand patiently waiting for him to continue—or dismiss him. He prayed for the latter.

"Why are you still here, Evans?" the duke asked, eyes narrowed on him.

"I shall take my leave, sir." Reuben turned to go.

"Not *here*." The duke sighed, obviously irritated. "In this house."

Reuben inhaled deeply and resumed his position facing the duke. "Her Grace requested that I remain."

"And why is that?" He persisted, stepping around the desk, coming toe to toe with Reuben.

"I cannot say, sir." Reuben held his ground. "Perhaps you should discuss it with the dowager duchess."

"I have." His gaze bored into Reuben's. "And I have told her I could find someone more suitable."

Reuben held his caustic response, tasting the blood again from holding his tongue. He would not let this man force his hand or encourage him to violence. Even if he deserved a good thrashing.

"While this is technically *my* home now, I have given my mother the liberty to do with it as she will until the day I take a bride." He clicked his tongue in disapproval. "I have been preoccupied as of late, but will rectify this immediately and discuss her staffing choices upon her return."

"Very good, sir." Reuben remained impassive. "Is there any other way I may be of assistance?"

"No." The duke waved his hand and resumed his seat behind the desk. "You may go."

Reuben retreated, running a string of curses through his mind that would make a sailor blush with shame. When he reached the door, the duke spoke.

"Evans."

Reuben came to a stop and turned. "Sir."

"Please ensure I am not disturbed." He shuffled some papers into a neat pile. "I do not wish to be interrupted until my mother has returned."

"As you wish, sir." Reuben closed the door behind him and frowned at the solid wood. *Ninnyhammer, indeed.*

In the hall, he came face to face with Mrs. Mercer, returned from her errand, and relayed the duke's instructions. She smoothed her hands over her skirts and nodded before setting back to work.

Things had become complicated. More so than Reuben was equipped to handle. He needed guidance, and fortunately, the young duke had given him the perfect opportunity to seek out some well-needed advice.

After retrieving his overcoat, hat, and his wallet, Reuben conveyed his need to step out to Mrs. Mercer and ventured out into the November air. He hailed a hansom and gave the driver the address of his destination.

During the ride, he allowed himself to ponder his situation more thoroughly. How could he explain it without sounding like a lovesick fool? No matter. Simon would see right through him. He always did.

One thing was certain, he needed to ask Her Grace outright if she knew of her husband's duplicity, even if it put his position in danger. The truth was more important than his comfort. And besides, he had enough money set aside; he could use it to take a ship to America and start anew if the need arose.

Just the thought of abandoning England—and the dowager duchess—left his stomach churning and sour. He *wanted* to stay with her. He wanted far more than that, if he allowed himself to be honest. But it was impossible. Even if she felt some small measure of affection for him, a dowager duchess and a butler engaged in a love affair? The scandal would be too much to bear.

The hansom rolled to a stop in front of a familiar building just behind Westminster Cathedral. Soft threads of fading sunlight drifted through the buildings, casting the streets in ominous shadows. He paid the driver and pulled his coat tighter around him.

Tucked at the end of the alley lay a tall, brick building with the letter *B* set in the masonry. He knocked twice on the door, then another three times in quick succession.

The door opened, revealing a stoic butler with a thin mustache Reuben had known for years. "May I help you?" Finn asked.

"I need to speak with him." Reuben held his gaze firmly. "It is important."

"Very well." Finn stepped aside. "Wait in the drawing room." He gestured to the room to his right and disappeared down the hall.

Reuben paced the length of the room and back three times before the door opened. He spun and relief filled him. Simon stood taller than most men with long, raven hair pulled back into a queue and piercing eyes. His broad shoulders filled the doorway. The tailored suit he wore spoke of money, but this was no titled lord. He was an old friend.

Simon Oh, the Lord of Devil's Acre, was the most notorious crime lord in London and the leader of the Bloody Talons.

"Reuben." Simon gestured to the chair by the fire. "You must be desperate to come here."

"I am, sir." Reuben sat, his fingers thrumming on the arms of the chair.

"Would you like some whisky?" Simon asked, opening the decanter and pouring a glass.

"Yes, sir."

He poured a second glass and handed it to Reuben.

"To your health." Reuben saluted him and together, they drank.

"Now." Simon sat in the chair opposite him. "Why are you in my home, Reuben?" He arched a brow. "Have you found what you were searching for?"

"Not exactly."

Simon inclined his head. "When I gave you this opportunity all those years ago, Reuben, I did not think it would take you *seven* years."

"I know." Reuben hung his head.

"Why are you still there?" Simon asked, his words careful and measured. "Have you found something *more* valuable to you?"

Reuben's head snapped up at Simon's teasing remark. A smirk played on his typically stoic face. "What do you mean?"

Simon finished his whisky and set the glass aside. "Come now. Every one of my men would give their souls to work for the lovely Dowager Duchess of Tolland."

"Fuck." Reuben ran his fingers through his hair, tugging on the strands and savoring the pinch of pain. "Things have gotten... complicated."

Simon arched one dark brow. "You are her lover?"

"No." Reuben's blood heated at the thought.

"But you want to be." Simon snorted a laugh.

"What the hell am I going to do, sir?" He sighed. "I have searched the whole house, ripped it apart, and still nothing."

"Have you asked the dowager duchess?"

"Absolutely not. Even though I have thought about it, she would never believe me if I revealed the truth."

"Then perhaps seduction is your solution." Simon shrugged. "If she knows something, she will reveal it in her passion. Or—"

"Or what?"

"Or she knows nothing, and you can indulge in a torrid affair with the most coveted widow in London." Simon smirked. "Either way, you get something you want."

Reuben frowned. This was *not* the type of advice he'd been expecting when he'd come to the Lord of Devil's Acre. He sighed heavily, nodded, and stood. "I should go."

Simon rose to clap a hand on his shoulder. "My intention for placing you in that position was to acquire something we both desired. Closure, for yourself, and my assurance that the duke upheld his part of the agreement." His gaze narrowed. "Do you think the young duke knows of his father's debt...or his proclivities?"

"No, and nothing short of an act of God will convince him of the validity of such an accusation." Reuben frowned. "What do you hope to gain from this, Simon?"

A half-smile formed on Simon's lips. "I have my reasons for pursuing this outstanding debt. But for now, you should concern yourself only with *your duchess*."

Reuben sucked in a breath at the implication of those two words and nodded.

"Send word if you need anything further."

"I will. And thank you again." Reuben shook his hand. "Give my regards to Mrs. Oh."

This time, Simon smiled fully, glowing with pride and love for his wife. "I will."

When Reuben stepped back into the street, a newfound sense of purpose filled him. He could do this. Right?

Seduce Her Grace.

His blood heated at the promise of passion between them. He wanted it. Craved it more than anything in the world. But would it work? Or would he lose himself along with everything he had worked so hard for all these years?

Son of a bitch. Maybe he should sleep on it. After the tense encounter with the duke this afternoon, he could not trust himself completely. He needed to be in control of himself and his desires because God knew once she acquiesced—*if* she acquiesced—it would bring him to the edge of ruin.

And he would welcome it.

Chapter Four

WHEN CASSANDRA RETURNED from her afternoon outing, she hardly expected to be confronted by a ghost from her past.

Cassandra nearly fainted when she stepped through the doorway and glimpsed the shadow seated behind the ornate mahogany desk. For one heartbreaking moment, she thought it was James returned from beyond the grave to haunt her. The world around her began to crumble into darkness. She braced her hand against the doorframe and tightly closed her eyes.

It cannot be true. Her mind raced.

"Mother, are you well?" the shadowed figure asked, rising from his seat and rushing to her side. He rested his hand on her shoulder and eased her against him.

She stiffened at the movement, wrenching her eyes open and staring up into the face of her son, Phillip. His stature was so like James, it often left her with the striking similarities to her deceased husband, but as she studied his profile, she noted the gentle concern in his eyes, so like her own. The vise around her heart eased, and she gasped, inhaling deeply to fill her spasming lungs with air.

"Phillip." Cassandra forced a laugh. "You gave me a fright." She pressed her hand to her heart. "I was not expecting you, although this is your house, you may come and go as you please."

"My apologies, Mother." His grip softened, and she leaned into him as he led her to the chair beside the fire. "It was quite unexpected on my part. I have just returned from Paris and did not know you had gone out for the afternoon."

"You always stop by unexpectedly." She waved her hand. "I do wish you would give up your bachelor lodgings and take your place here. This house is far too big for me alone."

"Where did you venture off to today?" Phillip asked as he poured her a small dram of port and redirected the conversation. "Here, drink this. It will help your nerves."

Cassandra took the glass with a muttered thank you. As she sipped the rich liquor, she wondered if her son would think her too forward by joining a group of widows in their philanthropic endeavors. She dare not speak of their other discussions. Instead, she chose fragments of the truth.

"Lady Corby invited me over for tea." She twisted the glass in her hands. "Lady Winstead and Lady Amesbury were also in attendance."

Phillip's brow rose. "The Mayfair Widows."

She ignored the skeptical tone of his voice. "Yes, it seems they have asked me to join their ranks."

"As one of the infamous Widows of Mayfair?" He laughed and poured himself a glass of whisky.

"Do not believe everything you hear, my darling son." She narrowed her gaze on him as he sat across from her. "They are highly respected and cast a great deal of influence."

"Of that, I have no doubt." He lifted his glass in salute before taking a drink. "But I must ask, you have only just ceased mourning for father—"

Cassandra held her hand up and the words died half-formed. "I have done my duty to God and my queen. I mourned your father for two years, and I have decided it is best for me to rejoin society and allow my influence to help those in need."

"Mother, I did not mean any disrespect." He hung his head as a child shamed but quickly divested it and met her gaze. "It is my duty to ensure you are well cared for. That is all."

"I believe I know what is the best course for my own life, son."

Phillip downed the rest of the amber liquid in the crystal glass before speaking again. "Is that why you choose to retain the services of Evans?"

This time, Cassandra bristled instinctively, her smile disappearing in a nervous twitch. "Why are you asking this after two years? What does the butler have to do with this conversation?"

"Come now, Mother." Phillip scoffed. "What was wrong with Owens?"

"He was elderly and died shortly after retirement."

"And so you recommended father's valet to the position without a thought to how it may be perceived?"

"I highly doubt such a suggestion would have caused a scandal." She straightened and set aside her empty glass. "While this is your home, I was in need of a butler I could trust."

"And you trust Evans implicitly?" Phillip nearly choked on the question.

"As a servant in our employ for nearly seven years, he has given me no indication otherwise."

Phillip stood, crossing to the table and retrieving the ledger sitting open on the flat surface. He held it high and pointed to one of the entries. "Then explain to me why I pay him a king's ransom in wages per annum."

"You do no such thing." Cassandra stood and snatched the ledger from his hand, squinting down at the numbers. They were generous, to be sure, but nothing she—*her son* could not afford.

"Mother, this is more than what you paid Owens when he retired, and he was in our family's service for fifty years."

"Can we not afford it?" she asked, standing her ground.

"We can, but…" He tugged his hair in evident exasperation. "Mother, he is—"

"He is what?"

"He is young," Phillip relented with a groan. "We are but four years apart in age."

"Are you saying I cannot trust him to be responsible?" Cassandra listened to his argument and found it severely lacking. "You consider yourself to be responsible. He is not much older than you. Should your age define you with such finality?"

"No, Mother. I meant nothing of the sort." He inhaled deeply and exhaled in a long sigh as though trying to gather his thoughts. Cassandra waited patiently.

"Then will you not trust me in my decision to keep Evans as our butler?"

"Very well, Mother." Phillip set aside the ledger and collapsed in the chair behind the desk. "You may keep Evans on the books, but I reserve the right to interview the servants at my leisure."

"As the duke, you may do as you please." Cassandra smoothed her hands over her skirts, pleased with the direction of the conversation. Even though this was her son's home, she wanted to feel safe in it.

"If Father were here, he would have found a suitable butler to replace Owens."

"Evans *is* a suitable replacement. He far surpasses expectations." Cassandra frowned. "And your father is no longer the Duke of Tolland, *you* are."

"Yes, but I wish to do his memory proud by following in his footsteps."

Cassandra stiffened at his words. How could he say such a thing? James had been a horrible husband and a selfish lord. Everything he had ever done had been for his own personal gain and pleasure. The extensive gambling. The never-ending string of affairs with noblewomen and whores alike. She closed her eyes and took several deep breaths to steady herself.

Phillip knew nothing of his father's proclivities and vices. Cassandra had done her utmost to ensure he remained oblivious to his father's true nature. But now she understood that had been to her own detriment. He truly believed his father to be a paragon of virtue. Someone to whom he should aspire to be.

Her body trembled at the realization that she had inadvertently reinforced this picturesque, pristine version of her husband he had presented to the world. By keeping this secret, she risked ruining his sainted reputation and breaking her son's heart with its revelation. *Damn you, James.*

Tears pricked at the back of her eyelids, but she pushed them aside, swallowing the painful memories of abuse and torment.

Cassandra could not reveal the truth to her son. Doing so would shatter the memory he held of his father and possibly send him into denial. The last thing she wanted to do was drive her son away. She needed him. He was all she had left, and as the new Duke of Tolland, he was responsible for not only upholding the family name but supporting her as well.

With a delicate sniff, Cassandra held out her hands and he took them. "You are not your father, Phillip. You are your own man and must step into your own as the duke. I am proud of you."

"Thank you, Mother." He pulled her into a warm embrace, and she savored it.

Phillip was *not* his father, and if she had anything to say about it, she would *never* allow such evil to consume him.

"Now, tell me, have you called upon Miss Georgianna Sumner?" She led him back to the chairs by the fire. "You cannot dance with a young lady twice at the most coveted event of the year and not call upon her, only to disappear to Paris for a month."

"*Mother.*" Phillip sighed in evident exasperation, but he indulged her curiosity. The shift in conversation eased her conscience, and still, the uncertainty lingered.

Could she truly do as she wished now that she was no longer tethered to James? Within reason and at the behest of her son, of course, but if she truly wished for freedom, it would come at a financial cost. For years, she had feared his wrath and bent her will to his demands. She shoved aside any remaining thought of her dead husband and instead listened with delight to her son as he regaled her with tales of his time in Paris.

By the time Phillip left for the club, it was well after dark.

Cassandra rang for supper, hoping to see Evans, who had been conspicuously absent the entire afternoon. Concern tugged at her mind. Had he forgotten her?

The conversation with Phillip about Evans's presence in the household rose up in the back of her thoughts. Perhaps he had said something to Evans and caused some confusion.

She rang the bell again, and this time, the door to the study opened. But it was Mrs. Mercer, not Evans, who answered her call.

"Mrs. Mercer, where is Evans?" she asked, clasping her hands in front of her.

"He has not returned from his errand, Your Grace."

"'Errand'?"

"Yes, madam. He left shortly after the duke's arrival, saying he would be back this evening."

"Ah, I see. Would you please bring my supper? I will take it in the study."

"At once, madam." Mrs. Mercer curtsied and took her leave.

Cassandra occupied the seat behind the desk as a chambermaid set the fire in the hearth. She traced her fingers over the ledger columns indicating the household expenditures. *Reuben Evans*. His name stared up at her from the page as though it were highlighted in red ink.

When her supper arrived, Cassandra pushed it aside. She had no stomach for it. Her gut twisted and the scent of roasted meat only added to her discomfort. Whatever hunger she had vanished at Phillip's lingering concerns.

Foregoing the meal, she reached instead for the decanter of port.

Will he ever return? she wondered as she poured herself a strong measure of the liquid. Grabbing both the glass and the bottle, Cassandra retreated to the chair by the fire. It set perfectly aligned with the door. Should anyone disturb her solitude, she would know it.

Part of her knew she needed to speak with Evans directly about her son's observations. But even she did not fully understand why her son was so uncomfortable with Evans remaining in this house.

Why would she ruin a good thing by sharing Phillip's assertions with Evans? Why could they not go back to the way they had been before? A comfortable companionship. Mistress and servant, in harmony.

But Cassandra knew the truth, deep in the pit of her stomach. She wanted *more* than that, and she feared that was exactly the reason her son wanted to rid himself of Evans once and for all. He *knew* his mother wanted something elicit—forbidden.

Cassandra sipped her port and lost herself in the flames, praying for an answer. But only silence met her pleas.

Silence and a longing she dared not examine too closely, lest it steer her down a path of scandal and destruction.

LOST IN THOUGHT, Reuben wandered the streets of London as he made his way back to the duke's home in Mayfair. It afforded him some time to think upon the position in which he found himself. Torn between his own personal desires and his dedication to his mission.

Could he truly follow Simon's suggestion? Seducing the lovely widow would certainly not be a burden on him. He had harbored a deep affection for her for years, even while her husband had still been alive. But he had suppressed it. Out of duty or conscience, he could not discern.

Reuben stopped at the gate to the handsome mansion where he'd spent the last seven years in service. His gaze wandered the brick and stone, cast in shadow by the street lanterns. Several of the windows glowed with a warm light, welcoming with signs of life.

He spied the familiar glow of the gas lamps in the study along the side of the house and sighed. She had returned. Or so he hoped. If he entered the house and found the duke still seated behind his father's imposing desk, Reuben questioned whether he could refrain from making a spectacle of himself in front of the entire household.

Squaring his shoulders, Reuben took a deep breath. There was nothing for it. His course was set. With a muttered curse, he wove around the path to the rear of the house and the servants' entrance. Inside, he encountered animated chatter in the kitchen. Ignoring the others, he deposited his outer garments and bypassed the illuminated staircase, choosing the small, narrow entrance to the servants' stairs that led him directly to the first floor.

Reuben braced himself for whatever confrontation lay behind the study door. With one hand resting on the doorknob, he cleared his mind, intent on doing his duty and nothing more.

As he stepped over the threshold, he allowed his gaze to drift over the room, searching for an occupant. Fortunately, it seemed the duke had taken his leave. Reuben's shoulders relaxed, and he frowned at the realization he had been braced for another confrontation.

When he glanced at the fireplace, he paused, noting the familiar profile of Her Grace seated in one of the chairs. He'd known he would find her here. It had been her custom many evenings after her husband's death. Why she chose this room over all the others, he never quite understood.

"Your Gra—" The words died on his tongue as he stepped closer.

The dowager duchess was fast asleep tucked in the deep-seated wingback chair.

Reuben's heart twisted at the sight of her. So peaceful in her slumber. He admired the dark locks slowly unraveling from their mooring and the pronounced curve of her jaw. Her lips, full and kissable, parted as she moaned, burrowing deeper into herself as she tried to find a more comfortable position.

Reuben swore. A widow of her age should not have looked as tempting as she did. His mind returned to the conversation with Simon. Seduction had always been an option. But was it necessary? If he wished to survive the persistent desire pulsing through his body and making his cock harder than an oak at inconvenient moments, then yes, a time for seduction would come. But this was neither the time nor the place to be having such thoughts.

Loath to wake her, he could not allow her to remain here for the evening. Why had she not gone to bed? Had she been waiting for something—or someone? It mattered not.

With the utmost care, Reuben scooped her into his arms, allowing her weight to shift into him. Her sweet, teasing scent surrounded him, filling his mind with more sinful thoughts. The dowager duchess moaned, curling into him and burying her face against his neck.

Saints preserve me. This was wrong. He should wake her, have Sidlow escort her to her chamber, yet he did not have the heart to disturb her slumber.

With tender care, he carried the sleeping former duchess to her chamber, praying he would encounter no other servants as he did so. Every step proved pure torment. Her warmth against him. Her scent tempting him. She fit perfectly in his arms, as though she had been made for him alone.

Reuben cast aside the possessive thoughts as he entered her chamber. He gently laid her on the counterpane. She was still fully dressed, and he pondered if he should call the maid.

A gentle caress brushed his hand.

Startled, Reuben stiffened beneath the soft touch.

"You returned." The dowager duchess blinked up at him, her sleepy smile unsteady. "I waited for you." Her words wobbled.

Was she—intoxicated? Reuben sighed. It was not the first

time she'd indulged in too much liquor, but never before had she fallen asleep in the study. He removed his hand from beneath hers.

"Would you like me to fetch Sidlow, Your Grace?" Reuben asked, placing some formality between them once more.

The duchess slowly sat up, the loose tendrils of hair curling around her face. He longed to reach out and tuck it back. He wished for nothing more than to trace his fingertips along her pale skin, cradle her head in his hand, and claim her lips.

Reuben's hands clenched into fists at his sides. He dared not move, lest he give into the temptation.

"No, Evans." She shook her head before meeting his gaze. "I can manage."

He took two steps back as she climbed from the bed. The overly large room seemed quite small now with her in it.

With unsteady fingers, she began unfastening the buttons at the base of her throat.

Reuben went still, uncertain of the wisdom of remaining any longer. At the third button, he hastily retreated several steps.

"I shall leave you, then, madam." He turned, determined to exit with his dignity still intact. It would be wrong to take advantage of her in such a state. Seduction was fine, but only when both parties were willing and of sound mind. Her Grace was still under the spell of the liquor and could not make a rational decision in such a state.

"Do you not find me attractive, Evans?" Her question stopped him dead in the center of the room.

Heat filled him. If he responded, it would seal his demise. If he left, she would oust him at first light. Regardless, he *had* to face her.

"Madam, surely, you cannot expect me to answer such an inquiry." He held his ground, hands flexing by his sides.

A soft pressure fell on his arm. He closed his eyes for a brief moment before opening them to find her standing before him. Her dress unfastened to her waist, revealing the top of her corset and her chemise. What lay beneath peeked demurely over the top of the fabric. The soft curve of her breasts enticed him with the promise of what could be.

"You cannot hide it from me, Evans." She slid her hand over his chest. Her fingertips slid across the raspy stubble forming along his jaw. "I see the way you look at me."

"I—"

"Do not deny it." Her finger pressed lightly against his mouth to silence him.

Reuben's parted lips burned with her touch. He bit his tongue to keep not only from speaking, but tasting her. Teasing her. Provoking her to action. Instead, he remained as still as a statue, attention focused on the wall mirror.

Her hands returned to rest against his chest. Pressure rocked him as she took his lapels in her fists and pulled him closer. He relented, allowing her to draw him level with her.

Those lovely, dark eyes held his for a long moment before dipping to survey his mouth. Reuben held his breath knowing if she kissed him, he would lose all control.

"Your Grace," he whispered, a plea of submission. "Is this truly what you desire?"

The dowager duchess pressed her lips together as a flash of realization lit her eyes. She released him slowly, easing back several steps. "Evans—I—" Her face pinkened and she pulled her shirtwaist closed, effectively hiding herself from his view. She cleared her throat.

Reuben inhaled deeply, straightening his garments but maintaining his composure. "I shall leave you to your rest, madam."

With a shaky nod, the former duchess turned away, as if unable to bear the sight of him. Deflated, Reuben crossed to the door.

"Thank you, Evans." Her parting words stopped him briefly.

But when he glanced over his shoulder, he found her hand braced against the hearth with her back to him.

Reuben retreated from the room, nearly stumbling in his

haste. By the time he'd reached the bottom of the stairs, he kept going with only one destination in mind.

Inside the study, he closed the door, sliding the key into the lock and securing it. His heart pounded in his chest, his breath ragged and racing. Leaning against the door, he took several deep breaths. *Inhale. Exhale. In. Out.*

He had nearly lost control.

Had she kissed him—*fuck*. He would have surrendered to her completely. He leaned his head back against the door and swore aloud this time. Seduction. He scoffed. That had been Simon's suggestion. But who was seducing whom in this instance?

Reuben pushed away from the door, his steps taking him directly to the decanter and Her Grace's discarded glass. He poured himself twice the amount he should have and downed the port, letting it burn a path to his gut.

The warmth of the liquor infused him. Slowly, the uncertainty ebbed away. He stared into the fire, losing himself in thought. As much as he desired her, this was not *how* he wanted her.

Images of exactly how he wished to take her filled his lust-addled, port-enhanced fantasies. He would wrap his hand in her long, thick hair and trace her body with his mouth. He longed to commit every curve, every hollow to memory before devouring her sweet cunt until her cries filled the air, echoing off the walls. Then he would bend her over the bed and drive deep, sating the desires they both secretly harbored.

The clock on the mantel chimed the hour. He stared at the face of the gilded monstrosity and inclined his head. His brow furrowed. Was it truly eleven already?

Grumbling, Reuben reached into his pocket and pulled out his watch. It clicked open. His brows rose. According to his clock, it was only half past ten. One of them was wrong.

Quietly, Reuben unlocked the door and ventured toward the entryway where the grandfather clock stood in the hall. Half past ten. He clicked his pocket watch closed and returned to the study.

Once he'd closed and locked the door, he removed the clock

from the mantel and opened the back.

"Well, well, what have we here?" Excitement coursed through his veins as he removed a small key from inside the mechanism box.

Reuben moved closer to the light, inspecting the small key. On the depression he found an inscription. *Colver.* Wait, where had he seen that name before?

Pocketing the key, Reuben searched the entire room, including the books, for that name. High and low he searched, until he finally collapsed in the desk chair and hung his head. Perhaps he had been mistaken. He opened the desk to withdraw a piece of parchment and instead saw the brass plaque inside the drawer.

Colver and Sons. That was it! They were furniture makers.

He pulled open the drawers, feeling high and low for any hidden triggers or false bottoms. When he wrenched open the largest drawer, he saw it. The discrepancy. The drawer was shallower than it should have been. He took the letter opener and pried the bottom until it finally popped free.

He licked his lips, blood rushing in his ears as he opened the compartment. A lockbox by the same furniture makers. Quickly, he removed it, placing it on the desk. After wiping his damp palms on his trousers, he placed the key in the lock and turned it.

It clicked open.

Reuben held his breath as he lifted the lid. The stack of papers and folded letters lay in a neat bundle tied with a red string. He lifted it out and cut them free.

As he read, Reuben's grin grew wider. *Finally,* he thought. *Everything I need and more.* The papers within this lockbox would bring closure and justice to all the wrongs done to him—to those he loved.

He tucked the papers back in the box and eyed the empty drawer. Guilt pricked along his neck, sinking its teeth into his conscience.

Tell her. The still-small voice inside of him whispered. *She deserves to know the truth.*

Reuben swore and raked his fingers through his hair. He had everything he needed. There was no reason to involve her.

Only there was. She'd suffered at the hands of the same man who'd stolen everything from Evans. He'd uncovered the truth, the proof of her husband's sordid dealings. If he revealed it to the world, she would be embroiled in the scandal. What *was* he going to do with the information he now possessed?

Fuck.

Reuben had everything he needed, but he could not bring himself to bring ruin to the woman he had come to care for. A woman who deserved nothing but compassion for those wasted years married to that horrid bastard.

But should he show her?

The true question was: could he trust her?

Locking the box, he tucked it back into the drawer, but he did not hide it beneath the secret panel. With a sigh, he left the key in the lock and closed the drawer.

She would find it. All he had to do was wait.

Chapter Five

UPON RISING, CASSANDRA realized two things. First, that she should *not* indulge in more than two glasses of port in one sitting. And second, that she had made an absolute fool of herself.

With a groan, she tore herself from her bed, only to come face to face with Sidlow. Her willowy maid's smile and exuberance grated against Cassandra's already fragile temper.

"Your Grace." Sidlow dipped into a low curtsey.

Cassandra waved her hand. "It is far too early and my head feels as though it has been kicked by a runaway horse."

Sidlow's smile disappeared. "Of course, madam."

"Once I have dressed, I shall require a very large pot of strong tea." Cassandra rubbed her temples.

After the maid's quick acquiescence, blissful silence filled the room. The occasional rustle of fabric or a creaking groan from the floorboards punctuated their movements. Upon seeing Sidlow's stoic expression, Cassandra shifted uncomfortably as guilt needled at her conscience.

"I fear I am quite out of sorts today, Sidlow." Cassandra cleared her throat. "Forgive me."

A small smile returned to the young maid's face, but she remained silent and continued working. As she pinned the final strands of hair into place, Cassandra inspected her reflection.

The skin beneath her eyes showed the effects of the poor quality of sleep. She pinched her cheeks to bring some life back to her pale face.

"Would you like some powder and rouge?" Sidlow offered.

"No, this will suffice for the moment." Cassandra stood. "I will take my tea in the study, Sidlow."

"At once, madam."

"If you happen to see Evans in passing, please relay my request that he join me in the study."

"He stepped out on an errand this morning, madam." Sidlow paused at the door.

"Oh," Cassandra muttered, wondering if his mysterious disappearance this morning could be attributed to their encounter from the night before. She barely registered when the maid curtsied again and slipped from the room.

The details of her actions the previous evening remained enshrouded in a port-induced haze. Had she really thrown herself at him in such a wanton display of recklessness? She hung her head and groaned. It was no wonder Evans had decided to put some distance between them. Not that she could blame him. Her behavior had been terribly unladylike. She pressed her eyes together and tried to shake the only vivid image that remained from the night before.

Evans staring at her in utter horror as she'd begun disrobing.

That had been the moment that had solidified her embarrassment. Not only had she offered herself to him, but she'd bared more than her soul in doing so. How in the devil could she face him now?

Cassandra straightened and smoothed a hand over her bodice. This was not the first time she had found herself in a compromising situation in his presence. Evans had shown no judgment on those previous occasions, so it maintained that he would not upon this blunder.

After fetching her wrap, Cassandra found her way to the study, where a lovely tray of tea, warm scones, clotted cream, and preserves waited on the desk. She muttered a prayer of thanks for Mrs. Mercer, who possessed the patience of a saint.

Cassandra basked in the relative silence as she poured a cup of the warm brew. It reminded her to send an invitation to Lady Corby and the other widows to join her for tea the following day. She set her cup aside to cool and opened the bottom desk drawer to retrieve some paper.

But the paper was not there. In its place sat a box with a key nestled in the lock. Curious, she removed the box and placed it on the desk. This had not been there last week when she'd looked in that drawer. Beneath the desk lay a thin slab of wood. It slid perfectly into the drawer, resting on small indentations along the sides and hiding the space where the box sat. But who had removed it?

Had it been her son? If Phillip had unearthed this treasure, then surely, he would have told her upon their conversation yesterday evening.

With a trembling hand, Cassandra slowly unlocked the box. Inside, she found documents. Letters. Her heart seized. *Photographs*.

She laid the pile on the desk, setting the lockbox back in the drawer. As she leafed through the papers, bile rose in her throat. Legal documents. Properties obtained. The hunting lodge in Scotland appeared frequently in the paperwork. Financial tabulations. Gambling debts. She gasped, covering her mouth with her hand. Lewd photographs, and a compiled collection of James's sordid investments. Horrified, she skimmed the text, glimpsing only a passing implication of what this revealed.

Cassandra opened an envelope and tucked inside were newspaper clippings—of various crimes. No—of *murders*.

The stack of clippings slid from her hand, scattering across the ground.

A soft knock echoed somewhere in the background. "Your Grace."

Cassandra jumped at the sudden interruption. Her gaze

snapped up in time to see Evans closing the door behind him.

"Are you we—?" The words died on his lips as his attention shifted from her face to the horrid pile on the desk before her. Evans straightened, clasping his hands behind him.

"Are you well?" he asked softly, gauging her reaction.

"Wh-What is the meaning of this, Evans?" Her hands shook as she dropped them in her lap and stood.

Evans gazed toward the heavens for a brief moment before meeting her eyes again. Gone was the stoic, impassive expression, replaced with a calculating confidence.

"It seems you have finally uncovered the full complexity of your husband's depravity." Evans took a step closer.

"I do not understand." Cassandra maintained her ground, keeping the desk between them. "These papers—what are they?"

"Proof." Evans rounded the desk, but Cassandra shifted, stumbling backward to keep distance between them.

"Proof of what?" Tears pricked at her eyes. "That he gambled. That he lied. I already knew these things."

"He gambled. He lied. But more than that…" Evans crept closer, his measured steps bringing him within arm's reach. "He stole."

"Everyone steals in some manner when it benefits them." Cassandra collided with the back of the chair near the fireplace. "He was a rotten blackguard. How is this proof of anything?"

"It shows his intent. His ruthlessness." Evans took a deep breath, his pupils consuming the handsome color of his eyes. "It proves he is a *murderer*."

Cassandra scoffed and it bubbled into a wild laughter. This was madness. Utter lunacy. "You have no proof of that claim. These"—she gestured to the pile of clippings sitting on the desk, out of reach—"are a collection of papers. Letters and articles that prove *nothing* of the sort."

Evans stood, still as a statue, regarding her with absolute stoic calm.

"You expect me to believe that a man I was married to for

nearly thirty years could keep such horrid secrets from me?" Cassandra's voice wobbled. The truth was, she knew very little about her late husband other than some of his vices and proclivities. But murder—that was ridiculous.

"You knew even less about him than you know about me," Evans responded, his voice even.

"I know practically nothing about you." Cassandra gripped the chair harder. Her mind begged her to flee, but the temptation to remain won.

"Exactly." Evans's wicked smile blurred her self-preservation. "And yet you would throw yourself at a man you do not know to compensate for a man you knew even less."

"Do not pretend to know my inner thoughts," she hissed. "Your audacity has reached its limit. I insist you leave at once."

"That is not what you truly desire, is it, madam?" Evans asked.

"It is." She glared at him, regret filling her mind as it warred with lust. "I order you to leave this house. *Now.*"

Evans tutted. "And if I refuse?"

"I shall have you arrested."

His laughter filled the space between them, infuriating her further, and still the fire in the pit of her stomach blazed hotter. "I would like to see you attempt it."

"Are you threatening me?" Her teeth ground together.

"Hardly." Evans's eyes sparkled in the light filtering through the windows. "If you truly viewed me as a threat, you never would have tried to seduce me last evening."

"I—" She scowled as the words died in her throat and heat rose into her cheeks. He baited her with his teasing—his lies. "Do not turn this on me."

"Is that why you attempted to kiss me? To entrap me into some offense where you could have me carted off to prison? To claim I took advantage of you?"

"You bastard." Cassandra raised her hand to him, palm flat, aiming for the side of his face.

With the reflexes of an alley cat, Evans caught her wrist in his hand, enclosing it like a manacle binding her to him. He tugged, pulling her against him.

"Oof." She collided with the solid wall of his chest. As she fought against his hold, his arm banded around her waist, firmly keeping her in place. No matter how hard she struggled, Cassandra could not break free. His iron grip softened slightly the moment she stilled.

Although her mind raged against the intrusion, her heart pounded deep in her chest with both desire and fury.

Evans hooked a finger beneath her chin, forcing her to lift her gaze and meet his amused expression. His eyes darkened, and those sinful lips parted. She wanted to hate him, but after years of longing—of desperate need for some scrap of physical affection—she could not bring herself to hate him. No. Cassandra wanted him—wanted this.

Then his lips covered hers.

Surprise flared inside her chest and turned to molten flame as his lips parted over hers, his tongue darting over the seam, begging entrance. She surrendered, and her sigh mingled with his groan of pleasure.

Cassandra had never been kissed like this in her entire life, as though she were being explored and savored. She grasped his coat, desperate to hold on to something to keep her grounded.

Evans kissed her with the patience of a man who took pride in his mastery. He teased her lips, her tongue—even his breaths brought her pleasure and torment. She melted into his embrace, desperate for more. There had to be more.

When Evans drew back, breaking the kiss, Cassandra moaned her disappointment. He searched her face with a bemused expression, his eyes midnight and his lips tilted in a roguish smile.

"Who are you?" Cassandra asked, her voice shaking and her limbs weak.

"Does that truly matter?" He brushed his thumb along her jaw.

Trembling from the lingering fury and the rush of desire that left her breathless, Cassandra nodded. "It does."

"Only to you." He stepped away, releasing her. "I should go."

Cassandra swayed before bracing herself against the chair. She rushed forward, catching his arm as he strode toward the door.

"Evans, where are you going?"

He turned, his brow arched. "You asked me to leave."

"You dare kiss me like that then abandon me in such a state?"

Evans grinned. "What state would that be, madam?"

"Forget I said anything." She sniffed, releasing his arm. "Go."

"I am afraid I cannot." Evans reached behind him and locked the door.

Cassandra took a startled step back, maintaining some distance between them. "Wha-What are you doing?"

Her heart raced with a mixture of fear and excitement as he prowled closer. She thought she knew this man. Thought he cared for her. Heavens, she had practically *begged* him to seduce her. But having him here like this unleashed something inside her she had never even pondered.

"What I should have done years ago," he growled.

What have I done?

THE DOWAGER DUCHESS blinked at him with wide eyes. Where there should have been fear—disgust—lay only desire. He crept closer, slowly closing the gap between them, ensuring no escape for his quarry.

"Evans—I—You misunderstand."

Reuben inclined his head, taking note of her rapid breathing, the flushed pallor on her cheeks, the generous swell of her kiss-bruised lips. "I do not believe I misunderstood at all."

The dowager duchess's backside hit the desk, and Reuben seized the opportunity to cage her in, trapping her. His hands splayed on the desk surface, nails digging into the wood as the ache to touch her consumed him. He knew what she felt like in his arms. Knew the singular taste of her lips. Now that he possessed this knowledge, nothing save death could stop him from craving it with every fiber of his being. It was wrong, given their stations and his history, but God help him, he could not find the conscience to care.

"How could I possibly misunderstand when you taste like heaven and torment me as though I were bound in the depths of hell." Reuben inhaled deeply, savoring the sweet scent of lilac and citrus combined with the heat of her skin and the effervescent hint of her arousal. "I have dreamed of this since the moment I crossed that threshold, madam." His gaze bored into hers. "And now that I have indulged in the forbidden, I will surrender to the damnation, whatever the consequence."

Her gasp made him smile. *Good.* Surely, if he must live through this torment, then she must feel the same.

"Wh-Who are you?" the dowager duchess asked again, her voice breathless.

"I am no one of consequence, madam. No one of means or title." His lips teased along the curve of her jaw, and she trembled beneath the whisper-soft touch. "But I am a man entranced. A man devoted. Obsessed." The last word left his lips on a growl. "And I desire none as I do you."

"Eva—" His name died on her lips as a moan tore from her throat.

He traced the column of her throat with his mouth, committing every detail to memory. The softness of her skin. The heady aroma of her presence. The pliant curves of her body. Throwing all reservations aside, Reuben grasped her waist and lifted, placing her on the desk.

The dowager duchess sucked in a surprised breath and clung, both hands, to his arms to steady herself as she rocked on the desk surface. Shifting, she cupped his face in his hands, forcing him to meet her gaze. Eyes glassy, hazed with need, she searched his face and licked her lips.

"Allow me to give you the attention and care you deserve, madam."

With a shaky nod, she loosened her hold.

He slid his hand over her hip, down to her thigh, where he gathered handfuls of her skirt in his hand and tugged them up. Her breath hitched as the fabric slid along her legs. He allowed his gaze to wander to the exposed skin, clad in silk stockings. When his fingertips brushed the delicate, pale skin along the hem of her drawers, she swayed against him.

"Whatever you do, madam, do not let go." He held her gaze, desperate to see every flush of pleasure wash over her lovely face as he explored her.

Slowly, he trailed his fingers higher until they met the silken center of her. He nudged her legs apart with his hips, creating a delicious friction. She sighed, and he longed to capture those whimpers on his tongue. *Not yet*, he chided himself. *Patience.*

Reuben's cock throbbed. He had barely touched her and he nearly fucking came at the thought of being the first man to bring her pleasure. He knew the old duke had merely done his part and sired an heir. There had never been any passion between them. In Reuben's years of service, she had been faithful to the old bastard, even though he took every opportunity to shame and abuse her. The old man had been a damned fool for neglecting such a prized treasure. The duchess deserved pleasure, passion, and love. And if he could bring her two of those things, he would do it without hesitation.

The first brush of his fingers across her pussy made his cock twitch. Her sighing gasp echoed in the study. As much as he longed to hear her cry out with every touch, he could not risk the other servants hearing. Reuben kissed her—hard—devouring her moans and sighs as he gently stroked along her folds, slipping his fingers deeper with every deliberate stroke.

Reuben consumed every moan, letting it break upon his tongue as he explored her. His kiss deepened as he pressed two fingers inside her slick channel. She arched her hips, taking him deeper, allowing him to stroke a perfect rhythm against her most sensitive spots. When he pressed his thumb to the swollen nub at the apex of her thighs, she broke the kiss, crying out.

"That's it, darling." Reuben coaxed her, moving his fingers faster. "Take me. *Use* me."

Her Grace held tight, her lips parted, hips pliant. Strands of her hair pulled loose from the intricate knot her maid had created. Blush stained her cheeks and neck, marring her pale skin. She clung to him as her desperate pants played a melody to his ears. He basked in the knowledge that he so thoroughly unraveled her delicate composure. That he *made* her feel *something*.

"Evans," she pleaded. "Please."

"We are beyond propriety, madam," he murmured against her ear. "My given name is Reuben."

"I—know." She groaned as he thrust deeper with three fingers, clutching his clothes in ironclad fists. "Reuben, I beg of you—end this torment."

"As you wish, madam." He kissed her again, hard and punishing, as his palm ground against her mound, and his fingers sought to ease the tenuous need pulsing inside of her.

If this was to be his only chance, Reuben would never forego the opportunity to taste her fully, to hear her sweet mewling cries of desire. He pulled back and dropped to his knees, drawing her to the edge of the desk.

Her sex glistened in the ambient sunlight drifting through the windows. *Magnificent*, he thought as he grasped her hips, pinning her in place.

"Wha—" Her exclamation died on her lips as he licked her slickened cunt. "Reuben," she sighed, burying her fingers in his hair.

There had never been anything more decadent on his tongue, more satisfying than this moment. He had dreamed of it. Fantasized about it. And yet nothing came close to the actuality of him being on his knees, worshipping this woman in the way

God intended. She clutched at his scalp, holding his hair in fistfuls as he laved her sweet essence at his convenience, determined to show her the meaning of *pleasure*.

"Reuben, saints, please, I beg you."

Her panted pleas reached his ears and he reveled in the desperation hidden beneath her command. He quickened his pace, savoring every moment.

As he moved, she echoed the momentum, meeting him thrust for thrust, groan for groan. Until she reached the pinnacle of her pleasure. Her body tensed beneath his touch. His hands gripped tighter. His mouth closed around her aching bud, and he suckled, milking every simpering whimper from her lips. Every delightful twitch. He delighted in his successful seduction.

The dowager duchess now knew the meaning of the word *pleasure*.

With attentive care, Reuben teased her, allowing every moan and sigh to guide him. When he slid two fingers inside her, she swore. Pride suffused him at the knowledge that he unraveled her propriety with such a simple stroke. Gently, he fucked her, alternating the pressure between his mouth and digits. His other hand gripped her thigh, holding her open and bracing her against the desk.

Her body arched against him, back bowed as her soft cries filled the study. He hissed in a breath when her fingers tangled in his hair, tugging the strands into her fists.

"Reuben," she panted, her breaths quickening. She rocked her hips, encouraging his momentum, urging him on. It would take very little to push her over the edge into blissful abandon.

He suckled, drawing her sweet center into his mouth as he thrust deeper, harder, faster.

The dowager duchess shattered beneath his touch. A choked cry tore from her throat as she found her release. Her shaking hands held tight as the waves of pleasure consumed her. She clenched around his fingers, and for a flickering moment, he wished it was his cock buried inside her. He shook those thoughts away and focused instead on her.

Slowly, he withdrew his hand and rocked back on his heels. Gazing up at her, Reuben grinned at the disheveled duchess spread like a feast on the desk. Saints, how he wanted her. Wanted to take her fully, drive deep into her slickened cunt and claim her completely. She would be his.

"Well, then," she murmured, her voice shaky. "That was—illuminating."

Reuben rose to his feet, gently rearranging her skirts to hide the temptation to cross the line even further. "I am honored to be of service, madam."

Her brow furrowed. "What do you—"

A tentative knock startled them, and Her Grace's eyes widened as she realized the precarious situation in which she found herself. She slid from the desk, rearranging her skirts and patting the sides of her hair, cursing beneath her breath when she realized it had come loose.

"See to that, Evans." She turned away, pressing a hand to her chest.

Guilt stabbed at him. He cursed himself and whoever had knocked. The moment between them was gone, lost to the harsh presence of reality.

He opened the door to find Mrs. Mercer standing on the other side, wringing her hands. "What is it, Mrs. Mercer?"

"The dowager duchess has visitors in the parlor." She handed him their calling cards.

"Visitors, you say?" The dowager duchess appeared by his side, and he opened the door further, putting distance between them. She took the cards from his hand, her eyes widening.

"Mrs. Mercer, please send Sidlow to assist me in my chambers." Her Grace turned to Reuben. "Please attend my guests and inform them I will be present momentarily."

Reuben gave a curt nod and watched the dowager duchess lead the way to her chamber. Mrs. Mercer followed closely behind. The moment they were out of sight, he slumped against the door frame.

His cock ached, pressing insistently against his trousers. How could he attend to her guests in this state? Taking several deep, steadying breaths, he imagined the least-arousing things his mind could conjure. Once he was certain his arousal was under control, he attempted to clear his mind of the simmering conflict still unresolved between himself and the dowager duchess.

Fuck. How much more complicated could it possibly get? *Later. I shall resolve it later.*

After straightening his coat, he slipped into the wash closet to clean himself properly and don a new pair of gloves before proceeding to the parlor. No one would be the wiser.

Chapter Six

CASSANDRA MANAGED TO regain her wits, scraping together some semblance of composure. But inside, she burned with questions and confusion. As Sidlow silently worked resetting the pins in her hair, Cassandra stared at her reflection, noting the flushed glow of her skin and the spark of life in the depths of her eyes.

What in the devil had she done?

Reuben Evans was not who he appeared to be. His absurd claims about James had left her shaken and hollow, but she'd *known* her late husband had had secrets buried with him. Never in her wildest imagination had she thought they would rise from beyond the grave to haunt her still. But Evans had known exactly where and how to uncover these threads of her husband's past. What else did he know and how? More importantly, she longed to understand his motivation behind his obsession with her husband.

Was it his intention to bring ruin upon her family? Upon her son? The sins of the father would certainly be irrevocably harmful to her son if they came to light. The scandal alone would tarnish his legacy. Fear permeated her very soul.

Evans held the power to reveal her husband's sordid past. But would he?

Conflicted between fear and self-preservation, Cassandra had meant it when she'd told him to leave. But deep in her heart, she felt the stirring of indecision and torment. In all the years Evans had worked in their household, he'd never once indicated that he'd had any intention of causing harm or bringing ruin upon them. Quite the contrary.

Evans had always made her feel safe and protected. He cared for her in ways no one else seemed capable of doing. Her skin warmed at the memory of his touch. His kiss. The pleasure he'd wrought from her with no expectations—no regrets.

Or did he regret what they had done?

Cassandra bit her lip, letting the pressure of her teeth pinch the tender skin. How could she be sure without talking to him?

"Your guests await, Your Grace," Sidlow said, stepping away.

She had not even realized the maid had finished resetting her hair. If Sidlow knew what had transpired between herself and Evans, she gave no indication. With a bow, Sidlow left the room, giving Cassandra an opportunity to compose her thoughts.

There would be time enough this evening to speak with Evans about what she'd uncovered in the study. Not only about her late husband, but herself.

Standing, Cassandra smoothed her hands over her bodice and skirts. To the casual observer, nothing seemed amiss. But glimpsing herself in a new light, Cassandra felt the residual hum of pleasure and desire. Her stomach fluttered at the vivid memories lingering in her mind.

Evans ignited a flame inside her. A passion she'd never believed existed. The entirety of her marriage had been dedicated to conceding to her husband's will, to *his* pleasures. But Evans had taken something she'd long believed absent and brought it into the light. Cassandra burned with this new revelation and it left her unsteady.

How could she possibly face the other widows in such a conflicted state? It was not something she could share openly. But was she alone in this? How did the others cope with their unspoken desires? Or did they even recognize them?

With a soft curse, Cassandra snatched up her gloves and a fan. As she ventured toward the parlor, she focused on steadying her breath and schooling her features into a more dignified demeanor.

Evans had left her with more questions than answers and a sense of hyper awareness.

Pausing outside the parlor, Cassandra inhaled deeply and purged him from her mind. Inside the room, three curious faces turned in her direction. The ladies rose to their feet and curtsied.

"Lady Corby. Lady Winstead. Lady Amesbury." Cassandra inclined her head in greeting. "Please forgive my tardiness. The time completely escaped me." She gestured to sit. "Welcome."

"Thank you for the invitation, Your Grace." Lady Corby sat first, her hands demurely in her lap. "We were delighted when we received it." She offered Cassandra a small bouquet of flowers. "From my conservatory."

"How thoughtful." Cassandra smiled at the unfamiliar kindness. No one had ever recognized her for herself. It had always been for her station, her connections, her *husband*.

"Have we arrived too soon?" Lady Winstead asked. "You seem a bit preoccupied."

"Oh." Cassandra waved her hand. "Not at all. You are a welcome distraction."

"'Distraction'?" Lady Corby selected the word with care. "Has something happened?"

Cassandra silently regarded the three ladies in turn before sighing. She could not bear the burden alone. Surely, they might have some insight, some words of wisdom to impart to soothe her flustered state.

"I have recently uncovered some rather"—Cassandra cleared her throat and shifted slightly, twisting her hands together—"*disturbing* documents in my husband's private collection."

The three ladies exchanged glances, wrinkling their noses and shifting closer. Finally, Lady Corby spoke.

"And these documents, are they of a sensitive nature?" she asked softly.

"Quite." The burden of the knowledge sat heavily on Cassandra's heart. She dropped her gaze to her hands.

"And has anyone, aside from yourself, seen these documents?" Lady Corby continued.

"Not to my knowledge," Cassandra lied. She could not implicate Evans. Not when there was so much left unspoken between them.

"If these documents were to come to light, they would cause an issue for the Duke of Tolland?" Lady Winstead asked.

"My son can never know." Cassandra stiffened. "It would devastate him and bring ruin to our family."

All three nodded in solidarity. They understood the gravity of the situation, the implications that lay heavily in the revelation of such a secret.

"How did you uncover it?" Lady Amesbury asked.

"In a lockbox I hadn't seen before," Cassandra replied. "What am I to do?"

"Nothing." Lady Corby smiled kindly. "There is nothing you *can* do, madam. What is done is done, and no one can alter the past."

Cassandra blinked at her reply. She was right, and yet the weight of the knowledge still hung over her head, threatening to crush her.

"Burn the documents," Lady Amesbury added. "Start anew."

"But what if someone comes looking for them? What if someone *knows* the truth?" Cassandra studied each of them in turn and found nothing to indicate deception or manipulation.

"There is always a risk." Lady Corby sighed. "But you cannot worry about that over which you have no control."

Cassandra's heart sank. Before she could reply, the door opened, revealing Evans, who bore a tray laden with tea and madeleines. Her flailing heart lurched at the sight of his handsome face.

"Pardon the interruption, Your Grace." He placed the tea on the table before her. "Mrs. Mercer asked me to deliver the tea, as it proved a bit unsteady."

"How unconventional," Lady Corby noted. "Your housekeeper is blessed to have such a flexible butler."

"Thank you, Evans." Cassandra watched him straighten, noting the broad outline of his strong shoulders. Her gaze lingered on his mouth. His wicked mouth and the sinful way he'd used it to bring her to climax. She shook her head and turned away, her face warming. "That will be all."

Evans bowed and exited the room.

"Allow me to serve the tea," Lady Amesbury offered as she reached for the pot.

Cassandra smiled. "That would be lovely."

Slowly, the tension ebbed away. Evans's presence affected her more than she thought. Curse him for having this power over her.

"Such a handsome man," Lady Winstead commented.

Cassandra startled at the comment but quickly adapted. "Yes. He has been invaluable in his service."

"How lovely." Lady Amesbury presented the tea to her.

The conversation lapsed to more suitable topics, including the Mayberry Academy for Young Ladies, the upcoming holiday season, and their personal hobbies. Cassandra fell into a comfortable rhythm, adding in only where she felt able, but the other ladies did not seem to mind. They welcomed her insight.

By the end of their visit, Cassandra was more at ease with her new companions.

The small confession she'd made upon their arrival had been reckless, but it left her with a consolation that she was not alone. Perhaps this newfound company would heal those parts of her that would otherwise fester in the shadows of loneliness.

When her guests rose to take their leave, Lady Corby came alongside Cassandra. "Might I have a word, madam?"

"Of course." Cassandra motioned for her to follow her. They

stopped by the window overlooking Grosvenor Street.

"If I may be so bold," Lady Corby said, keeping her voice low, "I cannot help but notice a certain shift in the air when Evans entered the room." She rested her hand on Cassandra's arm. "Is there something amiss?"

"Whatever do you mean?" Cassandra asked in confusion. Was the tension between them so obvious? She pressed her hands to her cheeks to cool them. Surely, it was not *blatantly* obvious.

"As a widow, I have found it is best to keep those around me whom I trust implicitly," Lady Corby explained. "If Evans has done or said anything to make you uncomfortable, madam, then I suggest you inform your son and find a suitable replacement post haste."

Lady Corby's concern for Cassandra's well-being warmed her heart. "I thank you for your concern, but there is no need to worry on that count."

Lady Corby's furrowed brow transformed to a knowing smile. "I see. Well, then forget I even brought it up." She stepped back. "Thank you for a lovely tea."

"You are welcome to join me whenever you are in the vicinity." Cassandra walked her to the door, noting Evans's absence. The footmen aided the other two ladies in donning their coats in the hall.

"Likewise, madam." Lady Corby curtsied before joining the other ladies.

With parting smiles, the trio left Cassandra standing in the hallway as Mrs. Mercer held the door for them. She glanced behind her, eyeing the door to the study.

Burn the documents.

Infused with newfound fortitude, Cassandra strode into the room. She hesitated only for a moment when she saw the desk and the rush of desire returned with more force than she'd expected. She paused, leaning her hands against the wood, and took a steadying breath.

Burn it all.

Had she not left the documents here on the desk? Confusion clouded her mind. Perhaps she had placed them back in the drawer in her haste.

Cassandra rounded the desk and tore open the drawer where she had found the incriminating evidence. Her confusion turned to ire as her stomach twisted in knots.

They were gone. Everything. Vanished. The lockbox was empty.

REUBEN NOTED THE moment the clock on the mantel struck nine. The slow, simmering anticipation curdled in his gut as yet another hour passed with the continued absence of the dowager duchess.

After her guests had taken their leave, Her Grace had vacated the premises with a haste that left him curious and concerned. Their encounter in the study that morning burned in his mind. He could still feel her—taste her. The lingering sensations tormented him, as there were still many words left unspoken between them.

His rash decision to confiscate the documents left him with a twinge of guilt. But Simon would ensure their safety until they were needed. While Reuben had neither the time nor the presence of mind to sort through the documents himself, he placed them in a leather satchel and slipped from the house to deliver them to Simon personally.

It was during this time he found the dowager duchess had left, giving no indication to Mrs. Mercer as to her destination. He doubted Mrs. Mercer believed his excuse of feeling ill and needing some air. The whole household had noted his absence, but he refused to allow it to affect him. Those files needed to be delivered and he trusted no one to do it for him.

Reuben paced the floor before the fire, his stomach twisted in knots. Surely, she would return and confront him. Where had she gone? She had no invitations, no pressing engagements for the afternoon or the evening. He could only surmise her desire to leave had something to do with *his* actions. Either that or a lifetime of deceit had finally caught up with him and he could not even trust his own intuition any longer.

The clock chimed quarter past the hour, and still no sign of the dowager duchess. No one knew the details of her destination? Should he search for her?

The lady is none of your concern, his conscience reminded him. *Know your place.*

Irritation prickled inside his mind. His hands flexed, desperate to be put to use. He had busied himself with his duties and gone over the schedule with Mrs. Mercer, but Her Grace's continued absence left him agitated. She was not his responsibility, and yet he *longed* for some connection between them.

"Goddamn it," he swore, raking his fingers through his hair for the hundredth time.

"Such vulgarity has a time and a place, but this is neither."

Reuben spun to find the dowager duchess standing in the doorway, shrouded in darkness. He had been so distracted, he'd failed to hear her arrival. "My apologies, Your Grace."

"I believe we firmly crossed the bounds of propriety, Reuben." She stepped into the light and closed the door behind her. "When we are alone, you may call me by my given name."

With pride, he swallowed an inappropriate response, carefully treading the broken shards of trust lying betwixt them. "As you command, Cassandra."

The flicker of light from the gas lamps along the walls played over her features. Had her eyes just darkened or was it merely a play of the shadows? He clasped his hands before him.

"I believe we have some unfinished business," Cassandra said, rounding the small table where the decanter of port and empty glasses sat untouched. She traced her fingertips over the edge of the desk where he'd sampled her just that morning.

Reuben licked his lips and cleared his throat. "I am at your service."

"There are many questions left unanswered, Reuben." She glanced at him over her shoulder as she circled the room. "I believe you have been keeping secrets."

His unease grew as she prowled the study, her cadence measured, as if her confidence had been restored in her time alone. Reuben could not help but feel as though he were the prey and she were the hungry predator. He inhaled sharply as she came closer, stopping just within reach. Holding his ground, he waited, heart pounding in his chest.

"I dislike secrets, Reuben." She tutted. "In fact, I abhor them with a grand passion."

Reuben could only nod in understanding. Her scent teased him and arousal, unbidden, spiked through his blood. He ignored it, but desire permeated the thick tension building between them. He clenched his hands into fists to keep from reaching for her.

"Do you know why that is?" Her gaze flitted across his face, lingering on his lips briefly.

He shook his head, unwilling to trust his own voice not to break. Curse his body for betraying him.

"Oh, come now. You know precisely the reason." She reached out, tracing her fingertip along his jaw. His breath stuttered. "My late husband kept secrets from me. Many secrets, some revealed to me this very day. Did you leave those papers for me to find, Reuben?"

"I did," he managed the meager response, fighting against his desire and self-preservation.

"And once my guests arrived, did you remove them from the study?"

"Yes." He met the intensity of her scrutiny with his own determination.

"What purpose do they serve you?" The corner of her mouth hitched into a sardonic smile. "You never told me the truth, Reuben, about who you are."

"I am no one," he replied in truth, but it rang hollow.

"I doubt that highly." Cassandra slid her fingers around his necktie, holding him like a dog on a leash. He swallowed hard. "All this time, you have been keeping secrets. Now is your opportunity to confess...to cleanse your conscience."

"Would you have me tell you all my sins, Cassandra?" He turned the tables, unable to bear the tension a moment longer. "How I cannot purge the taste of you from my mind. How I long to hear you cry my name as I bring you pleasure."

Red lips parted in an O. Her grip on him faltered for a moment, only to tighten as she regained her composure. "And would you seduce me to procure what you need for your own ends?"

"I will not refute my obvious desires."

"We cannot continue on as we have been, Reuben." She drew her tongue across her lower lip. "I refuse to be a pawn any longer. If your intentions are disingenuous, tell me now and perhaps I shall show leniency and merely turn you out of this house instead of informing the authorities."

"What crime have I committed?"

"The documents are gone, Reuben." Cassandra's gaze bore into him, relentless. "You were the only other person who knew of their existence and location. You even confessed to taking them."

"If that is so, you should have me arrested." Reuben grinned, and the simple response made her eyes widen. "You may be a dowager duchess, but your lot are not the only ones with power."

"State your demands, then, and have done." Cassandra dropped her hands and stepped back, scowling. "What could you possibly want?"

"Vengeance."

"On whom? My late husband?" She laughed and gestured to the room around them. "I am the only one who remains."

"Your husband may be dead, but his debt remains."

"My son has inherited the dukedom and I made sure he

cleared any outstanding debts." She folded her arms across her chest.

"Not all of them," Reuben replied.

"How would you even know anything about this estate's finances, Evans? My husband never let anyone but his steward and solicitor see his books. He would certainly not impart such information to his valet."

He shook his head. "I know about *this* debt."

"Tell me: who holds this debt? I shall speak to them."

"There is nothing *you* can do to clear this debt."

Cassandra's visible frustration turned to indignant fury. "I shall be the judge of that. Now, tell me who holds it."

Reuben marked her strength and sighed. There would be no dissuading her. She was right; they could not go back to as they had been. The winds had shifted, threatening to blow him off course.

"The Lord of Devil's Acre."

Cassandra gasped, covering her mouth with her hand. She spun away, stalking the length of the room to pause beside the fire. After a moment, she turned back, eyes wide.

"You work for him."

Reuben's soft nod made her swear. He liked the rough sound of the indelicate words on her elegant tongue.

"James said he won your services in a game of cards"—she clenched her hand into a fist—"from the Earl of Winterbourne."

"A favor between lords." Reuben simplified the agreement. No need for her to know the full extent of the friendship between Edmund Reddington, the Earl of Winterbourne, and Simon Oh, the Lord of Devil's Acre and notorious criminal mastermind.

"He placed you here—to do what?" She glared at him, every word bringing her a step closer. "To engage in espionage and extortion?"

"To ensure the duke maintained his end of the bargain." Reuben braced himself for her ire as she pushed harder.

"What bargain?" she asked, her eyes blazing.

"That, I cannot say."

"You *cannot* because you do not know, or you *will* not reveal it?"

As much as he wished to reveal the truth, the bargain itself struck between the late duke and the Lord of Devil's Acre was not his revelation to make.

"I am merely a humble servant who has been entrusted with a task."

"I doubt that entirely." Cassandra scoffed. "Fine. Then I wish to meet with him."

"With whom?" Reuben asked in surprise.

"Your employer. The Lord of Devil's Acre."

All humor fled. This was an unexpected turn of events. If she met with Simon, he would reveal the truth of her husband's depravity and the debt it had incurred. There were none who could repay it fully. Not without revealing the truth to her son—who would never believe it. The late duke had shrouded himself in secrets, using them to his own advantage. His entitlement and cruelty had been well marked by the Bloody Talons, but they had been well-hidden from those in society. Even Cassandra, who'd endured his abuse and torment firsthand, could not stomach the veracity of the late duke's past atrocities.

"Do you believe that wise?" Reuben asked.

"You would have me defer to my son?" Cassandra arched her brow.

Frowning, Reuben bit his tongue. His Grace was as strong and proud as his father, but he seemed to lack the same cruel predisposition, even if he was rude and childish. He sighed and shook his head, knowing Cassandra's involvement would ensure the young duke's cooperation.

"You will arrange a meeting and escort me." Her smile returned, but it lacked any warmth. "I doubt the Lord of Devil's Acre will allow any harm to befall me. If he had wished me ill, it would not have taken this long for me to uncover my husband's secrets."

He could not fault her logic. "I shall make the necessary arrangements, madam."

Cassandra wrapped her hand around his tie and tugged him closer. His heart lurched and thundered with need. He held his breath.

"I much prefer my name on your lips, Reuben." Her eyes glittered with something he could not place. "The nature of our association has shifted with such *intimacies* shared—on this, we can agree."

He groaned at the implication of her words. "Yes, Yo—"

She tugged on the fabric, bringing his mouth dangerously close to hers.

"Cassandra."

"Good boy," she murmured. "Perhaps you can still be of use to me."

Blood pounded in his ears. He wanted to fight it, but years of longing softened him toward this woman. He would surrender to her completely if he knew something beneficial would come of it. But it was hopeless.

Nothing would come from their passion. Nothing but pain and heartbreak and sorrow.

"Will that be all?" he asked, holding fast to his resolve.

Gently, Cassandra released him, and he straightened, adjusting his tie and smoothing his hair.

"Yes, that will be all." She retreated behind the desk and sat down.

Reuben bowed before turning to leave the study. He needed to put distance between them. If he remained any longer, he would finish what they'd begun that morning. He would take her on the desk and show her the meaning of the word *pleasure*.

"Reuben." The sound of his name stopped him just as he reached for the doorknob. He turned.

"Yes, Cassandra?"

"I expect you to bring those documents to the meeting as well." She tapped her fingers on the desk. "If you have not already delivered them to your employer."

"Of course. They are already in his possession." Reuben noted the heat in her gaze, even as her lips pressed together tightly.

Never in his duration as a servant in this house had he seen such determination and grit in Her Grace. He took pride in knowing that he brought out this new side of her.

He took an even greater pride in knowing that the tension between them was not a figment of his imagination. She desired him just as much as he craved her. His fear, however, was founded.

A dowager duchess could take a lover. Whomever she desired. But it would never be anything more than a fleeting passion should she choose him.

Reuben needed to remind himself of this daily.

Chapter Seven

There had always been a banked fire of independent will deep within Cassandra. Who could have foreseen it would be stoked to life at the hands of a servant?

Although Reuben Evans was not merely a servant.

As she fixed her cloak, Cassandra stole a quiet glance at the man waiting by the door. Reuben's stiff posture and grim expression gave her no comfort that this was the correct course of action. She had been the one to demand to meet with the Lord of Devil's Acre. What madness had gripped her to agree to such an arrangement?

Reuben had refused to give her any details of the agreement between her late husband and the notorious crime lord. He denied any knowledge of the particulars, and yet Cassandra could read the subtle shift in Reuben's demeanor when she'd pressed him for details. He knew more than he admitted.

Which only solidified her determination to have the truth directly from the source.

After Cassandra had found the documents had mysteriously vanished at the same time as Reuben's absence, she'd decided not to confront Reuben on the details of his past. Instead, she'd taken it upon herself to forge a new path.

A quiet afternoon stroll through Kensington Gardens had

done wonders for her mental wellbeing. There'd been no prying eyes, no forced pleasantries, and a labyrinth of tree-lined avenues where she could wander without interruption. It gave her ample time to ponder her position and this frightening new revelation. Cassandra had known nearly nothing about James when they'd married, and even less as the years had passed during their union. But to uncover such secrets after his death had left her in a deep state of confusion—and dread. There were now more questions than answers, and Cassandra was determined to uncover them all.

After an hour in the gardens, she stopped at a small bakery to warm herself with some hot chocolate and then returned home, ready to confront Reuben. But what she had not expected was to find him waiting for her in the study where they had indulged in reckless carnal delight.

Reuben caught her gaze, and she warmed—mostly from the layers she wore in preparation to step out into the November chill.

"Our carriage awaits, Your Grace." Reuben stepped aside as the footman opened the door.

With a sniff, she exited the house with a resolute determination. No matter what transpired during this meeting, she would remain composed and keep her wits about her. Whispers of the Bloody Talons abounded through the dark streets of London finding their way to the papers and gossip rags. Their reputation was fearsome, and none would dare cross them.

Reuben dismissed the footman and stepped forward to hold the carriage door and help her into the conveyance. Even through two layers of fabric, her skin burned at his touch. When he closed the door, she frowned at his decision to ride outside the carriage.

His insistence to maintain a strained semblance of decorum nagged at the back of her mind. While it was wise for them to not be seen in public together in such an obvious manner, part of her wanted his presence—his companionship. Even though Reuben infuriated her with his secrets, he had given her no reason to doubt his loyalty.

A loyalty she would soon realize could be tested. Would he choose her or the Lord of Devil's Acre? She shook her head to clear the burning thoughts as the carriage wove through the streets heading toward Westminster.

Cassandra stared, unseeing, out the carriage window. Her mind raced with questions and possibilities. A nervous flutter began in the pit of her stomach, leaving her with doubts as to the wisdom of this confrontation. By the time the carriage had stopped, she swore.

There could be nothing for it. She would face this devil head-on and demand answers.

The door swung open, revealing Reuben's stony expression. The flutter of nerves disappeared, transitioning into a delightful kettle of warmth that radiated through her body. Even twisted in this mask of displeasure and indifference, the man was stunningly handsome. To the point of distraction.

"Into the lion's den?" he asked as she stepped down beside him.

Her grip on his hand tightened. A gentle squeeze in response eased her uncertainty.

"Lead the way, Evans." Cassandra released his hand, and disappointment flooded her.

Reuben took the lead, keeping two steps ahead. They stopped on the steps of an innocuous brick building tucked into the twisting streets of Devil's Acre. He knocked twice, paused, then knocked three more times.

Cassandra shivered, pulling her cloak tighter around her shoulders as they waited on the landing. What madness had brought her so low? She cursed James just as the door opened.

Inside, the hall seemed warm and comfortable, not unwelcoming, even with the dark woods and distinctive lack of artistic ornamentation.

"He is waiting in the parlor," the somber butler said with a bow, gesturing to the room on his right. "I shall bring tea."

"Thank you, Finn." Reuben nodded and the man ventured down the dark hall, leaving them alone. He glanced at Cassandra. "Are you certain you wish to do this?"

"There shall be no more secrets." Cassandra unclasped her cloak and handed it to the footman.

A smile broke through his stoic expression. "As you wish, madam." He watched the footman place their outer garments on a rack by the front door before joining her. "After you," he said, gesturing to the room where the Lord of Devil's Acre waited for their arrival.

A tall man stood before the fireplace. His long, raven-black hair was pulled back into a tidy queue at the nape of his neck. Broad shoulders fit in the finest tailored suit. He turned, his eyes piercing, fixing on her face with curiosity. With an incline of his head, he acknowledged her presence. The Lord of Devil's Acre cut an imposing figure full of mystery and intrigue. She could not help but wonder if the whispers of his ruthless and violent nature were to be believed.

"Sir." Reuben cleared his throat. "Her Grace, Cassandra Sterling, Dowager Duchess of Tolland."

"I know who she is." Their host bowed. "An honor to finally meet you in person, Your Grace."

"Likewise." Cassandra regarded him for a long moment before nodding. "I see no reason to stand on ceremony. What business did you have with my late husband?"

The *lord* seemed stunned by her abrupt question, but he recovered quickly. "I heard you were quick of wit and as sharp as a rapier. How delightful that the rumors were true."

"If I were to believe the rumors about the indomitable Lord of Devil's Acre, I would have expected the heads of your enemies to line the walls and your face to be smeared with blood." She forced a smile to hide her false bravado. "I am quite disappointed."

The Lord of Devil's Acre bowed in respect, and Cassandra found herself momentarily stunned by the mysterious man with the reprehensible reputation. By the saints, why was he so handsome?

"Come, sit." The lord indicated the settee beside the fire.

The butler appeared with tea and an assortment of cakes, placing them on the table before the dowager duchess. Once he'd taken his leave, Cassandra sat, eyeing both Reuben and his other employer.

Reuben remained standing beside her, his presence comforting in a strange way. Her host sat on the chair opposite. He poured tea for her, preparing it to her exact liking without even asking her preference. She sipped the brew, enjoying the rich beverage and allowing the warmth to fortify her courage.

"Now, then." The lord leaned back in his chair. "Pose your questions."

"What business dealings did you have with the previous Duke of Tolland?"

"Are you sure you wish to know the answer to that, madam?"

Cassandra squared her shoulders and set her tea aside. "Seeing as you found it necessary to place a spy in my home, where he resided for the past seven years, then yes, I believe I am entitled to know."

The lord regarded Reuben for a brief moment before nodding. "Very well. Your late husband incurred several debts that he could not pay. He came to me in desperation, requesting I consolidate them and extend the terms of the debt to give him more time to repay. I did, but I also took the necessary steps to ensure that my leniency was not abused."

"Reuben Evans." Cassandra remained firm, unable to look at the man beside her. But this response was too simple, too tidy. "I surmised as much." Her gaze narrowed on the crime lord. "But that does nothing to explain the documents and clippings I found in my husband's desk."

The lord shifted, straightening in the chair, his gaze fixed on her face, searching—assessing. "What conclusion did you draw from these items?"

"My husband was not a kind or gentle man. He—well, the details matter not, but it would not surprise me in the slightest if he had indiscretions that left him vulnerable to blackmail or worse."

The lord stroked his jaw, his expression indifferent. "You are perceptive."

"I tire of the secrets and lies, sir. Tell me the truth."

His brow arched. "Are you certain you are strong enough to bear the burden of it?"

"I am." Cassandra nodded firmly.

"Your late husband brokered some unsavory alliances in his life. He pursued his pleasures where he could find them, and in some instances, the results were—deadly."

Cassandra stifled a gasp. It should not have surprised her, but hearing the words aloud from someone other than Reuben solidified their truth in her mind. She folded her trembling hands in her lap.

"In these instances, it became apparent his title and status guaranteed him immunity from the consequences of his actions. And yet there were those who sought to exploit their knowledge of his misdeeds. He ensured these *inconveniences* were removed."

Closing her eyes, Cassandra took several deep, soothing breaths. When she'd regained her composure, she met his gaze once more, steadfast and unwavering. "And what was your role in this? Did he hire you to remove his inconveniences?"

"He proposed an agreement for such an arrangement, but I declined. I answer to no one," the lord replied. "Our transaction was purely financial. However, his debts continued to grow, as did his destructive tendencies."

"And Evans's role in this?" Cassandra asked.

"Ensure the duke accrued no further debts and report any suspicious activity."

"You mean blackmail?" Cassandra glanced at Reuben, who remained silent and steadfast in his post.

"I view it as more of a protective measure to ensure any

further loss of life," Simon clarified.

"That does nothing to explain why Evans remained *after* my husband's death. Am I expected to repay his debts?"

"You? Of course not." The lord leaned forward. "But your son, the new Duke of Tolland, well, that's an entirely different conversation."

She nearly choked. "You expect my *son* to bear the burden of his father's indiscretions?"

"A debt is a debt and it must be repaid."

"But—" Cassandra shifted as unease crept along her spine and tendrils of fear curled their clawed fingers around her heart. "My son knows *nothing* of his father's true nature—of his—*indiscretions* as you so delicately refer to them."

"He is a man fully grown. Perhaps it is time he also learned the truth."

"I—You cannot expect him to understand. He is—" *A child*, she wanted to say, but she held her tongue, cursing herself as silly to even have thought it. "He will never believe you."

"Shall I summon him? Reveal the truth myself and spare you the pain?"

"He will despise me regardless."

"Why would he despise his own mother for trying to protect him by keeping the truth hidden?" the lord asked. "You do him no favors by withholding these things. As you yourself said, the time for secrets has passed."

Cassandra hung her head, trying to suppress the tears stinging her eyes and burning her throat. She had not expected such an onslaught of emotion. How could she bear the thought of her husband's past, but the idea of revealing his true nature to their son seemed an inconceivable assault on her very soul?

"In order to fulfill the debt, I require the fealty of the new Duke of Tolland." The lord regarded her with an indulgent smile. "If you can persuade him to listen to reason and reveal the extent of your husband's true nature, then I will have mercy on him and forgive the financial debt."

"And if I fail to convince him?" Fear clung to her throat, making it difficult to form the words. How could she be expected to convince her son of anything? He was as stubborn as his father, but thank heavens he had not inherited his cruelty.

"Failure is not an option, madam."

"And what of your *spy*?" Cassandra asked, noting the harsh way the words left her tongue and ignoring the guilt pricking along her conscience.

"Evans will remain in your son's service until he sees fit to relieve him of his post." He inclined his head thoughtfully. "I leave *his* presence at you and your son's discretion."

Reuben stiffened beside her, but she could not bear to look at him. Not now. The wounds were too fresh, too raw, and her clouded mind refused to be logical while her heart demanded the opposite. She would confront him *after* they left.

"The documents will remain in my possession for safekeeping until he agrees to meet with me, where I will relinquish them. You have until the first of January." The lord stood, inclining his head. "Do we have an agreement?"

Cassandra rose and nodded firmly. "The first of January."

"Excellent." He bowed.

A coalescing wave of mixed emotions washed over her. What madness was this? Striking a bargain with the Lord of Devil's Acre. She swayed as her confidence waned.

When she turned her back on both the lord and Reuben, Cassandra breathed deeply, attempting to gather back some of the courage she had when she'd entered the room earlier. But it had vanished—replaced with a sinking sense of dread.

She'd made a deal with the devil, but she was not afraid of losing her soul. She feared for her son's soul. Hers was already lost—as was her heart.

Madness, indeed. A dowager duchess caught between expectation and desire, tangled in a web of secrets and lies. And the only ally she possessed had led her into the belly of the beast.

CONFUSION AND FRUSTRATION twisted inside of Reuben as he followed Cassandra out of the house. The moment they'd stepped into the street, a gust of cold wind brushed against his skin, forcing him to bury his face behind the wool of his coat.

Simon knew him. Trusted him. But in those few moments with the dowager duchess, Simon had betrayed him. Not completely, but enough to reveal the true intent of those surrounding him.

The carriage rolled forward, stopping just as they reached the street. Reuben opened the door for his mistress, biting back the words burning like bile in the back of his throat.

As she stepped into the carriage, she turned abruptly. Her gaze narrowed. "Join me."

Reuben nodded, if only to get out of the biting November wind. He gave the driver direction as well as another coin in payment for his discretion. Should anyone see him in the carriage with her—well, there would be a bounty of rumors for the ton.

Once she'd settled in the cushioned seat, he climbed into the carriage, sitting opposite and giving her a wide berth. He tapped the roof before settling back against the cushion and crossing his arms.

Cassandra regarded him with a wary expression for several long moments as the carriage rattled down the street. A long pause stretched between them, and silence lingered like an omen revealing more to the complexities of unfolding events.

Five years he'd served the previous Duke of Tolland. Two years after the duke's death, Reuben had remained in the service of his son. All of that time, Reuben had believed to be in pursuit of the truth. The horrible reality of his true mission had haunted him for years, and in a few short moments, Simon had placed his future in the hands of the woman who both desired and despised him.

He admired her spirit, but she knew nothing of his past—of his passion for vengeance.

"You are upset with me."

He knew it was a statement, not a question, so he responded with a nod.

"Why?" she asked with a delicate tilt of her head. Her keen gaze fixed on him. "If either of us has a right to be upset, I maintain my position. But..." She pursed her lips in thought. "I believe there is something missing. Some piece of information that is crucial to understanding this entire farce, and yet you refuse to reveal it to me."

"Astute as ever, madam."

"Sarcasm is quite unnecessary, Reuben." Cassandra sighed. "I am trying to understand the intricacies of this whole charade. But how do you expect me to help you when you refuse to trust me?"

"What would you have me say?" he asked, his tone biting. At her startled look, he swore. "My apologies." After a deep breath, he continued, "I hardly see how my role promotes your current situation, madam."

"I shall find a way to deal with my son and the bargain I made with the devil." She sniffed, turning to gaze out the carriage window.

Guilt sank its teeth into Reuben's conscience. It had not been his intention to hurt her, but the thought of allowing her into his confidence seemed more intimate than those few stolen moments when he'd tasted her cunt laid upon her husband's desk and made her cry out in pleasure.

"Fuck." He groaned.

Cassandra's gaze fixed on him again, her mouth pursed into a delicate circle of surprise.

"My apologies, madam."

"None required, Reuben." A soft smile curved her sensual lips. "And please, call me 'Cassandra' when it is just the two of us."

"So, you will advocate to keep me on the staff?" He pondered the duke's personal dislike of his presence and wondered if he would uphold his mother's request.

"Of course." Her smile brightened. "I quite like having someone in whom I can confide."

"You still trust me?" he asked, surprised.

"Not completely, but as the secrets unravel, I find it comforting to know I am not alone."

"Your trust may be misplaced, Cassandra." He smirked.

"Tell me." She leaned across the carriage, resting her hand on his knee. "Would you allow harm to befall me?"

His heart thundered in his chest as blood raged through him in a torrential pulse of awareness. Heat blossomed beneath her hand as it rested on his leg.

"Never," he murmured with a confidence that left him stunned.

"Then my trust is well-founded." She retracted her touch and leaned back, resting her head against the cushion.

"While I would protect you with my life, I cannot pretend to be the man you wish me to be, Cassandra," Reuben said, his heart still racing at the phantom touch lingering on his leg.

"You may be right, Reuben. I know you care about me, but your silence is concerning," Cassandra responded evenly. "Throughout the entirety of the meeting with the Lord of Devil's Acre, you said nothing. Not even in your own defense."

"And that infers that I still harbor secrets from you?"

"Does it not?"

Reuben bit his tongue. *Damn.* He had hoped it presented more as a sign of respect than an admission of his guilt. There were things even Simon did not know about him and his past. Things he did not wish to share with another living soul. And yet when she confronted him, he wished for nothing more than to alleviate his conscience and reveal it.

He relented with a heavy sigh. "What is it you wish to know?"

"How did you come to be in the service of the Lord of Devil's

Acre?" she asked. "Were you a member of the Bloody Talons?"

"No. I was never a member of the Talons, but Simon always regarded me as part of his family."

"Why is that?" Her eyes sparkled, and the world around them fell away.

"When I was a child, my parents died, leaving me and my two brothers in the care of my eldest sister." His heart ached at the memory of his past, but it drove him forward, gave him purpose. She wished to know him—so he would not hide behind the secrets any longer. "We had no money. My sister worked hard to provide for us. To keep food in our bellies and provide shelter."

"A difficult task for such a young soul," Cassandra added, her voice soft.

"Yes, well, it did not last long." He swallowed past the lump in his throat, skimming over the details that had pained him for so many years. "She died suddenly, leaving us at the mercy of the cruel slums."

"Oh—" Cassandra fumbled with her words for a moment before growing silent.

"A bobby caught me picking some toff's pocket. Took mercy on me." He sighed. "His solution was to bring me to the Lord of Devil's Acre—not the current one, Simon. His grandfather."

"Just you?"

"No. My brothers and me. The old man took us in, and I quickly befriended Simon." A small smile appeared at the memory. "We grew up together. Same schools. Everything."

"An interesting turn of events, to be sure." Cassandra regarded him for a heartbeat before she smiled. "And your brothers, where are they now?"

"Successful. Independent." His smile faltered. "I ensured they excelled far beyond their station. One is a tailor in Paris, and the other is in America, making his own way."

"And what of yourself?" Her question echoed softly in the carriage, stinging his ears. "Why did you choose the life of a servant?"

"I did not choose this life." Reuben cleared his throat, shifting uncomfortably. "A debt needed to be repaid."

"Ah." Cassandra stiffened. "A debt."

He noted the quick alteration of her demeanor at the word. Still sensitive to the implications of Simon's agreement and the difficult path before her.

Reuben longed to reach for her, to take her in his arms and tell her not to worry. But he would not—could not. Their lives were never meant to intertwine, merely to run a course, side by side, until they parted ways, either by death or by the duke's design. It was the way of the world. He accepted it, even though it pained him to do so.

"Simon placed you in my home as a valet to spy on my husband's activities," Cassandra began slowly. "But that does not explain why you continued the charade."

"I told you. I wished to remain in your service." Reuben's blood heated. He'd stayed because he cared for her. More than he should.

Reuben bit his lip, dropping his gaze. The first time he'd seen her, he'd known he had never before seen a woman of such elegance and poise. She'd captivated him. When he'd glimpsed the bruises hidden under her sleeve, he'd paid closer attention. Then he'd seen the beast beneath the duke's cultured façade. Saw the hate he'd borne for his wife—and the indifference he'd shown his son. Reuben had sworn an oath on his sister's grave to protect Cassandra at all cost to himself.

Blush stained her cheeks as she glanced away. Reuben's thoughts drifted into silence as he refocused on the woman before him.

"I apologize for my harsh words, Reuben." She glanced at him again. "I am sorry for your loss."

"Thank you."

"May I—" Her words ended swiftly as the carriage rolled to a stop.

He reached for the handle, and her hand came to rest on his. She leaned closer, her breath mingling with his, and he wanted nothing more than to capture her mouth in a bruising kiss and steal her away for an uninterrupted night of pleasure. But guilt needled him hard, forcing him to push the desire aside.

"Pardon me, madam." Reuben opened the door and stepped from the carriage before he did something he would regret.

Like confess to murder.

Chapter Eight

THREE DAYS AFTER her introduction to the Lord of Devil's Acre, Cassandra accepted an invitation to join Lady Corby for tea. Finally, something to take her mind off the bargain and her butler.

Phillip had left London again and had not returned. His continued absence made her wonder as to his dedication to his duties. The moment he returned, she would follow through with her promise.

Reuben remained dutiful, not once allowing what had transpired between them to affect his daily tasks. He served faithfully and without question, but Cassandra noticed the way his gaze lingered when he believed they were alone. Her body ignited under his scrutiny. She longed to feel his touch once more, to lose herself in the pleasure she knew he could offer.

Reckless desire. That was precisely what it was, and it would only lead to ruin.

Bundled in her warmest woolen cloak and furs, she forewent the carriage and instead ventured on foot the several blocks to Lady Corby's residence on Bruton Street. The vigorous exercise did wonders for her mood. Even the biting cold and the overcast skies could not dampen it.

By the time she'd reached the lovely brick townhome, Cassandra felt the sting in her cheeks flushed with the exertion and her spirits lifted. A warm cup of tea and some friendly companionship would only compound the effects on her disposition.

The butler led her to the parlor, where a warm fire burned merrily in the hearth. Boughs of greenery hung over the stone mantel dotted with candles and paper flowers. A warm and welcoming scene awaited her arrival.

The dowager viscountess rose from her seat on the floral settee. "Your Grace, how lovely to see you."

"Likewise, Lady Corby. Thank you for the kind invitation."

"Heavens," Lady Corby exclaimed. "You are positively glowing."

"Oh, really?" Cassandra pressed the backs of her hands to her cheeks. "It must be the effects of exercise and the cold air."

"You walked here?" Lady Corby asked with muted surprise. "How bold of you to take on the cold. I myself enjoy walking, but I much prefer the warmth of the summer sun to the cold embrace of the winter air."

"Ah, yes." Cassandra nodded. "If I remember correctly, you enjoy spending time in your gardens with your namesake."

Lady Corby blushed and waved a hand. "I pride myself on my ability to nurture and foster growth. Plants are far more pliant than people, I've noticed."

"Very true. Although I do not count myself very fortunate with plants and flowers. They often wither when left in my care."

"Perhaps you have not found a plant suitable to your abilities," Lady Corby remarked as she poured the tea.

"Alas, I fear my talents are better directed elsewhere." Cassandra lifted the cup to her lips and the liquid warmed her from the inside. "Now, your invitation mentioned a fundraising event for the Mayberry Academy."

"Yes." Lady Corby set her tea aside and rested her hands in her lap. "As you know, most of the school's income rests on donations from ladies such as ourselves. Patronesses in search of a better future for young women of lesser means."

"Do our donations not cover the costs accrued? From what I gathered, the school houses a hundred girls and an adequate staff. Surely, our monthly donations cover the necessities." Cassandra had researched the school and discussed the opportunity with her solicitor. The amount set aside for the school would certainly aid in their education.

"Donations from the current patronesses do, in fact, cover the day-to-day function of the school, never fear. But…" She paused, her hands twisting together. "It is the building in which the problem lies. The owner has doubled the rent over the past few years and refuses to make any updates and repairs to the aging property. The other ladies and I think it would be wise to purchase the building outright and make the necessary repairs ourselves."

Cassandra frowned. She knew of men with souls compounded with greed, but she never had course to address such a situation. It had never been her place.

"Is it possible?" she asked, curiosity and concern growing in equal measure.

"We will have to utilize some more—*creative* methods, but I believe it is possible." Lady Corby averted her gaze.

"Why do I feel like you have already found a solution?" Cassandra asked, her gaze narrowing.

"Well, the method is a bit unorthodox, but I have been assured—if we can raise the funds to purchase the building, the rest will be handled without incident."

"I have two questions." Cassandra set her cup aside. "Firstly, how do you propose we raise the funds?"

Lady Corby grinned, her eyes sparkling. "A masquerade ball. It will be unlike any other event of the season. A veritable banquet of virtue and vice." She paused for effect. "The Sinners and Saints Masquerade."

Excitement pulsed through Cassandra's veins. A ball, but not just any ball—a masquerade, where even the most prestigious in society could pretend to be anything other than what they truly were. An opportunity for revelry and delights. She nodded as the idea took root in her mind.

"The cost of admission will pay for the event as well as add to the coffers for the purchase of the building." Lady Corby leaned forward in anticipation. "What do you think?"

"An excellent idea," Cassandra confessed with a smile.

"Wonderful." Lady Corby clapped her hands together. "I am so relieved you agree."

"But I have doubts on how you will succeed in purchasing the building once you have obtained the funds."

"Oh, that is but a trivial thing compared to obtaining the coin needed for the purchase."

"My second question." Cassandra arched her brow. "*Who* will be making the purchase? I doubt the owner will sell it to a group of widows or even a woman in general."

"Well…" Lady Corby's blush deepened to crimson. "That is a bit of a moral dilemma."

Cassandra straightened at the admission, a twinge of unease flowing through her.

"You see, madam, a widow of our acquaintance has offered the services of a most trusted friend and ally to purchase the building, and in return, he agreed to donate it to the society for the use as a school."

"A trusted friend." Cassandra tapped her finger on her chin. "And who is this widow of your acquaintance?"

"Mrs. Delilah Gallagher. The former Dowager Viscountess Everly."

Mrs. Gallagher had a reputation for being unruly and independent. Not that Cassandra saw anything wrong with that, but the ton had a way of shaming those who did not follow the rules of society.

Over the years, Cassandra had conversed with Mrs. Gallagher, the former viscountess, perhaps a dozen times, but there had never been any friendship forged during those encounters. It begged the question, what connections did the woman have that could aid in their endeavor?

"Mrs. Gallagher is one of the original donors of the school. She began before she married an American businessman, Warren Gallagher. Now they both invest heavily and wish for it to succeed," Lady Corby responded. "I have no reason to doubt their sincerity or integrity."

"This trusted friend of hers, have you met them?"

"No," Lady Corby's countenance dropped. "But I have it on the highest authority from Mrs. Gallagher that he can be trusted."

"Dare I ask who this mysterious benefactor is?" Cassandra asked with a laugh.

"The Lord of Devil's Acre."

Deep within her chest, Cassandra's heart ceased beating. "You cannot be serious."

"You must not believe the rumors surrounding him. Contrary to those salacious lies, he is an honest and loyal man who will uphold his end of any agreement."

The room began to spin. Cassandra gripped the arms of the chair to steady herself. She slammed her eyes closed. This could not be true. It was retribution for the sins of her husband. It had to be. There could be no other explanation for it. The Lord of Devil's Acre. Surely, this was a jest. Cassandra inhaled three deep breaths, exhaling slowly between each.

"Are you well, madam?" Lady Corby leaned closer. "Shall I fetch a doctor?"

"No, no. I-I am well," Cassandra stuttered. "Just—surprised."

"Such a shock is understandable." Lady Corby offered her some tea. "Drink this. It will help."

Cassandra sipped the brew, her mind spinning like a wheel on a racing carriage. Surely, this could be no coincidence. Perhaps she could use it to her advantage.

"This *man*," Cassandra said, refusing to use his cursed, illegitimate title, "is trustworthy?"

"I have it on the best authority from Mrs. Gallagher." Lady Corby nodded vigorously. "He is a man of his word and will do right by our organization."

"And what of *other* agreements he has made?" she asked, attempting to keep her voice even.

"Well, to that end, it would be wise to speak to Mrs. Gallagher directly. She can give you all the information you need to make an educated assessment of the man in question." Lady Corby relaxed, resting her arm on the edge of the settee.

"Well, that would be the best course of action, to be sure." Cassandra finished her tea. "Perhaps I shall call on her tomorrow. She can enlighten me as to the inner workings of this agreement." She paused. "Have Ladies Amesbury and Winstead agreed to this course of action?"

"Of course." Lady Corby's countenance brightened. "Once we have reached an accord, there will be no issues in creating a more secure foundation for these young ladies."

"Yes, I agree." The response came unbidden as Cassandra found her thoughts preoccupied by the connection between Mrs. Gallagher and the Lord of Devil's Acre.

The rest of the afternoon passed in a blur. Lady Corby's hospitality and direction shed new light on the unspoken conundrum in which Cassandra found herself mired. If she could uncover the true motives behind this bargain she'd made with the Lord of Devil's Acre, then surely, she could find some peace in reaching a more realistic solution.

On the walk home, Cassandra became lost in deep thought. Her son would never welcome an open dialog about his father's true nature, nor would he entertain a bargain with the most notorious crime lord in all of London. But if she could find a way to ensure both parties met with mutual understanding, then perhaps there could be a solution that benefited every party involved.

By the time Cassandra had reached the steps of her home, her head pounded and her limbs ached from the tension pulsing through her. How could she possibly be expected to find a solution? This was far more than she'd ever expected to undertake. Was she so ignorant that she had not seen the corroding flaws in her husband's character?

Sure enough, he'd been a heartless cad. A gambler and philanderer. He'd taken his anger out on her in any and every way. But in public, he'd been the epitome of a well-bred gentleman, living up to the standard expected of a duke.

Cassandra knew the truth. Her husband had been a brute and a bastard. The world, and she, were better off without him. But leaving their son to assume his debts with a notorious villain?

She shivered at the thought but blamed it on the cold as she escaped into the safe confines of her home. A meeting with Mrs. Gallagher would put her at ease. Tomorrow, she would call on the infamous lady and ascertain for certain whether Cassandra had just sold her soul to the devil or found redemption from a cursed existence.

FOR THE SECOND consecutive day, the dowager duchess left the confines of her home, leaving Reuben to tend to his duties without distraction. When she'd returned from her visit with Lady Corby the previous afternoon, she'd seemed to have regained her confidence. But still they maintained a distance between them.

Reuben did not have the heart to inquire further, lest he break the precarious truce. His feelings on the matter and for *her* specifically had not been altered. Until they reached a deeper understanding of their desires and their prospective goals, keeping to himself proved to be the wisest course of action.

Once Her Grace departed the house on her errand, Reuben breathed a sigh of relief. Remaining beneath the same roof after having tasted her, after experiencing such exquisite delight in bringing her pleasure, brought nothing but torment since he refused to allow himself to indulge again. Not while so much uncertainty remained.

After speaking with Mrs. Johnson, the cook, Reuben left the kitchen and climbed the servants' stairs at the rear of the house. He had just reached the second-floor landing when the sound of the front door closing echoed through the corridor.

It could not be the dowager returning so soon. She had only been gone for a little over an hour. Perhaps something had happened that necessitated an expedient return. Curious, Reuben crept forward to glimpse down the main staircase leading to the entryway.

A flash of black fabric caught his eye and the distinct outline of a gentleman's profile. He gritted his teeth. Only one man would enter the house unannounced as if he owned it—for he did. Reuben prayed for strength, knowing an encounter with His Grace would only lead to another disagreement and his possible dismissal.

The duke made no pretense about his feelings toward Reuben. In another life, they could have been amicable acquaintances passing on the street, but his current situation was not so simple and carefree. Reuben endured years of suspicion and loathing from the young duke. It took all of his restraint *not* to tell the entitled toff exactly what he thought of him.

Taking a deep breath, Reuben straightened his waistcoat and tie. There could be no positive outcome to this encounter, and yet he saw no logical way to avoid it. When the duke realized his mother was not at the residence, he would single out the person responsible for the household—which would be Reuben. Better to endure the daunting task than to prolong the inevitable.

With measured steps, Reuben descended the stairs. Deep inside his mind, he erected a barrier in which to confine his thoughts and emotions. He would *not* allow the duke to draw him out as he attempted to do on many occasions. It was as if His Grace took pleasure in his criticism of Reuben's presence in the house—both due to his age and past conflicts between them.

Pausing outside the study, Reuben transformed his expression into a mask of indifference. Only then did he cross the threshold.

"Your Grace." Reuben bowed upon entering the room to find the duke pouring himself a dram of whisky from the crystal decanter. "My apologies. I was unaware of your arrival."

"Evans. You are still employed here?" The duke scowled at him and took a drink. "Where is my mother?"

"Unfortunately, Her Grace had a prior engagement this afternoon." He stood at attention, his tone dispassionate. "I can pass on any message you have when she returns."

"And how can I trust that any message I leave with you will reach her?" The duke drained the contents of the glass and set it aside. "Considering it pertains to *you*."

Reuben's heartbeat quickened, but he maintained an easy calm. "I am certain I do not understand, sir."

"Why are you still here, Evans?" The duke slowly circled Reuben. "I made it clear to my mother that I was *displeased* with your presence in this house and yet she maintains you are irreplaceable."

"I am sure I do not know," Reuben replied, keeping his expression controlled while a storm raged inside of him. "Is there some reason you find my occupation of the current position unsuitable?"

"Yes, several, in fact." The duke rocked back on his heels, a slow grin spreading across his lips. "You know, for years, I could never quite pinpoint exactly what it was about you that nagged at the back of my conscience. I believed it was your age, but when I learned exactly *how* you came into my father's service, I began to question the validity of your training—and the references you provided."

"I made no secret of the fact that His Grace won my services in a game of chance among peers." Reuben stood tall, watching the duke with a wary eye. "My previous employer was a bit—*overextended* and offered my services in exchange for the debt. But if you speak to him, I am sure he will confirm both my references and credentials."

"See, now that's just the thing," the duke said, tapping his jaw with a finger. "I found the agreement tucked away in one of father's ledgers and took it upon myself to do a bit of research."

Reuben held his breath, terrified of what the man had uncovered. Guilt and uncertainty twisted into a thick knot in his gut, leaving him in physical discomfort. He inclined his head but said nothing in response, lest he contradict something inadvertently. This was an extremely dangerous game he played. Even though Her Grace knew of his agreement with Simon and his place in the house, her son did not. And she was not present to reveal it to him to ease the tension suddenly pulled tighter than a bowstring.

"And do you know what I discovered, Evans?" The duke leaned closer, his eyes glittering. He resembled his father in so many ways, it was terrifying to behold. Like a specter from the grave come to haunt him.

"Please, enlighten me." Reuben bit the inside of his cheek after he made the remark, knowing it sounded trite and laced with disdain.

"Your former employer, the Earl of Winterbourne, indeed confirmed your employment in his services for three years, but there is no trace of the Baron Rayne, your supposed employer before him, beyond a title that goes back to the fourteenth century whose line ended with no successor."

"I fail to see your concerns, sir." Reuben struggled to remain composed, but as his manufactured past slowly unraveled, he found it more difficult to breathe.

"I took my inquiry to a private investigator, who seemed decidedly eager," the duke said, his wicked grin unwavering, "and do you know what he discovered?"

Reuben held his tongue, knowing any word from him would constitute an admission of guilt or a blatant falsehood. So he waited for the man to continue.

The duke withdrew a piece of paper from his inside pocket folded neatly into thirds. "This is the result of his inquiry. Do you know what it says?"

"Reuben Evans. Born 1863 in Whitechapel. Brothers: Daniel and Jacob." The duke read the contents aloud, and Reuben flinched at the mention of his family. "Sister: Hannah. Prostitute. Died at the age of seventeen in 1878." The duke tutted. "A whore murdered in the streets of Whitechapel, how original."

Reuben dropped his gaze to the thick carpet beneath his feet. His hands clenched into fists. It would do him no good to lash out at the duke. Such a reaction would only garner him an immediate termination and imprisonment for assaulting a peer of the realm.

"I fail to see," Reuben said through gritted teeth, "how my current position is affected by the unfortunate circumstances of my birth."

"It is unfortunate, to be sure, but allow me to continue." The duke tapped the paper in his hand. "You and your brothers were taken in by the Lord of Devil's Acre." He folded it and tucked it back into his pocket. "Now, that is something I cannot abide. A criminal living beneath the same roof as my mother—in the service of my family."

The admission was dangerously close to what Her Grace had learned only days before, and yet there were details here that Reuben had chosen to omit in his confession to Cassandra. Most specifically the truth of his sister's profession. It had been neither the time nor place for him to reveal something that affected him so deeply. So intimately.

"What would you have me do?" Reuben asked.

The duke stood before him, shoulders squared, eyes burning with victory. "You will leave this house and never return."

"And if I refuse?"

"Then I will have no choice but to reveal the extent of your deception to my mother and have you forcibly removed from the house." The man's amusement faded, taking on an icy edge sharp enough to draw blood. "Then I will reveal your deception to all. You will never again find respectable work in England—or the Continent."

"I have done nothing illegal. Nothing to warrant such a

threat," Reuben retaliated, his anger reaching a fever pitch.

"It does not matter," The duke snarled. "Whom will they believe? A duke? Or an orphan of Whitechapel and the brother of a whore?"

Bastard! Reuben screamed inside his mind. Pivoting, he turned toward the window, unable to bear the persistent presence of the young duke. He took several deep breaths. *In. Out. In. Ou—*

A flash of crimson caught his eye out the window. The dowager duchess had returned. Reuben swore as he dragged his fingers through his hair. He could not allow her to see him thus.

"Damn! I'm late," the duke muttered. "Out of respect for my mother, who is overly fond of you, I shall give you a week to vacate the premises of your own volition. If you do not, I shall speak to my mother and all will be revealed. Tick tock, Evans."

Reuben stood as still as a statue, fury pouring through him like liquid flame. He cursed fate for putting him in such a position.

The sound of the front door opening drifted into the open study. In the distance, he heard the duke and Cassandra's low exchange of greetings and her son's promise to return for dinner the following week.

It was only when he heard the telltale click of the front door closing with finality that Reuben allowed himself to breathe fully. What had he done?

Cassandra already knew the truth of his ties to Simon, but he would not be able to bear the look of horror on her face when his secrets were revealed by her son with such obvious disdain.

Before him lay two choices, each more difficult than the last. He could leave and take his secret to the grave, but in doing so, abandon the one woman he cared for beyond reason.

Or Reuben could tell Cassandra the truth of his desire to find and punish the man who killed his sister in cold blood. To become that which he despised. He could only pray she did not look upon him in disgust.

He closed his eyes and held his breath, praying for guidance but knowing that only damnation waited for him.

Chapter Nine

A Few Hours Earlier

CASSANDRA KNEW VERY little about the enigmatic woman once known as the Dowager Viscountess Everly, save for the whispers of the society gossips and what little the other widows had told her. She'd expected to find opulence when she entered the former viscountess's home, but the rich and vibrant hardwoods mixed well with the exquisite art. Mrs. Gallagher embraced her style and taste with the pride of a man. The moment Cassandra stepped into her parlor and glimpsed the infamous widow clad in red silk and black velvet, she knew they would be fast friends.

"Your Grace." Mrs. Gallagher turned away from the fire and curtsied. "To what do I owe the honor of this visit?"

"I do hope I am not imposing." Cassandra took in the rich, green hues of the room. Plants lined the window, and a wall of books bracketed the door she had just entered.

"Not at all." Mrs. Gallagher gestured to the two chairs by the fire. "Shall I ring for tea?"

"That would be delightful. Thank you." Cassandra sat while her hostess summoned a servant and made the request.

"Tea is on the way," Mrs. Gallagher said, settling into the chair opposite.

"You have a lovely home," Cassandra said, admiring the

detailed scrollwork along the mantelpiece.

"Thank you, madam." Mrs. Gallagher folded her hands in her lap. "I know you did not come all this way to discuss my choice in ornamentation."

"They were right about you."

"Who?" Mrs. Gallagher smirked. "The gossipmongers?"

"Lady Corby, Lady Amesbury, and Lady Winstead."

"Ah," her hostess remarked with a laugh. "The Mayfair Widows. A divine trio, to be sure, quite unlike the rest of the peerage."

"Are they not friends of yours?" Cassandra asked, confused. "Lady Corby spoke quite highly of you on several occasions. I merely assumed..."

"Oh, yes, we are well acquainted. The four of us..." Mrs. Gallagher paused as the servant entered the room, placed the tray on the table, and left. "The four of us are patronesses of the Mayberry Academy for Young Ladies. Alas, since I met Warren, I have not been as active as I would like to be."

"Well, they have invited me to join them in their philanthropic endeavors." Cassandra elaborated as Mrs. Gallagher poured the tea.

"Excellent." Mrs. Gallagher handed her the cup. "I can think of no one more suited to the task of ensuring the school is a success."

"Well, that is one of the reasons I have come." Cassandra cradled the teacup in her hands. "According to Lady Corby, we have encountered a bit of a complication with the building's current landlord."

Mrs. Gallagher frowned. "Yes, it is quite unfortunate."

"She informs me that you have a solution for the problem at hand."

"I do." Mrs. Gallagher tapped her jaw. "But it seems you have reservations on my suggestion to purchase the building outright?"

"Once she explained the details, I admit is a wonderful idea." Cassandra paused. "I have considered asking my son to take on the task personally, but Lady Corby says there is another potential benefactor aligned to make the purchase on behalf of the school. The Lord of Devil's Acre, Mr. Simon Oh."

Mrs. Gallagher sighed and shook her head. "Simon." The simple word held a wealth of emotion. "They have finally decided to ask the Lord of Devil's Acre for help."

"How do you—?"

"We have a history." Mrs. Gallagher stood, retrieving a box off the mantel.

What past did the former dowager viscountess share with this man? Cassandra's curiosity grew exponentially.

"Do you mind if I partake?" Mrs. Gallagher held up a cigarette.

"Not at all." Cassandra sat stunned, a million questions burning through her mind. "I do not mean to pry, but might I inquire as to the nature of your association with *him*?"

"It is a long and rather complicated tale, madam." Mrs. Gallagher lit the tip and inhaled deeply, smoke curling around her head like a halo. "For the sake of brevity, I shall say only this. Simon saved me—on multiple occasions—both literally and figuratively. Without his aid, I would not be alive today."

"So, you trust him?"

"Implicitly." She held Cassandra's gaze, her eyes like sparkling jewels lit with flame. "There is not a man in the world I would place my trust in more than Simon—aside from Warren."

"Your—"

"Her husband." A deep voice rang behind her. "Pardon my interruption."

The cultured American accent struck her first, but when Cassandra turned, her breath caught. A handsome gentleman in a tailored suit with a silver waistcoat strode toward them. His dark hair fell in waves around his face, and silver graced his temples, giving him an air of sophistication. He carried himself with confidence, but Cassandra marked the roguish way he smiled at his wife.

"I shall only be a moment." He placed his hand on Mrs. Gallagher's waist and leaned close, whispering in her ear.

Her cheeks pinkened at his intimate attentions. "When I have finished here, I shall join you in the library."

He straightened with a nod and turned toward Cassandra, extending his hand. "Mr. Warren Gallagher."

"Cassandra Sterling, Duchess of Tolland." She stared at his outstretched hand for a long moment before she realized he wanted her to shake it.

"Do not mark his bad manners, madam." Mrs. Gallagher tutted with a smirk, nudging him with her hand. "He is American and has no patience for the rules of society."

"With all due respect, I find it quite tedious and antiquated," he said with a half-smile.

"And this is precisely why I first refused to marry you," Mrs. Gallagher murmured softly. "Now, go. I shall join you shortly."

Cassandra dropped her gaze to the fire and drank her tea, hiding her smile behind the cup. She envied their easy banter. It was quite obvious upon seeing them together that they were in love. Recklessly so.

For a titled widow to even consider another marriage to someone outside their social class, let alone a union with an American, well, it was unconventional, to be sure. But the threat of censure did not seem to deter Mrs. Gallagher.

The American tipped his head in respect. "Lovely to meet you, Your Grace."

"Likewise, Mr. Gallagher."

And with that, he left them.

"My apologies, madam." Mrs. Gallagher stubbed out the cigarette. "He is still unaccustomed to our ways, and despite my efforts to teach him, he remains stubborn and spirited."

"Yet you care deeply for him regardless," Cassandra said softly.

"I do." Mrs. Gallagher quickly recovered her composure. "Let us return to our previous conversation."

"Yes, your association with the Lord of Devil's Acre." Cassandra leaned forward. "Do you see any reason why he could not be trusted to keep his word?"

"None," Mrs. Gallagher vowed. "Despite his notorious and feared reputation, Simon is a man of his word and loyal to a fault. Any agreement made with him will be honored to the letter."

Sincerity rang in her declaration. Cassandra could not deny the conviction in her voice. If both Lady Corby and Mrs. Gallagher were convinced of the wisdom to include this man, then she should harbor no concerns. And yet this was not merely about the school.

Cassandra's bargain with the Lord of Devil's Acre concerning her husband's debts loomed like a dark cloud over her head. Could she truly place her trust in this crime lord as easily as Mrs. Gallagher had? There was more to that story, and she hoped this newfound friendship would allow her to learn more. The dowager viscountess had a strong, independent spirit and passion. It gave Cassandra hope of discovering her own.

"That certainly puts my mind at ease." Cassandra stood. "I thank you for your time and counsel."

"Of course." Mrs. Gallagher rose to join her. "You are welcome to return anytime."

Upon leaving the dowager, Cassandra pondered the exchange and the implications of this new information. When she returned home, she would speak with Evans. Confidence infused her as the carriage crept closer to her home.

They would work together to find a solution to this mess her husband had created. She doubted her son would listen. He was quite stubborn. If she was able to find adequate proof of her husband's hidden sins, then perhaps she stood a chance of convincing Phillip. There had been proof, but now it was gone. Could there be anything equally damning to convince Phillip aside from that?

The thought of tarnishing her son's memory of his father left her conflicted. He deserved to know the truth. James had been an absent father and a monstrous husband. How could she possibly reveal these things to her son and not expect him to lash out in disbelief and defiance?

Perhaps Reuben would have a solution. If only she had the documents he'd taken from the desk. Could she somehow persuade him to return them? Her face warmed at the thought of using a more... *seductive* method of persuasion.

Regardless of everything falling to pieces around her, she craved him. Desire never appealed to her, but now she had a taste of it—she longed for more.

By the time the carriage had reached the steps of her home, Cassandra needed the soft caress of the cold air to wash the heat from her skin. She ascended the stairs, taking measured breaths to keep from showing her impatience.

Inside the house, Cassandra nearly collided with Phillip in the entryway. He turned, pulling on his coat, his hat nearly slipping from his hand.

"Mother." He pressed a kiss to her cheek.

"Where are you off to in such a hurry?" she asked, flustered.

"I forgot, I have a previous engagement. I'm late." He pulled open the door. "I shall return for dinner next week. We have much to discuss."

"Very well," she called after him, but he was already gone, the door slamming in his wake.

Cassandra unfastened her cloak and handed it to the footman, who placed it on the rack, depositing her gloves and hat along with it. Where in the devil was Reuben? She smoothed her hands over her skirts as she ventured into the house.

A soft curse echoed through the crack in the study door. She pushed it open.

Reuben stood with his back to her, staring out the window overlooking the street.

"Reuben," she murmured as she stepped closer. He stiffened at the sound of his name.

When she came alongside him, she searched his handsome

profile, tracing the sharp edge of his jaw with her hungry gaze. He refused to look at her. His gaze fixed on some object in the distance.

"Is something wrong?" Cassandra rested her hand on his arm.

He glanced at her hand, then traced the length of her arm up until his eyes locked on hers.

"Everything is wrong." Reuben sighed, hanging his head and avoiding her gaze. "Cassandra, I have not been entirely honest with you."

Fear pierced her heart with the swiftness of an arrow loosed from a bow. She dropped her hand. "What do you mean?" Her voice hardened. "You promised—no more secrets."

"I know." He turned to face her fully. "I am not the man you think I am."

"Well, then I think you should start at the beginning." Cassandra inhaled deeply to quell the rising uncertainty and fear. Would the secrets and lies never end?

EVERYTHING HAD BUILT to this moment. Reuben had known this inevitability would arrive, and it would force his hand. He inhaled deeply before nodding.

"Perhaps we should sit," he said, gesturing to the chairs by the fire.

"I believe I shall remain as I am." Cassandra straightened where she stood.

Reuben groaned, his body humming with awareness at her proximity, but he saw the glint of steel in her eyes. She had demanded the truth. No secrets. But could he give her the answers she *needed* to hear without thinking the worst of him?

"Very well." He stood at attention, his hands by his sides. "You know of my association with the Lord of Devil's Acre, and how it came to be. But there is more to that tale."

Cassandra inclined her head, an indication for him to continue.

"As you know, I was born and raised in Whitechapel." He paused waiting for a reaction, but none came. Not even the flutter of an eyelash. Her gaze softened, but she said nothing, as though afraid if she would interrupt, he would end his tale. Instead, he continued.

"When my parents died, my sister cared for us. Work was scarce, and what we found often did not cover the expenses of our small family." He dropped his gaze. "I fell into a bad lot. A small band of thieves who would nick trinkets and money from those who were better off. Mostly toffs." He shrugged. "But my sister, she—well, she became a prostitute at the age of fourteen."

A soft gasp ripped from her parted lips.

"The pay was better than anything we had before, so she kept doing it." Reuben rubbed his hand across his forehead, wishing he could banish the memory of her drawn complexion, the bloodstains marring her perfect skin, the gaping wound at her throat. His voice cracked, "Until someone killed her."

"Dear merciful Lord," Cassandra muttered beneath her breath. "Reuben, I—" She bit her lip and contemplated her words carefully before speaking. "I am sorry for your loss."

He swallowed the lump in his throat and nodded, pushing the memories aside. "I was the one who found her, lying in an alley in Whitechapel, just two blocks from a gambling den where she'd worked as a whore."

Cassandra flinched at the revelation. "How old were you?"

"Fourteen." He flexed his fingers to keep them from balling into fists. The memories surrounded him, but he focused solely on telling his story without choking on the rising emotions. "Right after I found her, a bobby came round the corner. He saw my hands covered in blood and thought I'd done it. Until he noticed the fury and tears blinding me."

"What happened?" Cassandra asked, her tone soft and tender. "Did they find out who killed her?"

"No." Reuben shook his head, studying the patterns in the carpet beneath his feet for a long moment before lifting his gaze to meet hers. "The detectives had no leads, and they didn't care enough about Hannah to waste time searching for a mysterious killer. 'A victim of her trade,' they said." Bile stung the back of his throat.

"You cared for your brothers, then?" Cassandra pressed.

"I did. For a few months, at least." He scoffed. "Until the same bobby caught me nicking a toff's wallet on Bond Street." Reuben allowed a half-smile. "Instead of locking me up, he took mercy on me. He took me to the Lord of Devil's Acre."

"To save you from a life of crime he delivered you to the one man who'd mastered it?" Cassandra asked, blinking. "How could a bobby do something like that? Were there no better alternatives?"

"The Lord of Devil's Acre has far more influence than you realize. From those in society to the bobbies who walk the streets." Reuben nudged the topic back to himself. "The old man took all three of us in. Gave us an education. A chance to redeem ourselves."

"And he did this out of the goodness of his heart? A grand gesture of philanthropic proportions." She arched a brow.

Reuben shook his head, the weight of the past wearing heavily on his mind. "It was a debt to be repaid. One I took willingly so my brothers would never have to work for a dangerous organization with questionable morals."

"You bore the entirety of the debt to the Lord of Devil's Acre?" Cassandra asked, her voice solemn. "That must have been a hefty burden to bear for so long."

"It was."

"And do you still owe the debt?"

"Not in the same manner." Reuben rubbed his jaw. "Simon, the current lord, and I became friends. Attended the same schools. Our agreement continues the wishes of his grandfather, but I am free to make my own decisions on when and how I aid him—should he make a request."

"And you remained in my employment to acquiesce to his request?" Cassandra arched a brow. Curiosity burned in her question, and yet he sensed the hurt beneath the bold accusation.

"I remained *against* his recommendation."

"'Against' it?" The confession stunned her. "I do not understand. He placed you in my home strategically. Why would he suddenly change his mind?"

"Your husband's death," Reuben replied simply. "He felt there was more to lose if I remained. Until that point, I had done my diligence in keeping him abreast of the duke's activities."

"He now requires my son to bend the knee or take on his father's debt." Her gaze narrowed. "Why? After two years, what changed?"

"The documents." Reuben straightened. "Contained within them was a wealth of information concerning the duke's investments, interests, proclivities, and—well, there are some other incriminating elements that Simon must ensure do not continue down the family line."

"Are you insinuating that my son would indulge in such barbaric activities?" She protested, the fury in her voice highlighted by the flush of color rising in her cheeks. "He may be his father's son, but I did my part in raising him as well. He is a good man. Stubborn and entitled, but deep in his heart, he knows the difference between right and wrong. Phillip would *never* behave in such a manner."

"Would you stake your life on it?" he asked solemnly.

Cassandra bristled at the question. "I do not need to stake my life on it to know it is the truth."

"And that is why Simon requires your son's active participation and comprehension of the outstanding debt." Reuben inclined his head, gauging her reaction carefully. "But honestly, I believe your son is a lost cause. Simon would do best to cut his losses."

"How dare you?" Cassandra reeled, stumbling back as though

he had slapped her. "My son is *not* a lost cause! If we tell him the truth, explain things to him in a logical way, I am sure he will understand why this debt must be repaid, if only out of closure for the victims."

Reuben stepped closer, bringing them toe to toe. Her jaw tensed at the invasion. The sweet, familiar scent of her teased his senses and he inhaled deeply, savoring the way her heat surrounded them both. She intoxicated him.

"Why do you hate him so?" Cassandra asked, breaking through the haze of tormenting need. "What has my son done to you that you discount him so quickly?"

"Your son has made no secret of his contempt for me since the moment I took employment as your husband's valet." Reuben straightened and held her gaze. "I honestly do not know why he has indulged you and kept me in his employment while also elevating my position within the house. Perhaps he hoped I would fail and disparage myself enough to be rid of me permanently without guilt and blame."

"Why would he feel guilt? It is his right to do as he wishes with the house and the staff."

"But he knows how much you prefer my company." Reuben exhaled sharply. "And I remained solely at your request. To cast me aside without reason would only ruin the bond you share."

"He has said something to you?" Cassandra folded her arms across her chest, emphasizing her bosom and making it difficult to concentrate on the importance of their current conversation.

"Just before you returned this evening. The duke revealed that he had uncovered the truth of my birth, my past, and my intentions. Then he threatened to tell you all of it and ruin my reputation completely unless I abandoned my post with due haste."

Cassandra glanced away, as though reliving the exchange she'd had with her son only moments before. She turned back to Reuben. "Why did you not leave with your secrets intact?"

"Because those are not secrets. There is no dishonor in my

origins, in my poverty, in the way my sister provided for us." His tone softened. "But I could not bear the thought of abandoning you without revealing what he thought were secrets. It was my story to tell, and I could not allow you to hear the truth from anyone other than myself. You deserved that much."

"I see." Cassandra licked her lips. "I appreciate your honesty, although I wish it had come far sooner."

"I should have told you long ago, Your Grace. Forgive me." He bowed. "I shall pack my things and darken your door no longer." When he straightened, he turned, ready to follow through with his promise.

Her hand came to rest on his arm, stopping him. His body tensed at the innocent touch and burned for something more—*anything* to quell the longing simmering inside him.

"What of our agreement with the Lord of Devil's Acre?" Her question came on a broken sigh. "What am I to do about my son?"

"I will speak to Simon about your son." He covered her hand with his own. "This burden of revelation should not be yours. Your husband—the bloody coward—shall burn in hell for leaving the burden for you to bear alone."

Cassandra's hand drifted along his arm, up until her fingertips caressed his cheek. When she cradled his face in her hand, he leaned into the warmth.

"This is *my* burden to bear. *My* wrong to right." She took a deep breath. "I allowed him to persist in his cursed ways and leave a horrid legacy for my son."

"No." Reuben grasped her hand by the wrist and pulled it away.

"You view me through a rose-colored lens. I am no innocent in these criminal matters, even though I knew nothing of their existence. I must make an effort to right this injustice and bring it to a satisfactory conclusion. If there are aggrieved parties, I wish to see them properly compensated and cared for."

"He did not deserve you," Reuben whispered, his body tense

as she allowed him to draw her closer, his fingertips tightening on her wrist.

"How do you know what I deserve?" she asked.

He drew her hand to his lips, his breath teasing the delicate skin along the inside of her wrist. Reuben lifted his gaze enough to hold hers, noting the way her breath caught at the intensity pulsing between them.

"You deserve to experience life's little joys—and all the wondrous delights life has to offer." He kissed her wrist, allowing his lips to linger upon her pulse. "Like pleasure."

When she captured his lips in a ravenous kiss, Reuben knew it meant his complete surrender. And he did so. Willingly.

Chapter Ten

UPON HEARING REUBEN'S confession, something inside Cassandra snapped. She had fought against her desires for far too long and now they had reached a crescendo.

Kissing him felt like the last piece of herself had finally clicked into place. The smoldering embers from their previous encounter flared to life, creating an unstoppable inferno. She embraced the flames that had for too long threatened to consume her. If she survived, Cassandra would rise from the ashes like a phoenix, reborn into something new.

Reuben moaned against her lips. His arms encircled her waist, pulling her flush against his body. The hard length of him pressed against her stomach. A tremor of uncertainty and hesitation made her pause.

"I–If you wish for me to stop…" Reuben's whisper caressed her lips. When he tried to pull away, she held him tighter. Her fingers tangled in the fabric of his clothes. "Take your time." Reuben smiled, easing her tension. "Take whatever you need."

Whatever hesitation remained dissipated into the wind. Reuben was not James. She held his gaze steadily. "I *need* this."

They melted together, and for the first time in her life, Cassandra embraced the desire coursing through her.

Her tongue teased the seam of his lips, begging entrance. He obliged with a groan and tasted her. She wrapped her arms around his neck, fingers threading through his hair. Acting on pure impulse, she tightened her hands into fists, tugging on the silken strands.

"Fuck," Reuben growled into her mouth. "If you persist, I cannot be held responsible for what happens next."

"And what would that be?" Cassandra teased his lower lip with her teeth. "I want you to tell me *exactly* what you would do, Reuben."

His eyes darkened, as did his expression. A feral grin split his lips. "I would lay claim to that which has been denied to me for so long."

"Do not make promises you cannot keep," Cassandra murmured.

"From the first moment I saw you, I desired nothing more than an opportunity to pledge my loyalty to you alone." His grip on her waist tightened. "To worship you in every way. With my body. My mouth." He licked his lips. "I craved your presence. A hint of your scent. The briefest smile. A passing acknowledgment. You know not how I suffered being so close and not being able to act upon my desire."

Cassandra's face warmed. His words struck a chord deep within her. A life lived without passionate declarations and unrequited longing. Pride filled her knowing she possessed this power over him. Not because of her position or her status. No, he desired Cassandra as a woman. Heat blossomed within her, consuming every rational thought.

Reuben kissed her again, tenderly exploring the soft hollows of her throat with his lips, his breath on her sensitive skin sending her into a mindless spiral of hedonistic want. Her eyes drifted closed as he explored further.

His fingers slowly unfastened the buttons of her bodice. She shivered at the brush of his fingertips at the base of her throat. A groan of need tore free when he slipped his hand beneath the fabric, teasing the top of her breast.

"I have a confession," she breathed, lost in the moment.

"I long to hear it," Reuben murmured, his mouth burning her with every delicate pass over her bare skin. "Tell me, Cassandra. Allow me to unravel all your secrets."

"You..." She gasped when his teeth raked across her bare shoulder. "Your presence has tormented me since the moment James enlisted your services."

He drew back, smiling. "Did you know the extent of your desire for me then? Or was it an unhurried burn that slowly consumed you with an excruciating mounting tension?"

Cassandra blinked at him. The scoundrel. He knew exactly what he did to her and how long it had burdened her with guilt and shame. No longer. She refused to remain shackled to the unrealistic expectations of society—of marriage. James had treated her worse than he'd treated his horses, and he'd beat them regularly when they had not performed to his standards. Now, she found herself untethered from him—and his monstrous expectations. This was her moment to finally be free, to live by her own standards. And it felt wondrous.

"I refuse to live in the past a moment longer." Grasping his lapels, she met his gaze firmly. "The woman I was no longer resides within me."

"And what is your request of me, madam?" Reuben's hooded eyes belied his state of arousal. He craved her with a hunger she felt deep in her bones.

"I wish to take full advantage of you, Evans." She traced her finger across his lips. "I long to ruin you in every way conceivable."

He parted his lips, taking her finger in his mouth. The warmth of his tongue wrapped around the digit, and he suckled, teasing the length of it with his teeth. When she withdrew it, Cassandra blew out a shaky breath.

"No more conversation," Reuben said, his voice hoarse and strangled.

In a rush, he grabbed her by the waist, lifting her off the

ground. With two strides, he placed her on the desk, his hands impatient as he opened her bodice.

Cassandra gasped at the brute force, but her blood hummed with need. His hands skimmed over her shoulders and arms as he pushed the garment off. She fumbled with the knot of his tie as he pushed the fabric of her chemise down and freed her breasts.

"Saints, you are a vision." He lowered his head and took a nipple in his mouth.

She arched against his hold, burying her fingers in his hair as he laved each breast with attention. Pleasure spiked through her when he suckled and teased the sensitive buds.

"Evans, please." Cassandra tugged on his hair, and he broke free with a soft pop.

Reuben held her gaze as he lazily dragged his tongue over her. Then he pursed his lips, blowing gently against her skin.

Her body tensed at the flutter of sensation that coursed through her. With a deep, stuttering breath, she sighed.

"What do you need?" he asked, gathering a handful of her skirts and dragging them up. "Do you need me to touch you?" His fingers found the slit in her drawers. "Do you need me to taste you?" He stroked her slickened cunt. "So wet for me already, madam."

"*Evans.*" She damn near growled. "Cease your torment."

"Answer one question for me, and I will obey your every command."

"What—?" she gasped, unable to finish the thought.

"Have ever thought of me when you lie in your bed at night, aching and lonely, longing for release?" He slowly eased two fingers inside her. "Have you touched yourself, wishing it were me lying between your thighs, driving you mad with lust?"

The questions only amplified her desire. She closed her eyes, remembering the nights like the ones he described. Every time she'd found the temptation too great, she denied herself, unable to bear the disgrace should it come to light.

"I—I have never—" She licked her lips, panting as he slowly

fucked her with his fingers. Driving her mad with every measured stroke. "No." She gasped as he rubbed his thumb over the sensitive nub at the apex of her thighs. "But I imagined it—many times."

"Tell me, madam." He continued his blissful torment as he spoke in an even, seductive tone. "Tell me you watched me work while imagining what it would be like to bend me to your will. Did you want to corner me in the pantry, beg me to fuck you, to ease the ache between your thighs?"

"Heavens, yes." She moaned when he ground his palm against her center as he pleasured her. "Evans, I—I need—" Her pleas melted on her tongue when he drew back, leaving her empty and desperate for release.

"I have every intention of ravishing you in the way you deserve, madam." Evans freed himself from his trousers and stroked his cock.

Cassandra reached out and touched the head of it, catching a drop of his seed on her fingertip. She lifted it to her lips and licked the salty treat while holding his gaze.

"Fuck me, Evans." She arched a brow in challenge. "Show me exactly what I have been missing."

Without hesitation, Evans pulled her from the desk and spun her around. He wrapped one arm around her waist, holding her skirts in his fist. Then he arched her over the edge of the desk.

"Brace yourself," he whispered in her ear before drawing the lobe between his teeth.

Cassandra placed her elbows on the desk, thrusting her backside in the air. He arranged her skirts until she lay bare to him. He slid his fingers along her folds, parting them. She rocked against the touch, needing more, wanting everything he offered. Warmth unfurled deep in her chest as her breath hitched. Knowing her needs, her desires were at the forefront of his mind left her aching in anticipation. He cherished her, revered her. Every touch a gentle caress, a promise of safety and fulfillment. She craved more.

"Evans—" she pleaded.

His cock nudged her entrance, seeking her heat. Evans entered her slowly, his groan echoing off the walls and mingling with her sharp inhale of pleasure. He fit perfectly, stretching her to a full completion. She squirmed against him, wanting him to move, needing him to give her more.

"Patience, madam." He wrapped his free hand around her throat, drawing her up until her back melded with his torso. He squeezed with a hint of pressure at the base of her throat. With her pinned in place, she could do nothing but submit to him. To his control.

He isn't James, her heart reminded her. "Reuben…"

His grip eased and his hand dropped, fingertips splaying across her heart. "Trust me."

Peace filled her, and Cassandra surrendered.

With slow, deliberate but tentative strokes, he moved, but the momentum built with every caress, every thrust. Cassandra could barely catch her breath at the onslaught of sensations.

He fucked her with the confidence of a man who knew exactly how she liked it. But she knew nothing of what she liked or what she needed. All she knew was this man treasured her—valued her pleasure above all else. He was a man who *loved* her.

The thought alone left her trembling, but she could not dwell on it. Reuben shifted his other hand to settle between her thighs. He teased her, pushing her pleasure higher and higher until she came close to combustion.

Every thrust, every spiral of pressure, left her gasping and panting. Deep inside her, a powder keg came dangerously close to igniting. She ground her hips against him, arching back and withdrawing only to meet the pressure of his hand at the apex of her sex, teasing and stroking with unparalleled skill.

"Evans, I—" She crested, grasping her release as he drove deep again and again, even as she came apart, her body tense and pulsing with pleasure. He continued as though determined to wring every last drop from her willing body.

Evans withdrew quickly, stroking himself until he found his own release coating his hand.

Cassandra glanced at it with a sly smile. She took his hand and lifted it to her lips. Holding his gaze, she licked his fingers clean, savoring the taste of him and the stunned look on his face.

When she relinquished her hold, he pulled her in by the waist and kissed her.

Whatever this was, whatever happened next, Cassandra could not bring herself to worry. Reuben Evans had opened a door that neither of them wanted to close. And she would be damned if she did not thoroughly explore this new delight.

The duchess was pursuing her pleasure, and nothing could deter her from this newfound passion.

FINALLY. THE SINGLE word repeated over and over in his mind. After years of unrequited longing, he had finally claimed her. His duchess. His *dowager* duchess.

As the lust-induced haze slowly dissipated, Reuben's wits returned. Soft tendrils of hair lay against her cheek where they had pulled free from her coiffure. A gentle blush painted her skin in a delightful afterglow. He traced his finger along the curve of her neck down to her still-bared breasts, earning him a satisfied moan.

Cassandra was a goddess. An ethereal creature sent to lure him to sin. And he would gladly follow her into the depths of hell if she bade him. Whatever fascination he'd held for her before had now been solidified into a physical manifestation. He cared deeply for her. He loved her. But such a confession had no place in this moment—not yet, at least.

Reuben cleared his throat and readjusted his clothing. Cassandra frowned as he hid his cock from view.

"Have you finished with me?" she asked, slowly mimicking

his actions and repositioning her own garments.

He regarded her carefully before responding, noting how she easily readjusted her chemise to regain her modesty. Not as though she required it in his presence. He would have her naked at all hours of the day. Such beauty should never be hidden behind yards of muslin and wool.

"Hardly," he replied, keeping his other thoughts firmly hidden away.

"Excellent." She hooked a finger beneath his chin. "Come with me, Evans."

Reuben followed her into the hallway, which was thankfully vacant of servants. The last thing he needed was the house ablaze with gossip. Two steps behind her, he kept pace, up the stairs and into her private chambers.

Inside, Cassandra closed the door behind them and leaned against it. Her lips still bore the mark of their earlier passion. Her eyes darkened with hunger. He traced the curve of her down to the floor and back up, his imagination painting a vivid picture of her wearing nothing but the coy smile upon her full, beautiful lips.

"You have further use of me, madam?" Reuben asked, remaining as still as a marble statue.

"I believe we have moved beyond propriety, Reuben." She sauntered closer. "In this room, we are not mistress and servant. I am merely a woman and you are a man." Her hand came to rest on his chest just over his heart. Her lashes fluttered as she met his gaze. "I want to hear my name on your lips."

"Is that all, Cassandra?" His stance softened at the subtle hitch in her breath.

"No." She slipped his tie from the knot. "I want you to remove your clothes."

"Under one condition," he murmured, leaning closer.

Cassandra pulled the tie free, letting the fabric flutter to the floor. "I am listening."

"Allow me to remove yours first."

Heat flashed in her eyes as she nodded.

With agonizing patience, Reuben reached for her. As he peeled away the layers covering her body, he pressed reverent kisses to her pale skin. The gown pooled at her feet. He methodically unlaced her corset before slipping it free, leaving her in only a chemise, drawers, stockings, and shoes. His hands trailed over her curves as he knelt before her.

When his hand encircled her ankle, she caught her lip between her teeth and stifled a moan. Watching her reaction, he removed one boot then the other. His hands slid along the seam of her stockings, up and up, until they reached the garters tied at her thighs.

Cassandra's breath caught and shifted from measured to erratic. He reveled in the ability to elicit such a reaction from her. As he rolled the stockings down, he caressed the length of each leg, noting the soft skin and trembling heat beneath his touch. Only then did he remove her drawers.

"Reuben," she gasped as he gathered the hem of her chemise and drew it up, slowly rising to his feet.

Once he'd tugged it over her head and tossed it aside, Reuben lost all reasonable thought. His gaze raked over her. Down, then up, and back again. Words failed him. Cassandra was even more beautiful than he could have imagined. From her breasts to the soft swell of her stomach to the delicious bounty of her thighs and the delight he knew lay between them covered in downy hair. He licked his lips and a deep moan escaped him.

Uncertainty flickered in her eyes, but she made no move to cover herself. "I have done my part. Now you uphold your end of the agreement."

"As you wish." Reuben's cock stood at full attention as he removed his jacket and set it aside on a chair.

Cassandra's eyes sparkled with every flick of his wrist loosening the buttons along his waistcoat and then his shirt. He removed each item, placing it with the last. Silently, she watched with fascination as he stripped layer after layer. He toed off his shoes, leaving his trousers for last.

"Wait." Cassandra stopped him when he'd reached for them. "Allow me."

He lifted his hands in surrender, his cock aching from the slow torment.

Confidence infused every touch. She unfastened them with ease and slid them over his hips, allowing her fingertips to brush his cock, still covered by the thin fabric of his undergarments. She sank to her knees before him as he had with her. Once free of the garment as well as his underclothes, he stiffened.

Her hands rested on his hips. Her gaze fixed on his.

"Wha—?" The protest died in his throat as she took him in her mouth. "Fuck." He threaded his fingers through her hair as she took him deeper, sliding her tongue over the head of his cock and suckling. She cupped him, her fingers encircling the base of his cock and squeezing. Every stroke of her delicious mouth sent another wave of sensation through his body.

Pleasure radiated through him, echoing in the back of his mind. The warmth of her mouth pushed it higher and higher. He held her head steady, unhurried but with a building pressure. If she persisted, he would come. Part of him wished to prolong the torment, but he had little patience left. There would be time later.

"Cassandra," he ground out. His grip on her hair tightened when she refused to stop. He hissed when the gentle pressure of her teeth slid along the sensitive head. Finally, she relinquished her control. "As much as I enjoy this, I would much rather explore you."

A pout formed on her succulent lips.

"I promise, you may torment me in all the ways you desire *after* I have had a chance to worship you."

He aided her to her feet and swept her into his arms. Cassandra's surprised yelp echoed through the room. When he placed her on the bed, she sprawled out on the thick counterpane. His hunger intensified as he committed her to memory.

Naked and glowing, like a celestial being, she smiled. "You

wish to worship me?"

"In all ways." Reuben climbed onto the bed, hovering over her. He traced his fingers along the outside of her thigh, up over her hip, across her stomach, brushing a nipple with his thumb.

Cassandra inhaled sharply, her breasts trembling at the movement.

"Saints above, you are the most beautiful woman I have ever seen." He lowered his mouth to her breast, drawing the peak into his mouth.

Her moans filled the air around him like a chorus of pleasure urging him on. He pressed his body closer, savoring the delicious friction of his skin against hers, absorbing her heat, her very essence.

"I have dreamed of this for years," Reuben confessed as he continued to press gentle kisses along her bare torso. His fingertips kneaded the soft flesh of her hips and the swell of her stomach.

"As have I." She arched against him. "Reuben—more."

When he slid his fingers along her sex, her satisfied gasp made him grin. He loved this—her sweat-slickened body desperate for his attention. Her cunt dripped for him.

"Reuben, please—" She grasped his shoulders, pulling him up until they met eye to eye. He recognized the unspoken desire painted on her flushed cheeks and panting breaths.

Settled between her thighs, he teased her entrance with the head of his cock until she'd arched her hips. He slid deep with a single thrust, burying his head in the curve of her neck at the overwhelming pleasure.

Being inside her brought him a sense of completion unlike anything he had ever experienced in his life. He took two deep breaths while remaining perfectly still.

When she grasped his hips and slowly rocked hers, Reuben's restraint snapped. He fucked her, giving her exactly what she demanded. Their bodies melded as a delicious friction built between them. Warmth radiated from inside his chest, threatening to consume him with its intensity.

Whatever he gave her, she returned tenfold. Cassandra was no passive lover. Years of being imprisoned in a loveless marriage seemed to have left her with a burning, insatiable curiosity. He knew only of her limited experiences with her husband and had only assumed she knew nothing beyond it. Had he been wrong?

Cassandra stroked his cheek, bringing him back to the moment. Lost in her heavenly eyes, he knew none of it mattered. The only thing that existed was them bound in this moment of passion and pleasure.

Reuben thrust deeper, shifting his hips to open her wider for him.

Her cry of bliss made his heart soar. He pushed her, harder, faster—imploring her to take all of him as deep as she could.

She grasped the back of his head, pulling him in for an intoxicating kiss. Their tongues danced and the pressure escalated, rising with every thrust.

When he drew back and pressed his thumb to her sensitive pearl, she exploded beneath him. Her nails bit into his arms as she clung to him. Her cunt pulsed around his cock, tipping him over the edge.

Reuben withdrew and spilled across her stomach, admiring the glint of his seed marking her as his. A triumphant smile curved his lips.

"Proud of yourself?" Cassandra asked, her sated grin matching his own.

"I take pride in all I do." Reuben sank onto the bed beside her, propping himself up on an elbow to admire her beauty.

"As you should." She trailed her fingertips over his chest.

He chuckled as he climbed from the bed to retrieve a cloth he'd dampened in a washbasin.

Once he'd cleaned her thoroughly, he rejoined her on the bed. Cassandra curled up beside him, her head on his chest, her thigh thrown over his. He stroked her shoulder as they lay in silence, listening to the gentle crackle of the fire in the hearth.

"Are you hungry?" Reuben asked.

"Starving." Cassandra shifted to look down at him. "Reuben—we should discuss what happens next."

"Between us?" he asked, studying her somber expression.

"Well, yes, but also my son—and the Lord of Devil's Acre." She sighed. "There must be a solution."

"I agree." Reuben cupped her cheek. Her eyes fluttered closed at the caress. "But tonight, let us enjoy this moment. Tomorrow, we shall find a solution."

Hope blossomed in her eyes as she nodded.

"I shall retrieve something for us to eat." Reuben's wicked smile returned. "Then I fully intend to feast upon you until morning."

Cassandra made no protest, but her hand wrapped around his cock, gently squeezing. "This time, I will finish what I began."

"As you wish, You—" He gasped when she tightened her hold. "Cassandra."

"Good man." Cassandra kissed him thoroughly before she relinquished her hold.

Reuben dressed and escaped the room only to retrieve food and return. The servants would ask about it later, but he ignored them.

Tonight was for him and Cassandra. And he would make the most of his borrowed time.

Chapter Eleven

CASSANDRA WOKE ALONE. Disappointment cloaked her in shame until she found the note lying on the nightstand beside her bed.

Went out. Will return soon. ~ Reuben

While it quelled her initial fears, it did nothing for her lingering concerns. Their evening together had been—well, unexpected and amazing. But there were still so many unanswered questions.

Granted, falling into bed together had not been the wisest course, but she could not bring herself to care about the consequences of their dalliance. She enjoyed his company and his attentions. For years, she had poured everything into her son—her husband. Never before had she taken the time for herself. Cassandra deserved to explore the blissful delights of sex without the guilt society placed upon it. If men could indulge freely, why could women not do the same?

With a renewed vigor, Cassandra rose when Sidlow entered her chamber. No signs of Reuben's presence remained in her chamber, but still, she worried what it might look like to her other servants. Taking the butler as a lover was hardly condoned behavior for a dowager duchess. Part of her fretted that the gossip might spread, but she trusted her family's servants, who had been loyal to her through the years.

Cassandra spoke little, feigning a headache. The young woman nodded respectfully and set to work. Once Cassandra was adequately attired, she directed Sidlow to do a simple coiffure with loose pins in a fashionable style. It suited her well enough and showcased her newfound confidence.

"Have you seen Evans?" Cassandra asked.

"He stepped out this morning, Your Grace." Sidlow nodded. "I believe he said he would be back before midday."

"Very well." Cassandra stood. "My shawl, please, and I shall take my luncheon in the study. Thank you."

Once the warm shawl lay tucked against her shoulders, Cassandra dismissed the maid. She glanced at the clock on her mantel. It was nearly eleven. Surely, Reuben would have returned by now? She frowned. How could she possibly know where he'd ventured off to at such an hour?

Shaking her head, Cassandra retreated down to the main floor and took the chair closest to the hearth. One of the housemaids had already ensured that the fire was lit and burning brightly. She smiled when Mrs. Mercer appeared with her meal and a fresh pot of tea.

"Thank you, Mrs. Mercer."

"My pleasure, Your Grace." She placed the tray down on the table. "I was helping Mrs. Johnson in the kitchen after speaking to Evans about the day's schedule." Her brow furrowed. "Then he stepped out, something about an errand that could not wait. He was in quite an odd state this morning. Probably a poor night's sleep."

Cassandra shifted in her seat. "I see."

"No matter." With a smile and a curtsey, Mrs. Mercer left.

Cassandra poured her tea and sat back in her chair, ignoring the delicious sandwiches and scones lining the porcelain dish. The warm brew did wonders for her constitution, but it did nothing to ease her conscience.

She and Reuben had crossed a very delicate boundary. One

not only of class and propriety, but conscience. His presence in her son's home proved to be a complicated arrangement. He'd claimed it had originally been at the behest of the Lord of Devil's Acre, and yet he'd remained—because he cared for her.

A soft tendril of emotion unfurled in her chest at the thought. He had taken rather excellent care of her over the past two years. Even before this complicated mess of physical attraction had tempted her to indulge. Could it be possible that there was something more beneath the heat of passion between them? It would be madness to seek it out.

Then there was still the matter of her son and the outstanding debt with the Lord of Devil's Acre. How could she be expected to convince her son of anything, let alone reveal his father's tarnished legacy? Then there was the matter of Phillip's conversation with Reuben the previous day.

While Phillip was well within his rights as the duke and head of the household, Cassandra had never been more furious with her son. After all she had endured from James, she had hoped his death would have given her a chance to breathe. She should have insisted on taking a smaller home and keeping her own staff. Reuben included.

"I was hoping I would find you here." A familiar voice shook her from her thoughts.

Cassandra glanced up to find Reuben standing in the doorway with a brown box. His dark hair lay damp against his forehead, and his hazel eyes shone with an inner brilliance. The knot in her chest loosened at the sight of his handsome face, and heat flared in her cheeks at the memories of their amorous evening together.

"Am I interrupting?" he asked, stepping closer.

"Not at all." Cassandra gestured to the chair beside her. "Join me."

Reuben closed the door behind him before taking the seat she offered. He placed the box in his lap.

"What is that?" she asked, setting aside her tea.

"A gift." He offered it to her. "By way of an apology."

Cassandra regarded him thoughtfully as she opened the parcel. Inside, she found the stacks of papers and clippings that had gone missing from her husband's desk. A soft gasp escaped her.

"You chose to return them."

"I did." He clasped his hands together, sitting at attention. "They are yours to do with as you see fit."

Cassandra quickly skimmed some of the documents and shook her head. "You found nothing of importance?"

"There are things of great importance here, but I believe they would be better utilized to show your son the extent of his father's legacy. This is not merely about repayment. Once any deal is made with Mr. Oh, there is an understanding reached between both parties. In the duke's case, he will be required to reexamine the conditions of the original agreement Mr. Oh made with his father."

"What do you mean?" Cassandra asked, her voice trembling.

"The details of that agreement are particular to each, and I have not been informed of the specifics within the duke's contract with Mr. Oh." Reuben straightened. "I had hoped these documents would ease the process of revealing the debt he owed, but there is nothing concrete within those documents that will convince him of the severity of his father's actions or the consequences they would have on his son should his father's past come to light."

"How exactly will any of those things convince my son of the legitimacy of this contract? Are you attempting to disgrace his father's memory by threatening blackmail?" Cassandra tampered her frustration with a heavy sigh.

"My purpose lies only in revealing the truth of your husband's masochistic inclinations and ensure your son's proclivities do not match his father's." Reuben's gaze hardened. "Simon agrees."

"You do not think very highly of my son."

"To be quite honest, madam, I do not know him well, but I am inclined to believe the apple did not fall far from the tree." He arched a brow, allowing the implication to settle like a stone in her gut.

"Perhaps we can speak to Phillip without having to ruin his father's reputation and come to an agreement."

"After the conversation I had with him yesterday, I do not think such an agreement will be reached without evidence to support or allay Simon's concerns."

"What concerns would those be?" Cassandra sniffed.

"That your late husband indulged in random acts of violence, including murder, and hid the evidence," Reuben said simply.

"You have made this claim before, and I find it difficult to believe." Cassandra pressed her hand to her chest, mouth agape. "You have no proof of these accusations."

"I saw his temper myself. Saw him raise his hand to those he felt beneath him. I saw what he did to you." Reuben's gaze held hers steadily. "And I saw him kill Hannah."

A gasp tore from her as the air whooshed from her lungs. "You *saw* him kill your sister?" Deep inside her, a whirlwind of fear and panic twisted in her gut. "Are you certain it was him?"

"It was dark and secluded in the alley, but I saw him come out of the gaming hell just after her." The muscle in his jaw clenched as he recalled the memory. "I kept to the shadows as I followed them. By the time I'd caught up with them, she was lying in a pool of blood and he was running in the opposite direction."

Dropping her gaze, Cassandra cursed, knowing he believed it was the truth. Her heart ached, but in her mind, it fit. Had James truly done something so horrific? She inhaled deeply to steady her heartbeat. "I—I am sorry, Reuben. She deserved better—*you* deserved better."

He shook his head, throat working as though unable to speak the words.

Cassandra shifted the conversation back to the matter at hand. "What do you propose?"

"There were several properties mentioned in these documents." He pointed to the box in her lap. "Perhaps it would be wise to investigate those properties."

Cassandra scoffed. "You wish to visit my husband's country estate and his hunting lodge in the Scottish highlands?"

"If I must." Reuben nodded.

"What can you possibly hope to garner from such an excursion?" Cassandra set the box on the small table beside her. "We spent countless summers at the estate in Coventry, and the hunting lodge has not been utilized in more than fifteen years."

"When was the last time you visited the estate in Scotland?" Reuben asked.

The question struck her. Had she *ever* been to the hunting lodge in Scotland? Cassandra blinked twice. Had she ever even been to Scotland?

"I—I have never been."

A slow smile unfurled upon Reuben's tempting lips. "Then perhaps we should remedy that."

"What are you suggesting? We take the next train to Scotland?" Cassandra scoffed.

"Exactly." Reuben reached out and took her hand. "Come with me."

"I cannot just *leave* London on a whim." She hated how her heart fluttered at his touch and the promise in his eyes. "I have standing engagements. Events I must attend. Dinner with my son."

"It will only take a few days at the most." He rubbed his fingers over her knuckles before bringing them to his lips. "I vow it will be a delightful adventure." The delicate press of his mouth against her skin sent a tremor of need racing through her. She ignored the rising desire and instead focused on his suggestion.

"Even so, I cannot travel without Sidlow, and it would arouse even more suspicion if I joined my son's butler for any excursion." Cassandra paused, breathless at his touch. "How do you propose we travel together without raising suspicion?" she asked, her voice husky.

"As husband and wife, of course."

Cassandra laughed aloud. "Surely, you jest."

"I assure you I am quite serious." He grinned. "I do not mean a true marriage. We dress and act the part of a working-class married couple, and no one will be the wiser."

"You have too much faith in this plan." She eyed him with suspicion. "What makes you think it will work?"

"With the proper garments and a touch of theater, no one will suspect a thing." He squeezed her hand. "Most people are far too enraptured by their own lives to pay attention to anything else."

"Your confidence astounds me."

"And your hesitation gives me hope."

"Very well," Cassandra relented, feeling the weight of the undertaking resting on her shoulders. "When do you wish to leave?"

"Tomorrow. I shall purchase tickets for the first train to Inverness." Reuben pressed another kiss to her hand before relinquishing it and standing. "I shall make the necessary arrangements and procure the proper attire."

"I shall send a notice to the caretakers in preparation for our arrival." Cassandra rose, her purpose clear. "I must send a few letters before I depart to ensure there is no concern over my absence."

"A wise idea." Reuben stepped closer, resting his hand on her hip. "Think of this as a grand adventure, Cassandra."

"Difficult to do with such a weighted task hanging over my head." She softened in his embrace as he held her. "But I will make the best of it."

"Excellent, Your Grace." Reuben kissed her, stealing her breath and making her head spin. How could a man over ten years her junior be so damn alluring? She savored the heat of his mouth and the tender caress of his hand at her nape.

A hundred wicked thoughts crossed her mind, but she refused to dwell on them. There was too much at stake. Too many moving parts for her to adequately assess an outcome that suited everyone equally. Reuben seemed convinced he would find something of note. But Cassandra merely wished to find a way to keep Reuben close, despite her son's wishes. If she could uncover the dark secrets her husband had kept, then perhaps she could satisfy all parties involved. She cursed James for placing her in this situation, but without him, she would never have been in a position to meet Reuben and discover her own potential.

This was a very dangerous game they played. But Cassandra held out hope that they would find answers to bring resolution—including a happy ending to her star-crossed love affair. Only time would tell.

REUBEN REMAINED UNCONVINCED of the wisdom of his own plan. He'd merely prolonged the inevitable by persisting in his quest for some form of closure. For years, he knew the duke had a hand in the death of his sister, even though he had no physical evidence. But now, this demand for answers had become more than revenge or justice. He cared for Cassandra deeply and had for years.

In his own hubris, he'd convinced himself to stay—that she *needed* him. Reckless, foolish man. He cursed himself daily, and yet he could not bring himself to leave. Now, it was far too late. They were bound together with a common purpose.

By nightfall, he had purchased the tickets for the morning train to Inverness, secured adequate attire for both of them, and ensured Cassandra would not be missed over the course of their journey. When he retired for the evening, Reuben ensured the household knew nothing of their plans by relaying some simple falsehood about the dowager duchess visiting an ailing distant relative in Warwickshire. The supposed relative's illness required Cassandra to visit without Sidlow, so he gave the maid a week to visit her mother. He volunteered nothing about his own absence, other than his request for some time to take care of his own personal responsibilities.

The hardest part, however, was his decision to remain in his own bedchamber. It physically pained him to refrain from going to her after the servants were abed. He longed for nothing more than the next opportunity to take her in his arms and shower her with amorous attention.

Soon, he vowed to himself when he'd extinguished his lamp.

Morning took far too long to arrive for his liking. He barely slept a wink, his body twisted in a state of nervous terror and excitement. He rose before dawn, ensuring all of their items were safely packed and waiting by the door.

Before the morning sun broke the horizon, Cassandra descended the stairs, radiant in a plain navy wool day dress with a trimmed straw hat. The cream shirtwaist peeked from beneath the dark fabric, protecting the delicate column of her throat. It was simple and modest, but it did nothing to hide her lovely features from curious gazes.

Reuben licked his lips, wanting to tear it open and trace the contours of her body with his tongue. She ruined him for all others. Completely.

"I trust you slept well, madam," he murmured, offering her cloak.

The look she gave in reply spoke volumes to her current state. If one glance could kill, Reuben would cease to breathe. Instead of a response, she slipped the cloak over her shoulders and donned her warmest gloves before exiting the front door.

Reuben chuckled. He knew she disliked rising before nine; this hour was far from anything she was accustomed to. Once they settled on the train, she could rest.

Outside, her son's carriage waited for them. The footmen loaded their trunks as they climbed into the conveyance. He tipped them extra for their silence, including the driver. Once inside, they traveled in silence to the train station.

A thousand thoughts raced through his mind, but at the forefront, he could not help but wonder if this was the correct course of action. Pulling her deeper into his tangled web seemed disingenuous at the very least. But they needed answers—he needed them. If they uncovered them together, then perhaps they could both find peace and purpose.

In a flurry of commotion at the station, they managed to locate their compartment, reserved solely for themselves (a small indulgence on his part for her convenience). When the train finally lurched into motion, Reuben breathed a sigh of relief.

Cassandra leaned her head on his shoulder as they pulled away from the station and into the morning light. Within moments, her soft snores filled the cabin. He smiled. Perhaps it was for the best. She needed rest.

Reuben, however, found no rest in her presence. His body hummed, strung tightly like a coil, ready to release with the slightest provocation. He closed his eyes and breathed deeply, focusing his mind on anything but the woman curled against his side.

He wrapped his arm around her shoulder, drawing her closer and cradling her against his warmth. And thus he remained, still as a statue, set in his task like a loyal hunting hound.

The gentle sway of the train compartment and her relaxed breaths lulled him into a peaceful transfixion. Reuben surrendered to the peaceful embrace of slumber.

He dreamed of Hannah again. His sister lying in that dark alley, blood coating the cobblestones beneath her, spreading like vines into the darkness as the life drained from her. Vacant eyes and a silent scream painted a grim picture. Grief choked him.

A bobby pulled him back, shouting in the distance, the sound muffled in his ears. He whipped around, glaring at the intruder, only to find the alley empty. When he turned back to his sister—the alley was gone. Replaced by fine velvets, Persian carpet, and wooden accents. A familiar place. But his sister was gone.

In her place lay Cassandra. Her perfect lips parted in a final plea as her eyes stared up at him in horror. His heart lurched at the sight of the wound on her throat, the blood spilling in dark rivulets onto the thick carpet beneath her.

A familiar pain stabbed his chest, leaving him breathless and shaking. He pressed his fingers to the wound, only to find his actions compounded her agony—stealing her life even quicker. He choked on a sob and cursed. The last spark of defiance lit her eyes before she slipped into the embrace of death.

It mattered not what he did; there was no salvation. For either of them.

Reuben woke with a start, his breath catching in his chest.

"Are you well?" Cassandra asked, pulling him from the haze of his nightmare.

He glanced at the woman still tucked beneath his arm. His hand trembled as he rested it on her shoulder, drawing her closer. She came willingly and pressed her palm over his racing heart.

"It must have been a horrid dream to leave you in such a state." Cassandra rested her head upon his shoulder.

"Yes." Reuben refused to elaborate. The vivid images were still too fresh in his mind, too vibrant and violent for him to voice aloud. Instead of focusing on the details of his dream, he instead chose to center himself in this moment.

He inhaled deeply and marked her soft, steady breaths. The rhythmic pulse of her heartbeat. The warmth of her skin against his. She was here—alive. Reuben took comfort in that, even though he knew it could have ended much differently if—

No, he refused to think on it another moment.

"Shall I go secure us a table in the dining car?" Reuben asked, turning the subject toward something lighter.

Cassandra sat up, removing her gloves, and his arm slid from her shoulders as she turned toward him. "While I do have quite a hunger, I fear it may not be sated quite so easily."

Reuben stiffened at the gentle caress of her fingertips along his jaw. He wanted her. By the saints, he wanted her desperately. But this was neither the time nor the place for a dalliance. He rested his hand on hers, ceasing her curious torment.

"Would you deny me?" she asked, her voice a husky purr. She slowly removed his gloves.

"I could deny you nothing, Cassandra." He traced his fingers along the inside curve of her wrist before bringing it to his lips.

"Then allow me to indulge." She gasped when he suckled the pulse point into his mouth and grazed his teeth over the soft skin before allowing her sleeve to cover it once more. "Reuben."

When she whispered his name, his restraint evaporated like morning dew in the summer sun.

"Fuck," he muttered before grasping the back of her neck and pulling her in for a heated kiss. Her warmth consumed him. The sweetness of her lips mixed with the desperation only enhanced his desire.

She moaned as he pulled her across his lap, holding her close, cursing the thick skirts twisting around her legs and the narrow confines of the train car. Her fingers threaded through his hair and tightened their hold. He groaned at the delicious pressure.

One hand held her steady while the other slid along the inside of her calf beneath the cursed fabric. He shoved it aside as he trailed his hand higher, searching for the decadent center of her. When he finally reached the slick heat between her thighs, he grinned at her satisfied moan.

"Is this what you wanted?" he asked, teasing her with his questing fingers. "It must be." He nibbled his way along her jaw as her head tipped back. "Your body weeps for me, darling."

Reuben slid two fingers inside her heat, savoring the way she rocked her hips back to take him fully. Her grip on his shoulders tightened as he slowly fucked her with his digits. His thumb made slow, even circles over her delicate nub. Her soft gasps grew into louder and more insistent moans.

"That's it, darling." He murmured against her neck. "Take what you need."

He relished the effect he had on her, urging the desire to spill forth in a wanton display of pure, unbridled lust. She met his thrusts with a continuous roll of her hips. Back and forth, she took what she wanted, and he gave it willingly.

Every whimper, gasp, and moan sounded like a carefully orchestrated symphony to his ears, and he basked in every sweet note. This woman unraveled him.

He quickened his pace, eager to see her sated. Not because he wished to end this delightful moment. His cock ached with want, and he refused to pursue any pleasure of his own until they reached Scotland. Cassandra would be savored with reverence, and he wished to reserve her cries of pleasure for himself when he drove deep inside her.

Cassandra reached her climax in a rush of gasping breaths as she tightened around his fingers. With careful attention, he slowed his pace until he'd ceased completely and withdrew his hand from beneath her skirts.

She leaned back, holding his gaze, and smiled.

Reuben lifted his fingers to his mouth and licked them clean. He smirked at the sharp intake of breath as she watched him savor each digit. The action was meant to torment her, but it left his cock even harder than it had been before.

"I fully intend to finish what we began here once we reach your son's Scottish estate." Reuben savored the look of pure longing that crossed her lovely face before it disappeared into a poignant frown.

"You intend to make me wait that long."

"My intent, madam, is to ensure that we make it to Scotland without arousing suspicion, and I dare say, ravishing you on this train would rouse much more than curiosity." He kissed the base of her throat.

Cassandra shifted in his lap, making his uncomfortable position even more painful. He knew she did it purposefully, even though she brought no attention to it. She stopped a breath from his lips. Their gazes locked.

"I think your suggestion to visit this estate was merely an opportunity to get me out of London and far enough from the ton to avoid creating a scandal." Her lashes fluttered, but the look she wore was not the one of an innocent debutante. Cassandra knew precisely what she wanted—and how she wanted it. Judging from the hunger in her expression, Reuben knew he should be extremely concerned about what her intentions were.

But it only left him more aroused.

"I fear I underestimated you, Cassandra." He cupped her cheek in his hand and stroked his thumb over her lower lip. Her eyes darkened with need at the simple caress.

"Most do." She parted her lips and licked the tip of his thumb. He slid it past her teeth, allowing her tongue to dance across the sensitive tip.

"You will be the death of me, I swear." Reuben claimed her mouth in another punishing kiss.

She melted into him, grasping his lapels and teasing his senses into oblivion.

Reuben drew back knowing if he continued, he would not be able to harness enough restraint to stop. His labored breath matched hers.

"I shall reserve us a table for luncheon." He gently repositioned her on the bench beside him and stood.

Cassandra pouted but quickly tossed her head and gave an elegant shrug. "That sounds delightful."

Reuben knew a dismissal when he heard one, and while he disliked the sudden cool air of indifference she showed, he took it as the opportunity it was. A chance to put distance between them and allow their ardor to dissipate.

Less than a day should be simple enough. Then he remembered they were sharing a train compartment.

What in heaven's name had he been thinking?

Chapter Twelve

CASSANDRA KNEW NOW why she never chose to travel long distances. Even with a reasonably comfortable second-class compartment, the train to Inverness proved tedious and tiresome. But it became even more so when Reuben refused to relent on his decision to remain a respectable distance during the remainder of the trip.

By the time they'd reached the station, Cassandra thought she would lose her mind completely. Had she brought a book—something to occupy her mind during the trip—she would have been able to view Reuben with some semblance of comradery by this point. Instead, she longed to both strangle him and seduce him in equal measures.

The climate in Scotland left her longing for the warm comfort of her son's home in London. An icy chill blew in off the coast, drifting through the highlands and leaving her frozen to the bone. When they'd reached the small estate nestled in the mountains, the driver helped Reuben unload the trunks and returned to the village.

Cassandra whispered a small prayer of thanks. But those thanks vanished the moment they knocked on the door and no one answered.

"Did you not post the letter I wrote telling them of our arrival?" she asked Reuben, eyeing the setting sun dipping below the mountains.

"I did." His frown revealed the state of his frustration to match her own. "Perhaps we arrived before the missive."

"Is it unlocked?" Cassandra rubbed her hands together inside the warm mitt and sidled closer to his broad frame to block the relentless wind.

Reuben tried the handle. "Of course," he replied. Her sigh of relief echoed his own when the door swung open. "After you, madam."

Cassandra slipped into the darkened building, allowing her eyes a moment to adjust to the dim light. The manor looked much like a rustic rural estate on the outside, but the inside boasted all the amenities of a London townhome. This had been her husband's hunting lodge?

She turned, slowly taking in all the details, from the plush carpets beneath her feet to the array of mounted animal heads lining the entryway. It looked more like a gentlemen's club than a hunting haven.

Behind her, Reuben sprang into action. He handed her a lit lantern and set to work illuminating a path to the parlor, where he built a fire within moments. It was not as though no one had maintained the home since her husband's death two years ago. Not a speck of dust littered the wood furnishings or the heavy stone mantel over the hearth. Someone used this place regularly—but she could not imagine who that could possibly be.

Hartland Manor belonged to the Duke of Tolland's estate. Had her husband an arrangement with other lords to use the manor house? There was something off about it. Something she could not understand.

"I shall ready the house," Reuben said before he turned to leave.

"Wait." Cassandra rushed forward, guilt gnawing at her consciousness. "Let me help."

"How would you like to help?" Reuben regarded her with a

curious look. "Can you fetch firewood? Start fires in the bedchambers? Prepare a meal in the kitchen?"

Indignation rose up hot in her cheeks at his barrage of questions. "I—You act as though I were helpless and incapable of performing any tasks for myself."

"Forgive me. I did not mean to imply you were incapable of performing any of these tasks." He paused. "When was the last time you built a fire?"

"Never," Cassandra admitted, her confidence deflating.

"Have you made a bed?"

She pondered the question for a moment and shook her head. "No."

"Prepared a meal?"

"Fine. I see your point." Cassandra crossed her arms over her chest. "But just because I have never done any of those things does not mean I am incapable of learning. It seems those would be valuable skills to possess in such situations."

"They would," Reuben agreed.

Biting back her pride, Cassandra stepped closer. "Then teach me."

Reuben stared at her, amusement and surprise dancing in his eyes. "You wish for me to teach you how to care for yourself?"

"I wish to know how to do so should the occasion arise." She glanced around the room before facing him again. "And I believe there is no time like the present."

"Very well." Reuben took the lantern and held it aloft. "We shall start in the kitchen."

Together, they ventured down the servants' stairs and into the kitchens. Reuben took time instructing her on the proper protocol to build an adequate fire, starting small and adding bit by bit until the flame crackled in the hearth.

"We shall let this area warm while we prepare the bedchambers." Reuben led the way toward the narrow staircase at the back of the kitchen.

"Are we not sharing a room?" Cassandra asked as she followed closely behind him.

He paused at the top of the stairs and turned, his eyes dark, his face illuminated by the flickering lantern light. "You wish to *share* a room?"

Cassandra sighed. "We are lovers, are we not?"

"Yes, but I would never presume I would be welcome in your bed on a more... *permanent* basis."

"Well, then consider this a formal invitation." Cassandra nudged him to continue up the stairs. She caught a glimpse of his smile before he turned away.

Cassandra chose the first bedroom at the top of the stairs. Dark-blue damask fabrics covered the bed and hung in heavy drapes over the windows. The aged wooden floor creaked beneath their feet as they bustled through the room.

The linens were freshly changed, indicating a recent tenant. Cassandra made a note to speak with the couple who managed the estate. There were far too many questions unanswered for her liking.

Reuben allowed her to build the fire, gently instructing her on the process again. A sense of achievement flared to life as the fire burned brighter in the grate. She sat back, admiring her handiwork as the heat unfurled into the room.

"Very good, madam." Reuben offered his hand. "Shall we make something to eat?"

Cassandra took his hand and rose to her feet. He placed his hand on her waist to steady her on the uneven floorboards. A torrent of need consumed her at the innocent touch. She leaned into him, allowing his warmth to sink into her.

Losing herself in his gaze, Cassandra licked her lips. She recognized the flare of hunger in his eyes.

"I—I'm not hungry." Her confession lingered in the air between them, the implication clear.

A lopsided smile appeared on his lips. "If I kiss you, there will be nothing else. No supper. No bath. Nothing." His eyes darkened as he cupped her cheek in his palm. "I will ravage you until you scream with pleasure. The mountains will shudder beneath the force of it."

"And after that?" Cassandra preened under his possessive gaze. She loved it... *craved* it. Reuben's touch—his words—made her come alive.

"After that, I will bathe you in affection. Explore you with my mouth. Devour your pleas and cries. Then I will claim you again and again until you know that you belong to me."

Her heart beat like a thousand horses galloping through an open field. She clung to him tighter.

"Is that what you desire?"

"Yes," Cassandra murmured, threading her fingers through his hair and pulling him down for a ravenous kiss. "God, yes."

His lips covered hers and all thoughts flew from her mind. The heat and scent of him surrounded her in a comforting embrace. She tasted him, delving between his lips and running her tongue over his. He had tormented her on that train. Teased her to the point of combustion. Her grip on him tightened as he lifted her off her feet and carried her to the bed.

There were still too many clothes between them, and she scrabbled to pull her skirts up as he fumbled with his trousers.

"I need you, Reuben." She palmed him through the fabric. "Now."

"Fuck," was all he could manage. The word rasped against her throat as he raked his teeth over her pulse point.

A loud slam echoed in the distance, vibrating through the house and drifting in the open door.

Cassandra stilled beneath Reuben. Their panting breaths froze in unison at the intrusion.

"Hello?" A man's greeting rippled through the halls.

Reuben quickly disentangled himself from her embrace, fixing his trousers and suspenders before turning toward the door. Cassandra scrambled to right herself, tugging her skirts back into place and pressing her hands to her face to cool the heated flush.

"Where are you hiding?" another accented voice joined the

first. A woman."

Cassandra glanced at Reuben. "Perhaps your letter arrived after all."

"Come, let us join them before they seek us out." Reuben gestured for her to lead the way.

With a final breath to calm her racing heart, Cassandra stepped into the hall, determined to convey an air of confidence and poise, even though everything inside her rattled around like a basket of apples in a donkey cart. She rested her hand over her chest. *Breathe.*

At the base of the steps, she found the older couple placing several bags on the table near the door.

"Your Grace." The woman curtsied. "We had not expected you so quickly. Forgive us for not being here upon your arrival."

Her husband bowed. "We were visiting our children in the village when your missive arrived this afternoon." His bushy mustache twitched when he smiled. "The letter must have come on the same train as you."

"All is well. I apologize for arriving so unexpectedly, Mr. and Mrs. Mackenzie." Cassandra fell into a comfortable rhythm quickly.

"Allow me to prepare the bedrooms," Mrs. Mackenzie said with a warm grin.

"No need. I have already taken care of it," Reuben said, finally stepping forward.

"Oh, how wonderful. Thank you." Mrs. Mackenzie bowed her head in respect. "And you are?"

"Reuben Evans, ma'am." He nodded with a smile. "The duke has employed me to serve his mother and I escorted her from London."

"Very well. Lovely to meet you, Mr. Evans." Mrs. Mackenzie grabbed her bag by the door. "I shall set to work on some supper, then."

"Would you like some help?" Cassandra offered on a whim, startled by the thought of being left to her own devices as everyone else worked around her.

"Madam, tha—" The older woman cleared her throat. "That is kind of you to offer, but I can manage it."

Cassandra's countenance fell.

"But if you wish to keep me company, I would not mind a bit of chatter." Mrs. Mackenzie winked. "Come along, then."

Relief filled her. She glanced over her shoulder at Reuben, who watched with an impassive expression. When she smiled, he returned it, and she glimpsed the man beneath the servant's façade.

While Cassandra was upset at their intimate moment being interrupted, she knew he would make it up to her. Her stomach rumbled in protest as they stepped into the kitchen. Perhaps she was hungry for food, after all.

"Well, then." Mrs. Mackenzie patted a stool near the counter, where she set the bags. "Come, sit a while." Her lilting accent drew Cassandra closer.

"Would you care for a dram of whisky?" Mrs. Mackenzie asked with a knowing smile. "Guaranteed to dispel the chill on these cold nights."

"That would be lovely. Thank you."

Mrs. Mackenzie poured a healthy dram into a glass and set it on the counter beside Cassandra, then she poured herself some whisky. "To your health, madam."

Lifting the glass in salute, Cassandra acknowledged the toast and drank deeply. The strong whisky tasted of woodsmoke and cherries. Delicious. It warmed her through, and she sighed.

"Now, tell me true." Mrs. Mackenzie unpacked the bag, laying vegetables on the table with ease as she gave her full attention to Cassandra. "What brings Your Grace to the Scottish Highlands on such short notice?"

"W—*I have some questions about my late husband's estate.*" Cassandra held her ground, noting it would be best to be honest with the kind older woman. "Certain debts have come to light, and I wish to ensure that my son is properly protected."

"Ah, I see." Mrs. Mackenzie nodded. "You've naught to worry about. It has all been managed according to his wishes."

"My late husband?" Cassandra asked, confused.

"No, madam." The older woman beamed. "Your son, the duke. He visited on several occasions over the last year to discuss the care of the house and grounds. Bless me, he is a proper gentleman, and quite unlike his father. God rest his soul."

Cassandra blinked twice before she actually understood. "My son came to Scotland on multiple occasions?"

"Aye, madam. He stayed for a fortnight the first time to ensure the manor was well-maintained and able to be prepared at a moment's notice."

"I see." Cassandra tapped her finger on the edge of her glass, uncertain what this new information could possibly mean. Perhaps she needed to sit with her son and have a deeper conversation in which they both revealed some hidden truths.

"If you don't mind my saying so, madam..." Mrs. Mackenzie leaned closer. "I found it quite surprising that he chose not to sell it. Laird Blackwood offered him a king's ransom for the manor, far above what it was worth."

"Is that so?" Cassandra finished her whisky. It seemed some of the answers she sought were not in Scotland, but in London with her son.

James had kept part of his life shrouded from view, but it seemed her son was also of the same mentality. That gave her pause. Perhaps Mr. Oh and Reuben had been right to worry about Phillip.

Everyone was keeping secrets, and Cassandra was tired of remaining in the dark.

REUBEN CURSED THE unfortunate timing of the Mackenzies' arrival. While he had been surprised to find the manor dark and vacant when they had arrived, he'd relished the idea of having the lodge—and Cassandra—all to himself.

Mr. Mackenzie seemed eager to work, and Reuben volunteered his services in any way that would give him an opportunity to clear the desire simmering in his blood. He followed the older man out into the cold, highland air and retrieved firewood to last through the night. By the time they'd finished, a sheen of sweat slickened his skin, leaving him exhausted and desperate for a bath.

When they hung their coats in the entryway, Mrs. Mackenzie appeared. "Supper is on the table," she said with a smile, wiping her hands on her apron. "Her Grace has requested your presence, Mr. Evans."

"Would you prepare a bath for Her Grace to enjoy after her meal?" Reuben asked with a warm smile.

Mr. and Mrs. Mackenzie nodded and disappeared down the hall.

Reuben sent up a silent prayer of thanks. His stomach protested the lack of sustenance as he proceeded into the dining room.

Cassandra sat at the head of the table with her hands folded in her lap. Her eyes brightened at the sight of him, but she said nothing.

"You have settled in quickly," Reuben said, sitting in the empty chair beside Cassandra.

"Mrs. Mackenzie has been quite accommodating." She picked up her spoon and stirred her soup.

"Is that so?" Reuben inhaled the savory scent of the smoked meat and herbs rising from the steaming bowl before him.

Cassandra nodded before taking a bite.

Reuben tasted the stew and moaned with delight. A hunter's stew made with previously smoked meats and root vegetables. He tore off a piece of the sourdough bread and dunked it in the rich broth, savoring every bite.

"This is quite delicious," Cassandra murmured. "I doubt I could have made anything quite this hearty and flavorful."

"All it takes is practice." Reuben regarded her for a long moment, noting the somber silence that surrounded them. "Is something amiss, Your Grace?"

Her heavy sigh confirmed his suspicion. Something had transpired in his absence.

"Mrs. Mackenzie informed me that my son visited the estate several times this past year," she said thoughtfully. "It is his property now, and he can do with it as he pleases."

"Yet it bothers you that he did not inform you of this?" Reuben deduced.

"It should not, but I cannot help but think that my son is hiding something by not being forthright in his intentions with the hunting lodge." She pushed the stew around the bowl.

"Why do you say that?"

"Mrs. Mackenzie said Phillip was offered a significant sum to purchase this lodge and the land surrounding it." Cassandra's brow furrowed. "The estate possesses no significant importance. It was not part of the original dukedom holdings. James's father purchased it from a desperate laird years ago when Phillip was still a child."

"And His Grace refused to sell it?" Unease twisted in Reuben's gut. "Why? Such a sum could possibly repay the debts owed to Mr. Oh and give the duke an opportunity to invest the money in a more lucrative manner."

"My thoughts exactly." Cassandra took another tentative bite before pushing aside the stew. "I must speak with my son directly. This family has been plagued with far too many secrets and lies for it to continue. If I do not confront him on them, this unease and tension between all of us will persist."

Guilt stabbed him. While he had been honest with Cassandra about nearly everything, there were still a few details he'd omitted. Secrets that haunted him with every breath and could ruin every possibility of happiness—not just for him, but for her. The brazen truth would destroy Cassandra. Such a revelation would be dangerous for them both. Even so, she deserved to know *everything*. But now was not the moment for such a confession.

"Why would Phillip lie?" she asked, her voice cracking. "When I asked him to join me at the country estate for the summer, he told me he was traveling to the Continent. Venice, he told me." She scoffed. "Led astray by a mother's affection. I was a fool."

"You are not a fool." Reuben took her hand and held it firmly in his. "Your son is a man driven by desires and needs. Perhaps he chose not to tell you because he did not wish to upset you."

"That has worked out splendidly." Cassandra scoffed. "He is the duke, and he can do as he pleases. But I am still his *mother*." She frowned, the action marring her lovely face. "I endured far worse than he can imagine. I am stronger than he believes."

"You are the strongest woman I have ever met." Reuben kissed the back of her hand. "Perhaps it is time you told him."

"Tell him what?" Her eyes glistened with unshed tears.

"Everything," he replied, his tone gentle and sympathetic. "You cannot bear the burden of your husband's actions alone. His Grace deserves to know the extent of it. Only then will he understand the debt Simon holds and be able to assume responsibility for it."

"And what if it drives us apart?" she asked in a near whisper. "I cannot bear the thought of losing my son."

"It may be painful to hear, and it may take time for him to process such a startling revelation. But it will work out in the end." The irony of the parallel of his words to his own situation was not lost on him. He bit back the sting of his own conscience, knowing there was always that possibility she would not be as forgiving as he imagined.

"Perhaps you are right." Cassandra rose from her seat. "Perhaps I am overwrought from our journey and need some rest."

Reuben pushed aside his empty bowl and stood. "Is there anything else you require this evening, madam?"

"Are you not joining me?" She closed the gap between them

and brushed her fingers across his jaw. "I was hoping to finish what we had begun earlier."

The husky invitation lingered heavily in the air. Reuben swallowed hard, searching for any reason he might have *not* to indulge her request.

"Do you think that wise, madam?"

"The Mackenzies live in a small cottage on the grounds." She encircled her arm around his neck and leaned into him. The soft press of her curves against his body left him painfully hard. "We have the house to ourselves, Reuben."

"I am at your mercy." He caught her up in his arms and lifted her as a groom would his bride. With steady strides, he vacated the dining room and took to the stairs.

Cassandra's arms tightened around his neck and her breath teased his jaw.

When he reached her bedchamber, he kicked the door closed behind them and lowered her to her feet. She laughed, breathless, and swayed. He steadied her with his hands on her hips.

"I had the Mackenzies prepare a bath for you while we ate."

"That sounds delightful." Cassandra grinned as she reached for the buttons on her shirtwaist. "Will you join me?"

Reuben glanced through the doorway where the copper tub lay tucked out of sight. "I doubt it will fit both of us."

"I believe it will." She licked her lips, teasing the fabric free and exposing the glorious expanse of her bare skin. "There is only one way to find out."

With a growl, Reuben cast off his remaining restraint and tugged at his own garments. Her eyes darkened as he removed each item to mimic her own. Her shirtwaist joined his shirt on the floor, followed by his trousers and her skirts. She quickly loosened her corset, slipping it free until she stood before him wearing only her chemise, drawers, and stockings. Reuben knelt, still wearing his underclothes and slid her feet from her shoes before unclipping the garter belts and rolling the stockings off.

When he stood, she tugged the chemise over her head and let

it flutter like a flag on the wind as it fell to the floor. He admired the generous curves and pert nipples. His mouth watered, wanting nothing more than to sample their delights again.

Cassandra trailed her fingers over his stomach, making his body tense and his cock tent the fabric covering him. Her hand traveled lower, skimming over the hard ridge of his cock, making him suck in a shuddering breath.

He wrapped his hand around her wrist, ceasing her bold exploration. "Continue and I shall be forced to forego the bath and bend you over that bed."

The challenge flickered in her eyes, but she relinquished her hold, stepping back.

Reuben watched her disappear through the adjoining door. Saints preserve him. Her ass swayed in an alluring rhythm with every step. Her mere presence was a siren song that lured him into madness. And he surrendered willingly. He took a deep, steadying breath before following her.

She bent over the copper tub, running her fingers through the hot water scented with dried flowers. He leaned against the wall and waited as he admired her in such a state.

For years, he had desired her. But having her in such a vulnerable state of undress at his mercy left him emboldened. Reuben stripped off his remaining clothes.

He reached for the cloth towels on the shelf beside him and the soap. After placing them on the table beside the tub, he paused behind her. His hands rested on her hips, and her gasp made him grin. With the tub half full, she turned off the water and surrendered to his touch.

"Feel the effect you have on me, madam." He pressed his cock against the soft cleft of her ass. When she moaned, he rocked his hips forward, grinding himself against her as he held her firmly in place. His lips sought the shell of her ear. "You consume my thoughts. My dreams," he whispered. "I dwell in darkness without your light."

Cassandra arched against him, molding her back to his chest.

His hands slid around to her stomach and drifted higher, cupping her breasts in both palms. She filled his hands, spilling over in the best ways. He squeezed and savored the groan of pleasure that broke from her throat.

"Reuben, please—" Her plea died when he lifted her into the tub. He stepped in behind her, sank down, and pulled her on top of him to sit on his lap.

The hot water stung his flesh, but not nearly as much as her body burned him with the intimacy of the moment. She settled back against him, the water dangerously close to overflowing the tub. His palms cradled her breasts again as she leaned her head on his shoulder.

Gently, he teased her nipples with the pads of his thumbs, slowly circling with firm strokes until she squirmed against him. One hand drifted lower, over her stomach, until he cupped her sex in his hand. She gasped, shifting higher, panting with need.

He teased her pussy with his fingers, coaxing and stroking. Sliding deeper with each pass until he felt the slickness of her arousal beneath the water's surface. Her hips rocked against his hand, needing more friction—more pressure—and he obliged her, grinding the heel of his hand against the apex of her sex.

"Pl—Please," she begged as her gasps and moans pierced the air, filling the small room amid the sloshing of water.

Reuben shifted them both, placing her perfectly to take his cock. He slid deep with a single thrust and groaned at the pure bliss of her heat encasing him. She tightened around his cock as she gripped the sides of the tub.

Together, they found a rhythm, moving slowly at first and building momentum as the pleasure increased. Water splashed everywhere, spilling over the sides of the tub, but Reuben was lost in the moment. He wrapped his arms around her waist, thrusting to meet her desperate gyrations. She was close, and he was not far behind.

Reuben's fingers found her sweet center and gave her the pressure she sought. Circling the sensitive nub, he kissed the bare skin of her shoulder, urging her pleasure to the pinnacle.

Cassandra cried out as her climax struck with the force of a lightning bolt. She took him deep, grinding her hips against him and shuddering at the overwhelming sensations.

Reuben felt his own release rushing toward him. He tried to pull free, but she held him firmly beneath him. He growled against her skin as he came buried deep inside her wet heat and his hold tightened around her waist.

They stilled in the warm water as the storm settled around them. He rested his head against her damp skin. Reckless. Stupid. Wonderful.

He sighed. There was no escaping this. Cassandra captivated him. Body, heart, and soul. She knew not the power she wielded. No matter what transpired, he would always love her.

Even if she gave up her status and her place in society to be with him, she would never forgive him once she knew the truth of all he had done in the name of love.

Chapter Thirteen

CASSANDRA ROSE THE following morning with a renewed sense of purpose and determination. She had to admit, waking in Reuben's warm embrace proved even more enjoyable than sex. An immediate sense of calm washed over her in such a protective and intimate moment.

He woke when she placed a tender kiss on his forehead. Then he pulled her down onto the bed and slowly ravished her until she fell apart in his arms. Blissful domesticity. A woman could get used to this unfettered life.

But there was still a host of unanswered questions casting a shadow over her blossoming romance.

Once they'd retrieved new garments from their trunks, they dressed and descended to the main floor. Reuben pulled her into what she had now dubbed the trophy room, as it bore many of the taxidermized remains of the animals her husband had hunted over the years. She shivered at the glass gazes settling on her when she entered the room, convinced someone was watching.

"I abhor this room." Cassandra wrapped her arms around her torso, wishing she had her woolen wrap.

"Why?" he asked. "It is a lovely parlor of death." Reuben chuckled before encircling her with his warmth.

"I shall never understand it." She leaned against him, grateful for his grounding presence.

"Understand what?"

"The desire to hunt something with such majestic beauty, only to stuff it and mount it on the wall." She frowned at the handsome stag hanging over the mantel. "No one will see it. No one cares."

"Some crave the thrill of the hunt. Stalking their prey, securing the killing blow." Reuben stilled behind her, his voice steady and haunting. "These trophies are mementos."

"Well, if I had my say, I would burn the lot. All they do is remind me of a man I wish to forget."

Reuben spun her around to face him. "I would move the heavens and earth to remove the painful scars he left, Cassandra."

"If you did that, I would not be the woman before you." She cupped his cheek in her palm. "I cannot change the past, but I can adapt and grow."

His hand covered hers. "I do not deserve you."

Her heart constricted at his words. Why would he believe such a lie? Because of his birth, her rank, the disparity between them? Before she could formulate the question, he kissed her, and all thoughts fled from her mind.

A discreet cough shook them from the pleasurable interlude. Reuben drew away, facing the intruder and tucking Cassandra behind him to allow her a moment of composure.

"Pardon my intrusion, Your Grace." Mrs. Mackenzie bustled into the room, her eyes diverted and a hint of blush on her cheeks.

"Quite all right, Mrs. Mackenzie." Cassandra rounded her stalwart protector and smiled at the caretaker.

"After our conversation last evening, I got to thinking." Her lilting accent surrounded every word. "Not long after the duke, your son, left, I happened across this key tucked in the late duke's personal effects. I intended to give it to the new duke when he returned, but something tells me it would be best in your care."

Cassandra retrieved the key from Mrs. Mackenzie's open

palm. "What does it open?"

"I have tried every lock in the house, madam." The older woman shrugged. "It remains a mystery. Perhaps you can solve it."

"Thank you, Mrs. Mackenzie." Cassandra made a fist around the key.

"Did you require anything? Tea, perhaps? Or a hearty breakfast?" the caretaker asked, her smile warm and a bit teasing.

"Both would be lovely." Cassandra nodded.

"I shall prepare it directly and place it in the dining room." She paused. "Will Mr. Evans be joining you again?"

"Yes, he will. Thank you."

With a polite curtsy, the caretaker retreated, leaving Cassandra and Reuben alone once more. Cassandra turned to her lover and held the key up to the light. There was nothing special about the plain iron skeleton key. No markings. No indication as to what it unlocked.

"Have you ever seen this before?" Cassandra handed Reuben the key.

He turned it over, inspecting it closely. Brow furrowed, he shook his head. "I have not."

"What could it possibly open?" she asked. "A lockbox? A door?"

Reuben strode to the window, allowing the filtered sunlight to illuminate it. "It looks similar to a door key." He stroked his thumb across the metal. "I did not accompany him on that trip, as I was not yet in his employ. I remember the duke mentioning something about a missing key after he returned from Scotland. But this was when I first took the post as his valet. He never mentioned it again."

"What did he say specifically?" Cassandra asked, her heart pounding with anticipation.

"He was distraught over the absent key to the point of physical violence," Reuben murmured, lost in the memory. "He lashed out and shattered a crystal glass in the fireplace, cursing."

A shiver of unease shook Cassandra at the image that appeared unbidden in her mind of her late husband in a drunken rage looming over her in the darkness, taking what he wanted without—she shook her head, stopping the thought from coalescing into a full vision. Keeping her eyes closed, she took several steadying breaths in an attempt to ground herself.

"Cassandra." Reuben's gentle voice called down the long, dark corridor of her mind. "Cassandra, you're safe. Breathe, love. Breathe."

She opened her eyes to find herself in Reuben's firm embrace. His hand moved in circles over her back, slowly reviving her from the stupor. With a final trembling exhale, she slipped free from the chaotic spiral into madness.

"I—I'm well." Cassandra offered a hesitant smile after meeting his concerned gaze. "Just—lost in a memory."

Reuben cursed beneath his breath. "How can I help?"

"I—I wish I knew." She clung to him, leaning on his strength. Her gaze shifted to the mounted trophies on the wall, sliding over them one by one before dropping to the glass cases along the wall beneath them.

She slowly disentangled herself from Reuben and took a tentative step toward the barrister's bookcase. Inside lay a variety of weapons, knives, pistols, and medieval instruments of mayhem and torture. A macabre hobby, but certainly not uncommon among members of the aristocracy.

Her gaze drifted to the wall behind the case. Leaning closer, she examined the gap between the wall and the bookcase.

"What is it?" Reuben asked, coming alongside her.

"There is a door behind this bookcase." She pointed to the thin seam that nearly blended in with the raised wooden paneling.

Without prompting, Reuben pushed against the bookcase, grunting with effort at the sheer mass of the object. When he managed to shift it out of the way, they stepped back in awe at what they had uncovered.

There was a door built into the wall, carefully hidden with intricate details to hide the seams.

"Reuben, the key." Cassandra extended her hand, and he placed the skeleton key in her palm. Her hand trembled as she placed it in the lock and turned. The mechanism clicked, and the door popped free.

At her sharp inhale, she exchanged a knowing look with Reuben. Part of her longed to open the door and uncover this strange secret, but there was also the possibility that something horrid lay beyond that hidden door. She swallowed her fear, suppressing the desire to abandon her pursuit of the truth.

Reuben retrieved a small lantern and lit it. "Shall I go first?" he asked, as if sensing her hesitation.

"Yes," she whispered, her voice trembling.

Cassandra remained by his side as he pushed open the door and stepped over the threshold. The flicker of lantern light danced over the darkness, slowly revealing the contents of the room.

It was no bigger than a wardrobe, barely fitting the two of them side by side. A wall rose up before them with shelves stretching from the floor to the ceiling, heavily laden with glass jars. The light danced over the glass, revealing liquid inside them with the shifting reflection.

"What in the devil—?" Cassandra leaned closer, examining the contents of a large jar.

Someone stared back at her. A face, eyes wide and vacant, mouth open, twisted in pain, surrounded by thin hair suspended in the viscous liquid. It was a head. A severed human head.

Cassandra screamed.

Reuben wrapped his arms around her, offering the comfort of his shoulder against which she could bury her face. But it was too late. The image was seared into her brain. The horror almost too much to bear.

"Come, you do not need to see this." Reuben steered her toward the sunlit room behind them.

"No." She pushed against his hold. "I need to know."

He relinquished his hold but stood beside her, his hand resting on her waist.

Cassandra took the lantern from his hand and lifted it. Her gaze skimmed the jars. One by one. Noting the contents of each. A head. A hand. An ear. An eye. A finger. A toe. Each contained human remains.

"Wh-What is this?" she asked in horror, even though she knew the answer deep in her soul.

"Trophies."

Her stomach churned and she retreated, pushing past him and racing for the window. She pressed her face against the cool glass, allowing the sunlight to chase away the horror. For once, she was glad she had nothing in her stomach, for she would have spilled it. Her body heaved, and she closed her eyes, willing her heart to calm and the tension in her chest to ease.

When she'd finally managed to regain control, Cassandra pressed her hand to her stomach and turned.

Reuben stood in the center of the room, watching her. He made no move to console her.

"James—he collected those—" She could not bring herself to finish the statement.

Reuben nodded.

"You knew." Cassandra leaned on the chair beside her as the truth took root in her brain. "How long have you known?"

"I suspected," Reuben replied, his expression grim. "I wanted to tell you that night when I found the lockbox. The clippings. But I couldn't. I needed more proof than that. There had to be physical evidence of his violence."

"But how did you know it was James who committed these atrocities?" The question slipped free on a stunned whisper.

"My sister." Reuben's voice trembled with emotion and regret. "When I found her—I saw—" He swallowed hard, the confession choking him. "I saw him take—part of her."

"You—what?" Disbelief and rage flooded her.

"I was terrified. Horrified by what I encountered in that dark alley." His shoulders slumped in defeat. "I remained hidden until he left, but I saw his face—committed it to memory. When the bobbies found me with her body, they asked if I'd seen anything. I lied. I knew no one would believe me, and if they did, they would never bring the justice my sister deserved."

"Reuben." Cassandra's voice cracked as the tears came freely. She took a step toward him, but he held up his hand, determined to maintain a distance between them. Her heart ached for the young man who'd found his sister murdered in cold blood.

"The Lord of Devil's Acre not only took me in and raised me..." Reuben continued. "He believed me and confirmed my worst fears. The Duke of Tolland had done this before, although there had never been any witnesses willing to come forward. Willing to do anything about it.

"When the duke incurred a large debt, the Lord of Devil's Acre seized his opportunity to ensure both justice and an end to the murders." Reuben flexed his hands. "Simon ensured I was chosen as the duke's valet. An insurance policy of sorts to ensure the duke did not step out of line and take another life. Simon told him only that he would be watching and if he refused to comply, he would be forced to reveal the duke's proclivities to Scotland Yard."

Cassandra stared, unblinking at the man before her. It fit. All of it. Reuben's past, his pain, and his presence in their home—in her life. The Bloody Talons were notorious for their uncouth and dangerous behavior. The gang was feared among all who resided in London regardless of rank and title. A thousand questions swarmed her mind like angry bees, but one stood out among the rest.

"Did—" She swallowed past the lump rising in her throat. "Did he order you to kill my husband?"

"No." Reuben held her gaze, but those familiar depths held none of the warmth and kindness she had come to love. A knot of terror wrapped around her heart.

"But you sought your revenge." She whispered, "You killed him."

Reuben's jaw tensed, but he said nothing.

Overwhelmed with grief and horrified by the revelation, Cassandra gripped the chair tighter. Tears flowed, and she let them.

"Reuben—say something," her voice cracked beneath the strain.

He remained silent, keeping his attention fixed on the floor, unable to meet her gaze.

"Say something, damn you!" She lunged toward him, but he remained as still as a marble statue.

Finally, he looked at her, resignation in his eyes. "Forgive me."

Cassandra gasped, reeling as though he struck her. He had *murdered* her husband. Had that been his intent all along? Had he ever truly cared for her or had it all been an act? How could she possibly trust him? He had lied to her—again and again. And even now, he showed no remorse for his actions. Even though she knew her husband had been a heartless cur with no sympathy for anyone, could she love someone who also committed the same crimes even with the best of intentions?

She raced from the room, tears stinging her eyes and blurring her vision. Her sobs broke free, tearing apart her very soul. Rejection and betrayal clawed at her, shredding what remained of her strength.

She loved him, and he had used her, betrayed her.

Swiping at the tears, she stumbled and collided with a solid, warm body. A pair of strong arms encircled her.

"Reuben?" She glanced up, stiffening at the sight of the man holding her. *Phillip*. Relief filled her at the sight of him, quickly replaced by fear of reprisal for being here alone with Reuben. Of her son uncovering the horrors that they had just unearthed in the neighboring room. "Phillip? What are you doing here?" She glanced over her shoulder. Ripley, her son's valet, carried a trunk over his shoulder as he passed by in the hall.

"What happened?" Her son's concerned gaze slowly melted to anger at the sight of her disheveled and emotional state. "Where is he?" he growled.

"Phillip, please, I—" Cassandra sobbed as he set her firmly aside.

"No, Mother, enough." His jaw clenched. "I'm going to kill the bastard."

REUBEN WATCHED THE woman he loved shatter before his eyes. This was not how he'd intended to reveal it. He cursed himself for a heartless cad. Deep inside his chest, his heart twisted to the point of physical pain.

He had been a reckless fool to think he could hide something so volatile and damning. But he was completely naïve to hope there could be any future with Cassandra—even after such a heartbreaking revelation.

Cassandra believed him to be a coldhearted murderer. A man bent on vengeance for his sister's brutal death. But there was more to it than that. So much more. He needed to talk to her. Needed to set things right. She deserved to know the reason why he'd crossed that line. Why he had killed her husband. He could not bear the thought of her believing the worst of him without an opportunity to defend his actions.

With a growl of frustration, Reuben bolted from the room after her. He came to a halt, frozen in place when he spied Cassandra in the arms of another man.

Her son.

"I'm going to kill the bastard." The duke's words rang loud and clear through the hall.

Reuben's blood turned to ice. He held his ground when the duke's gaze met his. Hatred burned in their depths. For years, an unspoken tension had created conflict between them. Reuben had ignored it, avoided it, but there was no way to do so now. Not when fury consumed the duke in such a powerful way.

The duke stepped in front of his mother, blocking her from view. "What have you done to her?" It was more of an accusation than a question.

"I have done nothing." Reuben's voice remained calm, although his hands trembled in fists by his sides and his stomach roiled in protest.

"Lies!" The duke roared, advancing on him. He stopped short, braced for a fight. "I have tolerated your falsehoods for long enough. I warned you in London, and still you persisted by remaining in my service—and absconding to Scotland with my mother."

Reuben bit his tongue to keep from saying something that would escalate the situation even further. One swing at the duke would land him in prison for the rest of his life. But revealing his part in the death of the late duke would earn him a one-way ticket to hell.

"Phillip, enough." Cassandra came alongside him, tugging on his arm. Face ashen and shoulders tense, she turned to glance at Reuben. His heart shattered at the sight of her in such a wounded state. She blinked quickly and turned her attention to her son. "Please, you do not understand."

The duke scoffed, turning to Cassandra. "You believe yourself blameless in this, Mother."

She stumbled back, eyes wide, pressing a hand to her chest. "Wh—What are you implying?"

"Imagine my surprise when I arrived at my London home, only to find it vacated. When I asked the servants, they knew nothing of your true whereabouts, only that *he* had accompanied you." The duke snarled, unable to even say Reuben's name. "You did not take Sidlow as your traveling companion, and I inquired after your alibi, who confirmed your absence. From there, I managed to uncover your destination through simple logic."

"Phillip, I can explain. Ple—"

"Explain what, Mother?" the duke snapped. Cassandra flinched and pulled away, wrapping her arms around her torso. Reuben wanted to punch the insufferable cad. "Would you care to explain how you have been engaged in an illicit affair with the *butler*?" The duke's accusation compounded the pain on Cassandra's face.

Her mouth dropped open, and embarrassment stained her pale cheeks red. "I fail to see how that is any concern of yours."

"You are still a dowager duchess," the duke retaliated. "And are expected to behave like one."

Cassandra straightened, her hands falling to her sides. "So a duke may behave in any way he desires, gambling away his inheritance, whoring his way through London's brothels, taking mistresses and creating scandal without repudiation, but a *widowed former duchess* is expected to be demure in her composure, mindful in her actions, and remain chaste until her final breath?"

By the time she'd finished, Reuben saw the indignant fury rising around her like a shroud of protection. He remained silent. Whatever this had begun as had pivoted to something else entirely.

"Mother—that was not what I meant." The duke's tone softened.

"Then tell me what you meant *exactly*, Phillip." Cassandra rounded on her son. "Because I will not have you disparage myself or Reuben with your vile condescension. I may be a dowager duchess, but I am still a woman with needs and desires. If I choose to take a lover, then I will do so at my own discretion."

"He is not who he claims to be," the duke countered. "You cannot trust him."

"It seems I cannot trust anyone." Her gaze flickered between the men. "Both of you have lied to me."

"I never lied to you, Mother."

"Not with malicious intent, perhaps, but you kept secrets."

She glared at her only child. "Those are just as dangerous as lies, son."

"He has poisoned you against me." The duke pointed at Reuben, who blinked rapidly.

"Enough." Cassandra held her hand up. "I will not tolerate this a moment longer. Whatever cause you have to hate Reuben is your own concern, not mine."

"You traveled to Scotland together without telling a soul." The duke's scowl disappeared as his brows shot up, eyes wide. "Tell me you did not marry this lowborn bastard."

Cassandra gritted her teeth, eyes blazing. "If I choose to marry again, it is no concern of yours if I choose a stableboy or a king. Is that quite clear?"

The duke's brow furrowed, but he nodded once. "Why Scotland?"

"I believe this conversation requires a drink." Cassandra pushed past both men, heading for the parlor opposite the trophy room. "If you have quite finished, Phillip, I would have you join me. Reuben, would you be so kind as to have breakfast diverted to the parlor?"

Stunned by Cassandra's display of strength and resilience, Reuben could only nod in response to her request. Once she'd disappeared into the parlor, the duke spun on him.

"Whatever delusions you harbor about a future with my mother, I suggest you take a long, hard look at your prospects." He seethed. "If you value your life, you will take this opportunity to gather your belongings, vacate the premises, and never return. To *anywhere* my mother resides."

Reuben bristled at the command, but he also acknowledged the thread of truth within his assertion. Even if he desired to remain with Cassandra and managed to heal the wounds he'd inflicted, it would never last. Some things were never meant to be.

"I will leave, but not because you demanded it." Reuben growled, bringing himself eye to eye with His Grace. "But if you hurt her, I will hunt you to the ends of the earth."

"A haughty statement coming from a servant." The duke snorted. "And don't forget, she ran from you in tears—so if anyone should be punished for hurting my mother, it should be you." He sneered. "If you do it again, your punishment will be swift and severe."

Reuben squared his shoulders. "Your ignorance will be your downfall, Your Grace."

"And your foolhardy confidence will be yours." The duke spun away, leaving Reuben standing in the hallway alone.

Nothing remained. He had no reason to stay. His Grace had made his point clear, and Cassandra required time to repair the damage with her son. He only prayed she seized the opportunity to reveal the sinister truth behind her husband's legacy. But that was not his secret to share. He had done his part, and it was time to go.

After retreating to the kitchen, Reuben informed Mrs. Mackenzie of their new guest and the dowager duchess's request. Then he took his leave.

Once he'd gathered his meager belongings, he bundled in his warm overcoat and hat. Voices echoed from the parlor as he passed by. He slipped into the trophy room and beyond the hidden door. Selecting a jar from the grotesque menagerie, he cringed and placed it into the leather traveling bag.

He paused outside the parlor, debating the wisdom of leaving. But ultimately, he knew it was the proper course for everyone involved. Resolved in his decision, Reuben stepped out into the winter air and made his way toward the train station in the village on foot. Melancholy dogged every step, growing deeper with every passing moment she didn't appear. She had every right to want to distance herself from him. He was foolish to believe she would chase after him and beg him to return. But those fleeting hopes of her appearance disappeared by the time he reached the station.

By dark, he was on a train headed directly to London.

Lost in thought, he leaned his face against the cool glass, his gaze unfocused on the passing scenery beyond the train window. The rush of indignant anger and self-preservation faded into a heavy misery that settled deep in his chest weighing him down like a loadstone.

Had he done the right thing? It mattered little now, as it was done.

Once he returned to London, he would visit Simon and deliver the news personally, along with the physical proof required to finally lay his sister's memory to rest. He could only hope that Cassandra followed through on her bargain with Simon.

Even if she failed to do so, Reuben knew Simon's true nature. He would never allow any horror to fall upon an innocent woman. While the Lord of Devil's Acre had a fearsome reputation, he also bore a conscience and a soul. He only meted justice to those who deserved it. Simon would set it right. There was no need for Reuben to worry—or remain.

After he settled his affairs, he would seek a new position. Perhaps in America, where the streets were paved in gold and any man—even a lowborn servant—could make something of himself. Even with the promise of freedom and opportunity, Reuben's heart sank.

All the gold in the world was worthless without her. But he loved her too much to cause her any more pain. It was time to let her go.

Chapter Fourteen

Several Hours Earlier

CASSANDRA'S HANDS TREMBLED. Inside her mind, sense and horror warred in equal measure. Surely, this was a terrible nightmare. Even the knowledge of what that secret room contained left her stomach churning in revulsion.

She paced the length of the parlor, trying to regain control of her thoughts. Emotion ran hot through her blood. Seeing Reuben and Phillip locked in battle had nearly torn her heart in two. How could she choose a side when she knew both were guilty of harboring secrets and betraying her in their own ways?

Phillip's accusations rang in the back of her mind. The fact that he would use his position—his authority—in such a manner left her in anguish. Remnants of James lived in Phillip. Cassandra saw it in his mannerisms and his speech, but she'd never seen it in his actions toward another living creature before now.

"Mother," Phillip began as he entered the room. "Allow me to apologize."

"Apologize for what?" She stiffened.

"I should never have made such an assumption."

"You assumed a lot and made your opinion quite clear." Cassandra arched her brow. "Perhaps you should apologize for each offense independently."

Phillip slouched, looking more like a boy of ten than a duke of twenty-eight years. He sighed. "I apologize for assuming you were having an affair with a servant, for assuming you eloped to Scotland, for assuming you would live the rest of your life in chaste solitude." He met her gaze steadily. "Forgive me."

"I forgave you the moment you said those hurtful words out of spite and without thought." She saw the remorse in his eyes. Relief filled her.

He was *not* his father. But she had coddled him for far too long. He was not only a man, but a duke. It was past time for her to treat him as such.

"But do not make the mistake of thinking I will forget this transpired." She raised her chin and squared her shoulders, holding herself in a maternal and regal manner. "I expect better of you as the Duke of Tolland."

He inclined his head in acknowledgment. "Shall I pour you a drink?"

"Whisky, please."

His brow rose in question, but he said nothing as he moved to the sideboard and poured a drink for both of them. When he'd returned, he handed her the glass.

"Let us begin again," he said, lifting his glass in salute.

She met his toast and took a sip, letting the liquid infuse her with a courage she barely felt.

"Why did you come to Scotland?" Phillip asked.

Cassandra's heavy exhale did nothing to ease the pressure burning inside her chest. The weight of it nearly crushed her. "It is a complicated story."

"I have all the time in the world." Phillip smiled. "Humor me."

"Very well." Cassandra finished the whisky and set the glass aside. A coil of unease and uncertainty tightened around her heart. She detested the horrors she had to reveal, but it was the only way to make him see—to force him to understand. Mustering her courage, she began at the beginning. "Not long ago, I discovered some documents hidden in your father's desk.

Including letters mentioning this specific holding among other more unsettling details. All of which I will share with you upon our return to London."

"Why did you not ask me about the hunting lodge? Perhaps I could have answered your questions without having to travel so far." Phillip leaned against the chair.

"It was not quite so simple." Cassandra pressed forward, knowing the revelation would hurt him and in turn crush her. But it needed to be done. "It seems your father incurred some debts before his death."

"I took care of all his outstanding debts," Phillip said with pride. "And incurred none, I might add."

Cassandra shook her head. "There is one you have not addressed."

Phillip's brow creased with confusion. "With whom?"

"The Lord of Devil's Acre." Cassandra saw the moment of realization strike her son with the swift effectiveness of a bullet.

Phillip collapsed in the chair. "It cannot be true."

"It is." Cassandra sat on the chair opposite. "I have met with him and promised to ensure the debt is paid by the new Duke of Tolland."

His eyes widened and he shot out of the chair, raking his fingers through his hair in obvious panic. "*Mother*! How could you meet with such a man? He is the most notorious crime lord in London. How did you arrange such a meeting?"

"Reuben." Cassandra's simple response left Phillip swearing in multiple languages as he paced the room, his agitation palpable.

"I knew he was not to be trusted!" Phillip spat, pointing to the hallway where they had just been arguing. "That *bastard*."

Cassandra did not elaborate on Reuben's affiliation with the Lord of Devil's Acre or his own debt but instead chose her battles carefully. There would be time enough later to expand on the intricacies of the situation.

"What did he say?" Phillip asked, nostrils flaring.

"He requested a meeting with you after I explained the complexity of the arrangement and ensured that you were willing to acquiesce to his demands."

Phillip scoffed. "What demands?"

"I wager he meant the original terms of the agreement he held with your father." She folded her hands in her lap. "I was not privy to the intimate details of the bargain that was struck, but I was asked to ensure that you would be amenable to meeting with him and willing to negotiate the terms as the new duke."

"And why did you not tell me before now?" Phillip stared at her, jaw slack.

Tears filled her eyes. "I—I hadn't the heart to tell you the truth."

"The truth about what, Mother?"

"Your father was neither a good nor a kind man, Phillip." She hesitated for a moment but persisted, knowing this would give them both healing and closure. "He did horrible things. Wronged so many innocent people." The tears flowed freely.

Phillip knelt before her, taking her hand in his and offering a handkerchief. "He hurt you, didn't he?"

Cassandra nodded, and the dam broke free. She sobbed as the torrential emotions burst free from a lifetime of being hidden beneath the perfect veneer of a duchess and a wife.

"I knew it." Phillip cursed. "I mean, I suspected as much when I came home from school and found fresh bruises marking your arms and neck." He swore again. "I wanted to believe the best of him, but then I heard you both arguing one night and—well, I heard him strike you."

Cassandra gasped, choking on another sob. She had hidden it for so long, thinking her secret had been hers alone, and yet her son had borne the pain of it in his own silence. She rested her hand on his shoulder to offer him some measure of comfort.

"I wanted to kill him."

Phillip's admission rang in her ears and her blood ran cold. She shivered, suppressing the thoughts racing through her mind about Reuben's previous confession.

"I should have told you," Cassandra whispered. "You deserved to know."

"No, Mother, I should have protected you." He smoothed his hand over hers. "You never deserved to be treated in such a horrid manner. No one does."

"I am proud of you, Phillip." She smiled, grasping his hand in hers. "No matter what lies in our past, you can create something good from it."

"I will try."

"There is something else you should know about your father." Cassandra's smile faltered.

"What else could there possibly be?" Phillip asked.

"In the trophy room, you will find a secret door open along the north wall." She swallowed the fear pooling in her gut. "Go. See for yourself."

Phillip slowly rose to his feet and cast a concerned glance over his shoulder. But he gave a determined nod and exited the room.

Cassandra twisted her hands in her skirts. What had she done? This was too much. Phillip should never understand the depths of his father's depravity. Yes, he knew of the abuse. But to see the sick and twisted obsession with death firsthand was truly monstrous.

Minutes passed, but they felt like hours. Cassandra rose, poured herself another drink, and returned to her seat. An inhuman howl of rage echoed through the lodge. She trembled at the sound and wrapped her arms around her, sinking deeper into the chair.

When he returned, she recognized the disbelief and horror painted on his face. He bore the same expression she had earlier that morning.

"Mother, tell me that room is not what I think it is." He pointed in the general direction of the hidden closet. "Tell me this is a farce."

"I am afraid it is not, son." Cassandra rose and went to him. She wrapped her arms around him, holding him close. "I am as horrified as you at this revelation." Her voice dropped to a whisper. "He truly was a monster."

"This—This cannot be true." Phillip slumped against her, hiding his face. "Is it?"

"I fear it is, my darling." She stroked his head.

"When did you realize?" he asked, his voice unsteady.

"When you found me earlier, I had just discovered that room and the truth."

Phillip pulled away. "What of *him*?"

"He knew the truth as well." Cassandra sighed. "Long before the rest of us."

"But—how?"

"His sister, Lord rest her soul," she said softly, "was one of the victims."

Fury replaced grief in his eyes. "He knew, and he said nothing—did nothing."

"What could he do?" Cassandra's heart broke. "Who would believe him?"

"You did." Hatred poured from his lips. "Was this before or after you fucked him?"

"*Phillip!*" Wounded, Cassandra pulled away, putting distance between them. "How dare you ask me such a crass question?"

"So it *is* true." Phillip narrowed his gaze. "You slept with him."

"That has no bearing on the conversation regardless of my answer."

"Oh, but it does, Mother." Phillip cocked his head. "Did he tell you his story of woe *before* he seduced you or after?"

Cassandra gasped, indignation burning in the pit of her stomach.

"He used you, Mother." Phillip regarded her for a long moment. "He is no longer welcome in any of my houses, and if I ever see him again, I will kill him."

"You would never." Cassandra glared at him.

"I will. Mark my words." With that final stab into her already bleeding heart, Phillip left.

Cassandra collapsed into the chair, staring at the fire.

Mrs. Mackenzie entered the room silently, placing a tray on the table. No doubt she had heard the raised voices and understood most, if not all, of the conversation. Fortunately, she left the food and retreated from the room without a word, leaving Cassandra in peace.

Peace. An unfamiliar term.

Cassandra had lived her whole life in fear. In uncertainty. In pain. What was peace? She knew nothing of such a state of existence. But she craved it—with her whole heart.

Phillip had abandoned her, but where was Reuben?

She rose from the chair and wandered the house, searching for any sign of Reuben. But there was none.

Her son's words came to her in a haunting refrain. *"He is no longer welcome in any of my houses."*

Cassandra collapsed on the staircase and sobbed.

Reuben was gone.

UPON HIS RETURN to London, Reuben returned to the ducal mansion only to retrieve his meager belongings. Everything he owned fit neatly into one valise. He encountered none of the other servants, which proved to be a blessing in disguise as he detested farewells. When he left the house, he refused to indulge in one last look at the building where he had spent the last seven years.

As he walked, the cold November air bit his face, but it did not affect him. He was numb. The entirety of the train journey, Reuben had allowed the events of the last several weeks to replay in his mind. He wondered if he could have done things differently. Would it have produced a better outcome? Or was their relationship truly doomed from the beginning?

Cassandra's horror-stricken face had been imprinted on his memory. The duke's bitter, angry threat echoed in his mind. He wished he had pushed harder, fought for her. But the duke's status and fury stood like a mountain in his path hindering any possibility of repairing the damage he had done.

She now knew his darkest secret. He had killed James. If she chose to tell her son, Reuben's life would be forfeit. Her son would have him imprisoned and executed. Would she reveal it?

Reuben cut through St. James's Park. The sun hung low over the city as it sank into early evening. His stomach rumbled, craving something of more substance than a stale loaf of bread. But before he could find lodging and a meal, he needed to see Simon.

By the time he'd reached the front step outside Simon's home on the edge of Devil's Acre in Westminster, the sun had relinquished its hold on the sky, casting the city into haunting darkness. He knocked, fully expecting to meet an irritated and somber Simon.

The butler admitted him with a scowl, gesturing for him to wait in the parlor.

He placed his valise on the floor and the traveling bag beside it. Warming himself by the fire, Reuben carefully considered his precarious position.

"Reuben." Simon's voice pulled him from his thoughts. He turned to find his friend assessing him with an impassive expression. Simon's gaze found the two pieces of luggage, and his brow arched. "A new development?"

"Yes."

Simon crossed to the decanter of whisky and poured two glasses. He handed one to Reuben.

"Has the dowager duchess come to her senses?" Simon asked.

"The duke demanded my immediate resignation."

"I see." Simon took a drink. "Well, then, perhaps you should start at the beginning."

Reuben tossed back the liquor and launched into his tale. He picked up from the last time they had spoken, including a brief description of his blossoming affair with the dowager duchess for context. Simon said nothing as he revealed his confrontations with the duke, followed by the hasty trip to Scotland. The more he spoke, the more somber Simon became. The stunning revelation of the late duke's secret chamber and the contents within garnered a response.

"There were *jars* of human remains?" Simon snarled in distaste.

"Yes." Reuben retrieved his travel bag and pulled the small jar from deep inside. He held it up, allowing the light to filter through the murky contents.

Simon took the container and held it closer to the light. The sediment settled revealing the discolored remains of a human eye as it rotated suspended in the viscous liquid. Hannah's blue eye.

Simon scowled at the contents before a frown replaced it. He set the jar aside and retreated to the fireplace, then rested his hand on the mantel.

"How many?" Simon's question broke the silence.

"At least a hundred."

"And Her Grace's reaction?"

"Horrified." Reuben confirmed. "Then her son arrived."

Simon spun around, his brow furrowed. "He saw it?"

"I assume so." He shrugged. "I was told to leave before I could confirm that Her Grace had revealed the hidden room and its contents to her son."

"The duke asked you to leave?"

"Yes." Reuben cleared his throat. "I was also told in no uncertain terms that my presence was no longer welcome. That if I returned, I would be arrested."

"You uncovered the truth, revealed it to the light, and have found vindication after all these years." Simon regarded him thoughtfully. "But you have not found peace."

"This may have begun as vengeance, but—" Reuben began.

"But you have developed deeper feelings for the dowager."

"I have." Reuben dropped his gaze, almost ashamed by his confession. "Living in that house, seeing how he treated her, and knowing his penchant for inflicting pain and suffering... I had to protect her."

"Does she know the lengths to which you have gone in order to protect her?" Simon inclined his head, no doubt implying his role in the late duke's untimely death.

"She does. But she does not know that I did it for her." Reuben shrugged. "I tried to tell her, but I could not bring myself to rip her heart open any further."

"But she knows of your sister and her husband's role in her death?"

"Yes." Reuben ran his hand over his face. "She must believe I acted out of revenge—not love."

"You love her." A small smile appeared on Simon's lips.

"I do. Heaven help me, but I do." He groaned and paced the room. "I know I should let her go. I need to leave London, go to America. Start a new life." He pulled at his hair. "She deserves better than anything I can offer, and her son loathes me to the point he threatened my life should I return to her. But such a death would be well worth it to kiss her once more."

"I see." Simon stroked his jaw. "It sounds like you have a difficult decision to make."

Reuben hung his head in defeat, knowing whatever decision he made would alter the course of his life.

"I release you from your debt, Reuben. No longer are you bound to me and the Bloody Talons." He rested his hand on Reuben's shoulder. "Whatever choice you make, it will be the path you were meant to follow."

"I—Thank you, Simon." Reuben's voice cracked.

"Take this." Simon reached into his pocket and withdrew a roll of bills. "Use it to take the next steps."

"I cannot accept it." Reuben pushed his hand away. "You have already done so much for me and my brothers."

Simon tucked the money back into his pocket. "If you choose to go to America, I have connections in New York City. They can help you find a position."

"Another gang?" Reuben asked, unwilling to tie himself to another group with illegal activities.

"No. A businessman and friend," Simon assured him.

"Thank you." Reuben extended his hand, and Simon shook it.

"I wish you the best," Simon replied with sincerity.

With the jar in Simon's care and his debt resolved, Reuben took his leave. He hailed a hansom cab and gave the driver directions to Whitechapel.

As the carriage rolled down the streets of London, Reuben allowed his mind to venture into the dark recesses of his mind, where the bloody memories of his sister resided. No longer did the need for vengeance rule his life as they had for years. The truth had been brought to light, and Hannah's soul could finally rest in peace.

Reuben was finally free of his debt and his promise for revenge.

The carriage passed by the familiar row of small, decaying homes filled with poor families with no prospects of hope for a brighter future. He remembered what it was like living in a similar place with his sister and brothers. How they had scraped and begged and slaved just to survive.

Those days were gone. His sister finally at peace. His brothers successful and thriving. They did not need to be drawn into the past with his unexpected arrival, only to bid them farewell forever. No, he could finally let them go.

He paused, absorbed in examining his own life, and found it severely lacking with no direction. A life devoid of love and joy.

Reuben frowned. The time for change had arrived, and the world lay before him like a bag of coin ripe for the taking.

But all he could think of was how much he missed Cassandra.

Regret became his constant companion as he searched for a place to lay his head.

Chapter Fifteen

THE DEEP HUM of the train lulled Cassandra into a trancelike state of being. She felt nothing but the numbness of betrayal and rejection.

Phillip sat across from her in the narrow compartment with his arms crossed and pouted like a petulant child.

They'd left Inverness just after dawn heading directly for London. Not a word had passed between them over that duration of time. Cassandra possessed very little tolerance for her son's poisoned opinions of Reuben and his hereditary stubbornness.

"Are you hungry, Mother?" he asked, finally breaking the silence.

Cassandra gave him a pointed look but said nothing, afraid she might retaliate in a manner most unbecoming of the mother of a duke. Although at this juncture, it hardly mattered, as they were beyond polite manners and pleasantries.

"You cannot ignore me forever." Phillip sighed, slumping in his seat. "I am your son, after all."

"I did not raise my son to behave in such a vile and crass manner," Cassandra replied simply.

"If you expect me to apologize for my behavior, you may find the wait excruciating." Phillip sniffed.

"I cannot believe you cast Reuben out as though he were the

villain of this story." Cassandra scowled at him. Her heart ached at the thought of Reuben killing anyone—even if it was to save her and other innocents.

"He *is* a villain, Mother."

Cassandra bristled at his trite response. "You know nothing of his past—of what he endured."

"Is that so?" Phillip's condescending remark only compounded her fury. "Then perhaps you can enlighten me."

"If I believed you would listen with an open mind and a forgiving heart, I would."

"You think me callous and unfeeling to cast him aside without just cause?" Phillip's gaze narrowed. "I have my reasons for what I did, and I have no need to justify them because you developed an unhealthy relationship with a servant."

"You claim to know so much about his past." Cassandra inclined her head. "Tell me what it was that made him unfit to serve in our house."

"Aside from his obvious infatuation with you since the moment Father brought him into the house as his valet?"

Cassandra gasped. "He was not infatuated with me."

"He was—and still is." Phillip snarled. "We are only four years apart in age, Mother. It does not take a detective to decipher another man's intentions when it is as plain as the nose on my face."

"Evans never indicated any intentions toward me that could be misconstrued. He maintained decency even through mourning." Cassandra felt the heat rise in her cheeks. "If anyone is to blame for crossing that line, it is my own foolish folly that eroded his restraint."

"I have no wish to uncover the precise timeline of your romantic involvement." Phillip raised his hand to stop her from continuing. "But I maintain my statement. He remained in our service for the sole purpose of seducing you."

"Believe what you will," Cassandra relented, unconvinced of the wisdom of trying to explain anything to her son. Perhaps

Reuben had been right—Phillip would never see reason.

"Did he tell you of his childhood in the slums of Whitechapel? Of his sister's employment as a whore?" Phillip persisted in his attempts to tarnish Reuben's character.

"I have been aware of these facts for some time now." Cassandra maintained her composure at her son's obvious surprise. "His parents' deaths created a void that his sister filled with her sacrifice. One I'm not sure many women would be willing to make unless it meant survival."

Phillip pursed his lips in irritation but remained silent.

"She sold her soul to provide for her three younger brothers." Cassandra spoke with reverence out of respect. "And she paid the price with her life."

Phillip bowed his head. "Mother—I—" He stopped talking at her stern expression.

"He happened upon it, you know? His sister's murder in a dark alley in Whitechapel. He saw the violence and froze, unable to intervene. Unable to save her life." Her voice softened, tears filling her eyes. She couldn't say it. Couldn't choke out the words that Phillip's father was the one who had done it. "The bobbies found him with her."

"Sweet merciful God." Phillip rubbed his hand over his mouth and jaw, speechless.

"He survived and found his way, enabling him to care for his younger brothers. But it put him in debt with the Lord of Devil's Acre." She shook her head at the irony. "It seems you share that commonality."

"You knew of his ties to the Bloody Talons?"

"Not until recently, but yes, I did."

"And you allowed him to remain?" Phillip growled. "You allowed a criminal to remain in my home."

"He is not the monster you believe him to be." Cassandra bit out with a honed edge to her words. "Your father was the true monster."

"All you have are some questionable jars filled with—"

"Human remains." Cassandra finished for him. "I also have a witness to your father's reign of horror."

Realization struck him with the force of a physical blow making him reel. "You cannot mean—"

"Reuben Evans witnessed much more than his sister's death. He saw the man responsible."

"No. It's not possible." Phillip shot out of his seat.

"It is true whether you believe me or not." Cassandra folded her hands in her lap. "Your father maintained the illusion of a gentleman and a proper duke. He *hid* the monster within him, but he indulged in its demand to be sated."

Phillip stared at her jaw slack, eyes unblinking.

"Your father was a murderer." Cassandra let her tears flow, hoping this revelation would help heal the gaping wounds between them. "Evans knew the monster he was, and he chose to stay—to provide a small measure of security."

"Why did he remain after Father's death?" Phillip asked.

"I believe you answered that question yourself." Cassandra smiled sadly. "Evans cares deeply for me. As I care for him."

Phillip swore. "Mother, you cannot think this match prudent or proper."

"Love follows no rules or boundaries, son. It simply exists."

"You love him."

"I do." She wiped away her tears with a clean handkerchief. James had been a horrible man, an atrocious husband, and a murderer. He'd deserved to die. Even if Reuben had approached the man with the intent to end his life, Cassandra could not blame him for his actions. Not with so much pain marring his past and clouding his judgment. Reuben's actions had been out of love—for his sister. For her. And she loved him still.

With a sigh, Phillip sat on the bench beside her and took her hand in his, offering a small measure of comfort and understanding.

"Mother, I—I was wrong to act in such a manner. I merely wished to protect you." He lowered his gaze. "I see now how single-minded I was. We were all deceived." He met her gaze once more. "My only wish is to see you happy and safe. After all you have endured, you deserve to make the decisions that directly affect your life."

Cassandra squeezed his hand, feeling the burden of her past and her guilt lift like a cloistering shroud that had been keeping her in a dark, lonely place for so long. "Thank you."

"I may not like Evans, and I still do not approve of your union. But if he is the man you love, who am I to deny you that simple joy?"

"Speaking of unions…" A soft laugh escaped her at the perfect segue he'd provided. "When do you intend to take a wife? You require a suitable bride to step into my role."

"'A suitable bride'?" Phillip blushed, shaking his head.

"Yes," Cassandra said with a wry smile. "I find it hard to believe my son has not found a bride yet. You are nearly thirty. It is time."

"And would you have me ensure her pedigree like a horse or a hound?" Phillip teased.

"No. I would ensure you marry for love. No other reason will suffice." Cassandra spied the glowing heat rising in his cheeks, even though he tried to hide it. "Or have you found someone to take up my mantle already?"

"It is still too soon to tell, Mother." Phillip waved his hand. "But I assure you, when the time is right, I shall secure a proper introduction."

"This is a fairly recent development?"

"Yes, Mother. I cannot say whether it is love, but I do care for her—deeply."

Cassandra's heart gave a swoop of joy. "I am delighted to hear it."

"Do not make plans for the wedding just yet." Phillip laughed.

"I promise, I shall refrain from any such thoughts." Cassandra's eyes widened. "But what of the house? Should you wish to marry, your wife will want me to leave. I would not blame her."

"We will address that should the need arise." He patted her hand. "But if you require a place that better fits your needs and desires, we can begin the search for a more appropriate location. Perhaps something just outside the city, close enough to maintain your social duties, but isolated enough to give you a quiet existence if that is your preference."

Cassandra heard the undercurrent of the words he'd left unspoken. If she chose Evans, this would provide her the perfect opportunity to slowly retreat from a life in the spotlight. A promise of a life of her choosing without judgment.

"Thank you, Phillip." Cassandra leaned close and pressed a kiss to his cheek. She cradled his jaw in her hands as she had so many times when he'd been a little boy. The resemblance to James faded into obscurity, and she saw him in a new light unmarred by the blight of his father's sins. "I love you, my son."

"And I adore you, Mother."

Contentment settled around them. Finally, the broken pieces of the past began to knit together and heal. There would be scars and the occasional pain, but it would serve as a gentle reminder of their growth and the restoration of balance.

By the time they'd reached London, Cassandra bore a new purpose. She needed to find Reuben.

Phillip delivered her safely to the London home on Grosvenor Street, and with a bow, he took his leave.

Inside, Cassandra found no trace of Reuben, as she suspected, and none of the servants knew of his departure. Frustration filled her.

How on earth could she find him?

The Lord of Devil's Acre.

Cassandra sat at her desk and took up her pen. She wrote two letters. One to the Lord of Devil's Acre. And the other to the small band of widows she now considered close companions, calling for a meeting to discuss the upcoming masquerade ball.

It was time to reveal a deeper part of herself. She only hoped that the other ladies would see it for the opportunity it was. While it could very well cost her everything, Cassandra knew like love—friendship was also worth the risk.

THE SUMMONS ARRIVED three days after he'd returned to London and last spoken to Simon. Reuben had found a quiet flat in a respectable neighborhood buried among the working middle class. A place where he could blend in easily without suspicion or question. No one would find him here.

Yet Simon had.

It should not have surprised him. There was no place in London he could hide where the Lord of Devil's Acre could not find him. Even if he should travel to America *without* accepting his friend's help, he knew if Simon wished to contact him, he would.

When he arrived at Simon's home, Reuben was ushered directly into Simon's private study. His friend glanced up from his papers and set aside his pen.

"Thank you for coming." Simon gestured to the chair opposite the desk. "Please, sit."

"I see you kept a close watch on me," Reuben said simply.

"You should know I have an infinite network of reliable informants throughout the city." Simon smirked. "There is not a soul I cannot find should I have the need."

"A momentary lapse on my part," Reuben noted in good humor. "A mistake I will not make again."

"I dare you to *try* to hide. You, of all people, should know such a feat is impossible."

"I was not attempting to hide. I merely required a respite from my past." Reuben regarded his friend. "I have come when summoned. Is there something you require of me?"

"I require nothing of you," Simon said. He reached into the top drawer of his desk and withdrew a letter. "But there is someone who does."

Reuben's brow furrowed in confusion. "What is this?"

"A letter." Simon opened it. "From the dowager duchess."

Every nerve in his body ignited as though electrified at the mention of Cassandra. Reuben sat taller, leaning toward the desk. "She wrote to you?"

"Yes," Simon replied. "Shall I read it?"

He shifted uncomfortably. Was she meeting with him on behalf of her son? Had something happened that required his assistance? His heart ceased beating and an adequate verbal reply choked him. Reuben could only nod as Simon read the missive aloud.

"Dear Sir,

I am writing to formally request your assistance in a matter of extreme urgency.

I have spoken with my son, the Duke of Tolland, and informed him of the previous agreement made between yourself and my late husband. Since I have no knowledge of the intricacies of the debt and the delicate details contained within, I defer to you. I have instructed him to await your summons for a meeting to negotiate a path forward.

But for my true purpose, I will impose upon your kindness and request a personal favor.

Please direct me as to the whereabouts of Mr. Reuben Evans. It is important I speak with him directly concerning a private matter.

You may contact me directly at your discretion. Thank you.

Sincerely,
Cassandra Tolland'"

Reuben sat in stunned silence as the implication of those words took root in his mind. Not only had she spoken to her son about the debt, but she had arranged a meeting between him and Simon. Pride filled him. Her initiative and determination proved her resilience.

The second part of the letter hit him like a punch to the chest. Cassandra was searching for him.

"She wishes to speak with me?"

"It would seem so." Simon handed him the letter.

Reuben read it again and again until the words blurred together. Finally, he raised his head in confusion. The request was simple, straightforward. Anyone reading this could easily dismiss the importance of such a statement, but Reuben knew. And it broke his heart.

He passed the letter back to Simon.

"How shall I respond?" Simon asked, folding the letter and returning it to the desk drawer.

"Tell her you have no knowledge of my whereabouts, as our business has concluded." Reuben's chest ached at the response. He despised lying to her, but there was no helping it. It was for her own benefit that he maintained his distance. Her son's disdain, the crushing burden of society's judgment, not to mention the weight of her knowing his role in her husband's death. He could never put her through such agony. She deserved better than him, and in remaining, he would only increase her heartbreak tenfold.

Simon arched a brow. "If that is how you wish for me to respond, then I will respect your choice." He folded his hands and leaned on the desk. "But I must ask why you make the decision to reject her so adamantly. It's not because…?"

Simon shrugged. "Most men are changed when they take a life. Perhaps they find themselves unworthy of love. Especially when the man they killed is the husband—"

Reuben held up a hand. He had known Simon knew the truth, but there was no reason to discuss the matter further. "It's not that. Considering what that bastard did, I sleep soundly at the knowledge that my actions ended his reign of terror."

"Then why do you reject her?"

"She is a dowager duchess," Reuben replied simply. "I am no one."

Resigned, Simon leaned back in his chair. "Very well. If that is how you feel, I will respond as you requested."

"Thank you." Reuben stood, ignoring the persistent pain in his chest where his heart lay fractured like a broken window. "Is that all?"

"Yes." Simon rose to his feet and extended his hand. Clasping it firmly in his own, Reuben noted when Simon gripped it tighter. "There is always hope for redemption, my friend."

Reuben acknowledged the sentiment, but it did nothing to soothe the regret building inside him like a gathering storm. He relinquished Simon's hand and turned to leave.

Halfway down the hall, a familiar voice stopped him and a shiver of dread snaked down his spine. The Duke of Tolland stood just inside the door, speaking to the butler. The guest's gaze snapped up at Reuben's presence.

"Your Grace." Reuben bowed out of habit, not respect.

"Evans," the man said with evident distaste.

"I shall see if my lord is ready to receive you, Your Grace." Finn bowed and scuttled down the hall behind Reuben.

Reuben clenched his hands into fists as he faced the duke alone. Their previous encounter left him bitter and wounded. Still, he maintained pleasantries.

"I trust you are well, sir," Reuben said.

"I am." The duke's clipped response irritated him.

"And your mother?" Reuben asked, unable to contain his curiosity. "Is she well?"

The duke inhaled sharply, his nostrils flaring, but he quickly resumed a measure of composure, schooling his features into a calm repose. "She is quite well."

"A relief to hear." Reuben bowed once more. "If you will pardon me, sir, I must be on my way."

Eager to be away from the duke, Reuben edged around him, heading for the door. His hand gripped the doorknob when the man's response drew him up short.

"I do not approve," His Grace began, his tone brusque. "My

mother is a dowager duchess. Such an affair could leave her reputation irreparably damaged and my family name tarnished."

Reuben turned to face him. "I believe your family name is already blemished. Thanks to your father."

The pointed barb struck true, and the duke's cheeks turned red. Reuben paused, taking a deep breath and closing his eyes in an attempt to compose himself. When he opened them, the duke's gaze burned into his soul.

"I am not responsible for the sins of my father," the duke snarled. "But I will make damn sure that my mother is adequately protected from this moment on."

"Of that, I have no doubt," Reuben replied, feeling the weight of his vow.

"But..." The duke straightened, his tone leveling to a calm that belied his obvious internal conflict. "If my mother wishes to pursue a relationship outside of her class and status, I will not interfere. Even though society will tear her apart should it come to light, so I do not think I can give my blessing."

"Do you think I have not considered the implications of our relationship?" Reuben asked, his blood heated. "For years, I have struggled in vain to suppress my feelings, to contain my desires. And all of it to ensure her protection. The sacrifices made in her name are well worth the price I have paid in blood, sweat, and tears."

The duke reeled at the vehemence of his statement. "You love her."

"I have always loved her," Reuben snapped. "And I will until my dying breath."

Simon appeared in the distance, his eyes glinting in the dim light, a faint smile on his lips. He nodded once. Without waiting for the duke's response, Reuben retrieved his coat and hat, turned, and opened the door.

Out in the street, Reuben allowed himself to breathe. The cold November air stung his cheeks as he pulled on his coat and hat, bundling up tight against the winter chill.

He stalked toward Westminster Cathedral and around the corner until he'd reached the Thames. Staring out over the river, Reuben cursed himself for a fool.

In a pique of passion, he had tipped his hand in revealing his true feelings for Cassandra. Society would never sanction their relationship. This was no fairy tale. No happily ever after.

Broken and searching for connection, they had found each other, united by a common traumatic past. But they were from different worlds. Nothing could change that. Not to mention his role in her husband's death.

Cassandra Sterling, Dowager Duchess of Tolland, was the love of his life, but she was a star gleaming in the skies, far out of reach.

He hung his head and followed the path leading to the nearest pub. Perhaps a hearty meal and a pint would clear his head. But he doubted it.

There was no enjoyment in any of it. Not when his heart lay shattered on the cobblestones of Westminster.

Chapter Sixteen

WHEN HER THREE guests arrived, Cassandra stood to receive them. Her heart gave a nervous flutter, and her hands twitched. She folded them before her and smiled as Mrs. Mercer admitted the ladies into the parlor.

"Welcome to my home, Lady Winstead, Lady Amesbury, Lady Corby." Cassandra gestured with grace to the small sitting area already prepared with tea and a variety of pastries. "Please, make yourselves comfortable."

"Your Grace, thank you for your gracious invitation," Lady Corby said, leading the trio.

"Yes, what a lovely surprise, Your Grace." Lady Amesbury followed with a curtsey.

"So unexpected, Your Grace," Lady Winstead added with a kind smile before spying the desserts. "Are those macarons? Delicious."

"I appreciate you all coming on such short notice." Cassandra resumed her seat as the other ladies selected their own. "Tea?"

All three nodded in unison.

Cassandra poured the tea, playing the part of gracious host and dutiful dowager. But inside, her conscience warred with itself. *Patience*, she murmured internally.

As the ladies accepted their tea, they complimented her on

the ornamentation of the room and her silk gown. The typical, banal conversation Cassandra had been exposed to her whole life. Nothing of substance or interest, merely the casual inane dialog of the wealthy aristocracy. She longed for something more—something deeper.

She longed for true friendship. But could these women provide it?

The conversation shifted into an animated discussion about the upcoming masquerade ball in support of the girls' school. Lady Winstead and Lady Amesbury had already received their costumes, and Lady Corby was meeting with her seamstress that afternoon to finalize the details of her gown. All eyes turned to Cassandra as the conversation shifted to her.

"Have you selected your costume, madam?" Lady Corby asked, her gaze settling on Cassandra.

"Unfortunately, I have been quite occupied with some other matters and have not had the opportunity to even contemplate it." Cassandra smoothed her hand over her bodice. "I am sure I will procure something suitable in time for the event."

"It is a week hence!" Lady Winstead cried in shock.

"You must allow us to help you," Lady Amesbury added with a solemn nod. "We will ensure you are the belle of the ball."

Cassandra scoffed. "I am hardly a belle, and I do not require anything lavish. Surely, a simple domino mask will suffice with my gown."

"It will not do." Lady Corby shook her head. "You are the mother of a duke and as such are held in high regard. Guests will be clamoring for a glimpse of you as one of the hostesses of the event. The four of us will be at the center of it all, welcoming patrons and stirring interest in our charity. You *must* make your presence known, and the best way to do it is through your costume."

The other two ladies nodded in fervent agreement.

"Please, allow us to help you," Lady Winstead pleaded.

"I do not wish to impose," Cassandra slowly relented as a

warm glow of acceptance filled her.

"It is no imposition," Lady Amesbury said with unbridled excitement. "We would adore the opportunity to be of service."

"Very well," Cassandra said with a mild wave of relief. She had completely forgotten about procuring a costume for the event.

"Perfect." Lady Corby clapped her hands. "You can join me at the seamstress's tomorrow morning. The three of us will be there to offer support and advice. You will be the talk of the ton."

Cassandra's eyes widened at the thought of being the center of any scrutiny, especially after the revelations of the past few weeks. "I—I do not wish to steal the focus of the evening's events from its true purpose."

"It is merely a figure of speech, madam," Lady Amesbury assured her.

"Oh—yes, of course." Cassandra waved her hand in dismissal.

The conversation shifted from planning their costumes to scheduling their meeting the following morning before flowing into an easy discussion about their plans for the upcoming holiday. Christmas was approaching quickly, and it seemed they all had plans in some form or fashion. Cassandra sat quietly, enjoying the companionship but unsure of whether or not to add anything for fear of dampening their spirits with her melancholy.

"Is your butler well, madam?" Lady Corby set aside her tea. "I noticed his absence when we arrived earlier." She smiled kindly. "Such a handsome young man."

"Ah, yes." Cassandra cleared her throat, scrambling for some excuse. "Well, Evans is no longer under my son's employment."

The trio gasped, exchanging surprised glances.

"Oh, dear," Lady Corby said with a frown. "I am sorry to hear that. Such trustworthy help is so difficult to find."

"Yes, he will be sorely missed." Cassandra toyed with the hem of her sleeve, unable to meet their curious gazes.

"Madam, forgive me if this is indelicate, but I feel I must ask." Lady Corby's gentle voice broke the silence. "What caused his sudden departure?"

Cassandra could no longer bear the weight of it. Her carefully crafted façade crumbled. Tears flowed freely. She tried to stem them behind a handkerchief, but to no avail. The dam had been breached.

"I—I made a horrid mistake."

Lady Corby exchanged a solemn, knowing look with the Ladies Amesbury and Winstead.

"There, there, madam." Lady Corby came alongside her, offering another handkerchief. "We understand your reluctance to speak upon it, but we can assure you of our discretion. You are among friends. Nothing we speak of will leave this room. You have my word."

"No one should be left to suffer in silence," Lady Amesbury added. "We have all had our share of scandal. There are many things we hold deep inside, unable to reveal, whether it be for the sake of propriety or loyalty."

"Or shame," Lady Winstead contributed.

"I detest social engagements." Lady Amesbury straightened. "I would much rather retire to the country and spend my time with my horses."

The revelation left Cassandra stunned. The lovely dowager countess had always brought such life to all the social engagements she'd attended.

"I want to open my own pastry shop," Lady Winstead confessed with a blush.

"I could spend every day in the garden among my flowers." Lady Corby sighed, closing her eyes, as if imagining herself among the peonies and roses. "My children scold me constantly for my obsession."

Cassandra sniffled, her tears ceasing, but the revelations, the little glimpses behind each of their lives, gave her hope. Still, none of them harbored a desire quite like hers, and it left her conscientious.

"All of those are wonderful things that should never make

you feel shame." Cassandra regarded each lady in turn, admiring their courage to share such vulnerable parts of themselves. "But I fear my mistake is not as innocent and well-intentioned."

"Perhaps not, but it is a part of yourself you do not feel you can share with anyone." Lady Corby gestured to the other two ladies as well as herself. "We will listen, without judgment. Sometimes we must speak it aloud in order to find a solution."

"I fear there is no solution to this predicament." Cassandra inhaled deeply, suppressing her growing concern. What if this was a trick? A way to manipulate her? She shook her head. "You all led wonderful lives with happy marriages. I cannot burden you with my sorrowful tale."

"I married a childhood friend to escape an arranged union." Lady Amesbury spoke softly. "There was no joy in our marriage. Only a simple arrangement."

Cassandra stared at her, stunned.

"My marriage was a farce. We shared a home but never a bed. He loved food and drink more than he cared for me." Lady Winstead murmured, her confession startling. "This is why we never conceived an heir."

Disbelief filled Cassandra. These women were the shining stars of the aristocracy who had used their titles and privilege in positive ways. Yet they'd harbored the secrets of their loveless marriages for years. Cassandra could only blink, her mind caught up in their confessions.

"I devoted myself to my husband. I loved him and he loved me." Lady Corby twisted her hands together. "When I lost him so soon into our marriage, I vowed I would never love another as I loved him. I miss him desperately."

"There is no shame in that," Cassandra offered in comfort.

"No. I was fortunate to have him for the time I did. He gave me four wonderful children." Her eyes clouded with pain and sorrow. "When he died, part of me died with him. I was never the same. I poured my heart and soul into my children, but now they are grown—and I know nothing of who *I* am, aside from a still-grieving widow and a dowager viscountess."

The other ladies nodded in sympathy, and Cassandra agreed. Each of them had shared an intimate part of themselves, a part no one else saw. They'd shown their humanity beneath their title. The truth behind the silken veneer of the ton.

Cassandra's heart softened as they welcomed her into their confidences. They were her friends, her allies, and she knew in that moment, she could trust them.

"My husband indulged in prostitutes, gambling, and vices too horrid to mention." Cassandra took a deep breath. "He abused me. For years, he took his anger out on me, while hiding it from the world and our son. When he died, he left me broken and indebted."

The ladies surrounding her gasped, offering their words of outrage. When they fell silent, Cassandra continued. "But through it all, Evans remained a steadfast fixture. After my husband's death, he remained in my family's service.

"At first, I denied myself the ability to feel anything for him." She sighed. "I never thought I would find love or experience passion. These were foreign to me."

The Ladies Amesbury and Winstead nodded in evident understanding. Lady Corby took Cassandra's hand and squeezed gently, showing her solidarity.

"But—slowly, the desire consumed us until we conceded." Heat rose in her cheeks. "I love him."

"What happened?" Lady Amesbury asked, her voice tinged with sadness.

"My son." Cassandra cleared her throat, attempting to find the right words. "He discovered us and cast Reuben out of the house."

Indignation rose around her. Lady Amesbury glowered. Lady Winstead protested with a blustery huff. Lady Corby's brow furrowed and her mouth pulled into a tight frown.

"He was well within his right to terminate Reuben's employment." Cassandra defended her son, even though she was still hurt by his actions and his incorrect assertions.

"Yes, he is the duke, after all." Lady Corby nodded. "But have you explained things to him as you have to us?"

"I have." Cassandra's tears began anew. "He knows everything." She remembered the look of disbelief on his face when she'd told him that she loved Reuben. Her heart and her composure shattered. "But Reuben is gone."

"What would you do to have him return?" Lady Corby asked plainly, as if it were the most obvious question in the world.

"Anything." Cassandra nodded, sight blurred by tears.

"Such a path will not be easy or free of scandal," Lady Corby murmured. "But you were blessed with a chance to discover love, and that is worth the risk. Do you not agree, ladies?"

"Oh, yes." Lady Amesbury brightened.

"Absolutely." Lady Winstead grinned. "Tell us how we can be of help."

Cassandra nearly choked with relief. She swiped the tears from her eyes and met the supportive expressions of three loyal friends. "How did I get so fortunate?"

"You are not alone." Lady Corby beamed. "Such a burden was not meant to be borne by yourself. We must support each other in all ways. It is the only path to survive such a harrowing, but rewarding journey. To ensure a life worth living."

"How can I ever thank you, Lady Corby?" Cassandra asked, her soul elevated.

"First, you can address me as 'Hyacinth.'" She winked and pointed to Lady Amesbury. "Eleanor." And then to Lady Winstead. "Victoria."

"I believe we have breached the bounds of etiquette." Hyacinth chuckled. "You are now an official member of the Mayfair Widows."

"Thank you, sincerely. And you must call me 'Cassandra.'" The heavy weight upon her heart lifted, and Cassandra could breathe again.

"Now, what is to be done about the missing butler?" Hyacinth asked, tapping her chin.

"Well," Cassandra interjected, "I have already made an inquiry with someone who may know." She revealed his association with the Lord of Devil's Acre and the questions began again with fervor.

Cassandra revealed everything except for her husband's role in Reuben's sister's death, his penchant for murder, and Reuben's subsequential role in her husband's demise. But those details were inconsequential to the conversation at hand. She had no intention of revealing the latter to another living soul.

The ladies remained for another hour discussing all the possibilities and avenues with which they could help locate Reuben Evans. By the time they'd left, Cassandra was confident in her decision to entrust this burden to another.

They would find Reuben, and Cassandra could rest knowing she no longer had to bear the burden of her past in silence.

Finally, she was free.

DARKNESS SETTLED AROUND the small tavern beside the Thames, but Reuben had reached the point where time meant nothing. He gazed deep into the pint clutched in his hand, lost in the frothy liquid. Was this his fifth or sixth? To be honest, he had lost count. Not that it mattered. It was not as if his presence were required anywhere in any form.

He could do whatever he damn well pleased now, except for that which he wanted to do most.

Reuben took another mouthful and swallowed the bitter brew. There was no use in ruminating over something over which he had no control. He had made his decision and therefore had crossed the threshold of no return.

Lifting his gaze, Reuben steadied himself against the bar as the room swayed, hazing in and out of focus. Perhaps he was drunker than he'd realized. With a wave of his hand, he beckoned the barkeep closer, requesting a hearty stew with some bread to soak up the alcohol seeping into his body at an ungodly pace.

With a nod, the barkeep shuffled off, leaving Reuben alone in his corner of the dingy, poorly lit tavern. Reuben cradled the tankard in his hand and groaned.

Perhaps it would be better if he left England completely. America seemed bursting with opportunity, giving him a wider range of possibility when it came to making something of himself. But that would mean leaving everything he had ever known behind. His family. His friends. His connections.

His heart.

Reuben swore, downing the rest of the liquid in a single gulp.

He should leave, especially before he did something seriously idiotic in his inebriated state. Like go to her. That would be foolish. Even more so if he happened upon the duke in the process. He would be in shackles and tossed in the darkest, dankest cell in Scotland Yard before he could protest.

The chair beside him creaked as it dragged across the floor and a man plopped into it. Reuben ignored him, not wanting to engage in any niceties with strangers when he was in no mood to converse. He wanted only to drown himself in his misery and copious amounts of ale before retreating home to collapse in his bed and sleep—perhaps indefinitely. He cradled his empty tankard closer and hid his face.

"This is how you choose to squander your time?" the man asked.

Reuben bristled at the familiar voice and glared at the intruder. The Duke of Tolland's profile highlighted by the poor light left the sharp angles of his face cast in nefarious shadows.

"What the fuck do you want, *Your Grashe*?" Reuben slurred. "Have you come to twist the knife a little deeper?"

The duke sighed, and the sound left Reuben unsettled. "I have come to talk."

"'Talk'? About what?" He scoffed. "I believe you made your

sentiments quite clear upon our last meeting."

"I—" The duke shifted in his seat, seemingly uncomfortable at the situation or the thoughts in his head. "That is precisely what I wish to discuss. Perhaps I was a bit—*hasty* in my decision."

Reuben blinked twice, wondering if this was a drunken hallucination or if he had passed out and was dreaming. Either way, it could not possibly be real. He reached out and pushed his finger against the duke's shoulder.

The duke stared at him brow raised. "I assure you I am not a figment of your imagination."

"Are you apologizing to me?" Reuben narrowed his gaze. "Sir?"

"In a manner, yes." His Grace summoned the barkeep and ordered a pint.

When they were alone once more, the duke turned to Reuben. "I was wrong to misjudge you for your complicated past." He sighed. "I commend you for your strength and fortitude. Caring for siblings in such dire circumstances must be—terrifying and exhausting."

"An understatement." Reuben grumbled. "But thank you."

"My mother explained everything. Your unfortunate childhood. Your sister's death. Your bargain with the Lord of Devil's Acre." The duke paused as the barkeep approached. He took the proffered tankard and nodded to the barkeep, who was already retreating. "I was wrong to judge you so harshly after all you have endured."

"You had your reasons for reacting in such a protective manner." Reuben's heart broke at the thought of Cassandra defending him. He could not help but wonder if this meant Cassandra had kept his role in the duke's death a secret. "If it were my mother or sister, I would have done the same."

"I cannot retract my harsh words or my actions."

"I appreciate the acknowledgment, but it does not change our situation." Reuben straightened. "Regardless, I fully intend to respect your wishes."

"My 'wishes'?" the duke asked, inclining his head.

"Yes, you were merely trying to protect her, as was I." Reuben shrugged. "It is best for everyone if I walk away with what remains of my dignity. I intend to leave London—perhaps for America."

"So far?" The duke regarded him for a long moment. "That seems a bit drastic."

"Her Grace deserves to live her life as she sees fit, free to do as she pleases." He hung his head. "The best thing I can do is leave the country. I dare not remain. The pain is too great and I would never forgive myself if I inadvertently encountered her on the street and tore open such a wound."

"No matter where you go, you will always be a part of her." The duke took a drink as the words seeped into Reuben's alcohol-addled mind.

"What do you mean?" he finally asked.

"I have never seen my mother glow when she speaks of anything—or anyone—like she does when your name arises." The duke's gaze narrowed. "I may not be fond of how your relationship came to pass, or the recent revelations. However—" He sucked in a breath.

Reuben's bruised and battered heart ceased beating in anticipation.

"I am willing to overlook the indiscretion and insubordination if you vow, here and now, to do what is right." The duke's gaze hardened as he held Reuben's.

"What are you saying?" Reuben asked, his voice hoarse.

"You love her," the duke replied simply, as if the implication were obvious. "Therefore, continue to love her unconditionally. Protect her with your life." He scowled. "If you fail to do either of those things, I will kill you myself. Mark my words."

Hope unfurled in Reuben's chest, consuming him like the heat of a summer sunrise spreading across the land. But uncertainty clung to him like the deepest shadows, casting doubt on this wonderful gift. He squinted as the possibilities rolled through his mind.

What if it goes to hell? a small, persistent voice inside his head screamed. *Ahh, but what if it doesn't?* another equally desperate voice added from somewhere in the depths of his soul.

The barkeep returned with a bowl of beef and barley stew accompanied by a thick slice of fresh bread. He placed it in front of Reuben and removed the now-empty tankard from his grip.

Stunned, Reuben could only stare at the food, absorbing nothing but the implication of this tentative truce the duke had placed before him. More tempting than anything he had ever encountered in his life. The possibilities took flight, but fear kept his feet firmly grounded.

The duke placed several coins on the bar, and the barkeep took them without a word.

"What prompted this change of heart?" Reuben asked, unraveling the duke's purpose behind such an act of kindness and sympathy. "Did Simon see fit to forgive your father's debts?"

"What transpired between the Lord of Devil's Acre and myself is none of your concern. He has also sworn himself to that, so don't bother asking him."

"I would never." Reuben held up both hands. "If you have found a solution, then that is all that matters."

The duke eyed him warily. "Consider the matter settled."

"So...if not that, then what has changed?"

"I—" The man hung his head, but Reuben caught sight of the blush high on his cheeks. "I have, as of late, found myself in a situation quite similar." He exhaled heavily. "It has created a cause for deep contemplation of what I truly desire and if the risks are worth the reward."

"I see." Reuben could not help but smile. Perhaps they were not as dissimilar as he'd believed. "A woman."

"A woman." The duke groaned, raking his fingers through his hair. He straightened, composing himself quickly before glancing at Reuben. "But this conversation is not about me and my complicated courtship."

"Perhaps not, but sometimes it is best to discuss it with someone to best find a solution."

The duke eyed him warily. "We have just struck an accord of peace. Do not mistake it for a friendly invitation to meddle in my affairs."

"I would never be so presumptuous," Reuben replied. "But—should you ever find yourself in need…"

"I shall take it under consideration," the duke said, slowly rising from his chair. "But the question remains: do you still desire to pursue my mother's heart?"

Memories of Cassandra swarmed his mind, momentarily leaving him stunned and speechless. *I will always love you*, the entirety of his body screamed. But no sound emerged from his lips. As he stood paralyzed by a flood of emotion, the other man seemed to take his silence for indecision.

"I do not expect an answer." The duke took a card from his pocket and held it out between two fingers. "You have one week to decide which path you choose to take."

"What is this?" Reuben took the card, unable to read it properly.

"The name of my tailor. He is at your disposal."

Reuben's brow furrowed in confusion. "Why in the devil would I need your tailor?"

"To obtain suitable attire for the masquerade ball my mother and her friends are hosting next Saturday." The duke presented a sealed envelope. "You will need this."

"One week from today." Slowly, the pieces clicked into place like a gear sliding home and falling into synchronization. "One week to make my decision," he muttered to himself. "A grand gesture." He returned his questioning gaze to the duke, who merely shook his head.

"Perhaps you should sober up." The duke stood, donning his hat and coat. "Ale dulls your wits, and I much prefer you as sharp as a cutlass blade." He smirked. "A more worthy opponent for verbal sparring."

"I—" Reuben swallowed the emotion threatening to choke him. "Thank you, sir."

"Phillip," he replied. "We are beyond propriety at this point." He extended his hand.

Reuben took it firmly in his and shook. "Thank you, Phillip."

"Reuben." When they broke apart, Phillip gave him a lopsided smirk. "Until Saturday." He tipped his head and turned to make a hasty retreat, leaving Reuben to stare after him.

It took several long moments for his wits to return. Only then did he devour his meal and abandon his lonely post at the bar. Out in the biting cold, he wrapped himself deeper in his coat and ventured toward home, his hand clenched around the card in his pocket.

He needed sleep, for there was much to be done and only a week in which to accomplish it.

Chapter Seventeen

Cassandra surveyed the packed ballroom, a small grin tugging at her lips. An absolute crush. Every prominent house in London society was in attendance, their purses loose and willing. They had already surpassed their financial goals and were well on their way to providing enough funds to expand the school come the new year.

Their Sinners and Saints Masquerade was the talk of the ton. The event of the winter. Pride suffused her knowing her contribution led to a rousing success.

Standing on the elevated dais surrounded by the Ladies Winstead, Amesbury, and Corby, Cassandra watched the festivities progress. The four hostesses greeted their guests upon their arrival and mingled with the crowd briefly, but they retreated to their dais, content with their own company as the night wore on.

Evergreen garland crisscrossed the ceiling. Silver tinsel dangled from the deep-green boughs, like melting ice. Red and gold bows added a burst of color to the forest canopy overhead. Red velvet ribbon decked the walls. Holly and mistletoe hung from the arched doorways. Whorls of fluffy cotton wove beneath the refreshment tables resembling fresh snow.

Victoria had overseen the decoration of the ballroom, while Eleanor had ensured the refreshments were to her standard.

Cassandra and Hyacinth had taken great care in sending out invitations, ensuring every illustrious member of society had received one. The four of them worked well as a cohesive unit.

"A decidedly splendid affair," Hyacinth said, coming alongside her. "It will certainly be the talk of London tomorrow."

"One can hope." Cassandra regarded her companion, admiring her deep-amethyst gown flecked with crystals to make it sparkle in the light. The gilded demi mask she wore bore the intricate details of a floral bouquet, brimming with small hyacinth blossoms, carnations, and a solitary vibrant orange lily. "Your costume suits you perfectly."

"As does yours," Hyacinth said with a knowing smile. "My modiste has wonderful taste, but your ensemble is truly one of her best pieces to date. Who would have thought such a decadent color suited you?"

Cassandra smoothed her hands over the red silk bodice. The tiny, black beads accented the pleats across the bodice all the way to her shoulder, ending in an elegant plumage of vibrant red feathers. Self-conscious, she blushed, knowing this was a far cry from anything she would have chosen for herself. But it pleased her indeed to know that her friend had had enough foresight to give her such a gift.

"Cardinals are such lovely birds, but you far outshine them." Hyacinth winked.

"You are too kind, Hyacinth." Tugging at her black and red mask, Cassandra ensured it remained in place. "Thank you."

"This is what friends do, Cassandra." She placed a hand on Cassandra's and gave it a gentle squeeze. "It is an honor and a privilege to have you in our little circle."

The sentiment warmed Cassandra's heart. A year ago, no one could have told her that this was where she would have been. Eleanor and Victoria joined them as they admired the crowd dancing below and mingling in varying extravagant costumes.

"Who is that?" Eleanor asked, her voice trembling with excitement as she gestured to the main entrance.

A lone figure clad entirely in black stepped into the light.

Curious eyes darted around and whispers rippled through the crowd as it parted for the mysterious guest.

Cassandra stepped closer to the edge of the dais, her gaze following the tall figure. A man, most certainly, judging by his attire and his height. As he wove through the crowd, he turned his head, his eyes fixing on hers.

Her breath caught in her chest, and her heartbeat thundered, drowning out the sound around her. *It can't be.* Hope took flight, catching her up in the moment.

He nodded, a smile appearing beneath the edge of his black domino mask. A smile she would recognize in the midst of a raging inferno.

Reuben.

Everything faded into the background as she spun around, nearly knocking into Eleanor. She steadied herself against the railing as she descended to the main floor. *He came for me.*

Cassandra darted into the crowd, her gaze searching as the anticipation caught in her throat. Curious eyes fell upon her as she wove through the guests. They parted, watching her and whispering to each other. She ignored them. All of them. There were none who mattered in this room save for him.

A flash of black caught her eye. She turned in time to see his dark head disappearing through an archway leading to the conservatory.

Hiking her skirts in her hands, Cassandra rushed toward him. Breathless, she made her way across the room. When she'd reached the doorway, the light dimmed to the sparkling lanterns dotting the paved path snaking through the overgrown conservatory.

The music faded into the distance as she entered the silence of the tangled jungle. She wandered down the pathway, hands trembling as they held her skirts to keep from tripping over the uneven cobblestones. Her blood hummed, creating a delicious friction inside her. The hair on her arms rose at the eerie calm ahead mixing with the dying cacophony of the festivities behind her.

A few figures moved in the distance behind the greenery. Couples intent on stealing a few amorous moments alone in the midst of the revelry. They skittered in the opposite direction, heading back toward the glittering lights of the ballroom.

Cassandra quickened her pace, gaze darting back and forth, searching for any sign of Reuben. When she'd reached the far end of the conservatory, she frowned and groaned in frustration. *Where has he gone?*

A lone bench sat tucked in the corner, illuminated by a single lantern. She spun around, searching the isolated corner of the garden.

"Looking for someone?" A deep, comforting voice curled around her.

"Reuben." Cassandra gasped, relief spilling over into delight as she spun to face him.

He stood before her tall and broad, a specter shaded in black. His hazel eyes sparkled behind the dark mask. He removed it, and then hers.

"Why are you here?" she asked, her voice cracking, even though she longed to reach for him. "You were not invited."

"I could not stay away." His heated gaze raked down the length of her. "You look resplendent, Your Grace. A vision worthy of the masters."

"You flatter me." Cassandra took a step closer, her pulse pounding so loudly, she feared he would hear it. "But I have little use for your honeyed words."

"Would you have me on my knees, begging your forgiveness?" He slowly lowered himself to one knee, gazing up at her. "I am a fool, Cassandra. Forgive me."

Cassandra closed the distance between them and hooked a gloved finger beneath his chin. "No more pretty words." She leaned down, their lips dangerously close. "I tire of them."

"Then make your demand of me." His eyes flashed with

hunger. "I am at your mercy."

She grasped his chin, holding his jaw in her gloved hand. He arched into her touch in complete surrender. His reaction left her humming with desire. The ability to elicit such control over another was a heady feeling, but Cassandra did not wish to control Reuben. Quite the contrary.

"Why did you leave?" The simple question hung heavily in the air between them. She did not need to elaborate. He would know. He always knew. It was his skill—his gift—to predict his mistress's desires before she herself understood what she required.

"I could not remain." His lips parted as her grip tightened. "The duke commanded I leave immediately, never to return."

"You obeyed."

"I did what I believed was in the best interest of my mistress."

"Your *'mistress'*?" Cassandra purred.

"Yes."

"And if your mistress desired your company, what then?"

Reuben hesitated.

Cassandra teased him, her breath caressing his sinful lips. So close, she could taste his familiar kiss. "You left me, Reuben. When I needed you most."

"Forgive me, madam." His eyes drifted closed.

"I will—but only if you vow, here and now, to never abandon me again."

"I vow it, madam. Please—" Reuben's breath caught.

"Stand," she commanded.

He stood, her hand still resting upon his jaw. His eyes were wide open, locked in a silent battle with her own intense gaze. He loomed over her, intimidating and still, she found it erotically stimulating. She burned for him.

"Why did you leave?" she asked again.

"Because—I could not bear to see you torn between your son and myself."

"But that has been rectified. Has it not?"

"It has," Reuben replied, his gaze dropping.

"Why are you *here*?"

"I have seen the error of my ways, madam."

"Is that so?" Cassandra arched a brow.

"Yes, madam."

"Is that all I am to you, Reuben?" she murmured, tracing a finger along his cheek. "'Madam'? 'Your Grace'?"

"No—" He swallowed hard. "Cassandra."

A fire ignited inside her. "Tell me," she asked softly. "What am I to you?"

"My will to live. My purpose." He sighed, holding her gaze with an intensity that burned like the sun. "My reason for being."

Her heart clenched. "Is that why you murdered my husband?" she asked, her voice low.

Reuben met her gaze, his soul aflame. "I did what I must to ensure your protection."

"Not for revenge?" she asked as the knowledge washed over her, solidifying what she already knew deep in her soul.

"No." Reuben's jaw clenched, a steely determination etched upon his countenance.

"Why did you do it?" Cassandra could barely trust her voice, and yet the question flowed without hesitation.

"Because I love you. Beyond reason, beyond comprehension." He held his breath. "I love you, and I could not bear the thought of you enduring another moment of pain and torment beneath his tyranny."

Cassandra's heart ceased beating. "You—what?"

"I love you." Reuben's confession rang in her ears. "I have since the first moment I saw you."

Every ounce of hesitation fell away at his stalwart confession. Cassandra rushed him, wrapping her arms around his torso and clinging to him.

"I cannot live another moment without you, Cass," he whispered into her hair. "Be mine. Forever."

Her heart faded into oblivion as she melted into his embrace.

"I have always been yours."

Contentment settled around her even as the reality of their situation hovered in the distance. None of it mattered. All that she cared about lay here and now between the two of them. And nothing save the hand of God Himself could stop them.

Cassandra had finally found peace, and she would be damned if anyone tried to take it from her.

MINE. REUBEN HELD her tightly as a deep, soul-shattering sense of relief consumed him. *Finally.* He inhaled, allowing the sweet, floral scent of her to permanently capture this moment in his memory.

She drew back and cradled his face in her hands. Her tear-brightened eyes searched his.

"How did you know where to find me?" Cassandra whispered in awe.

"I will always find you," he replied, half-serious. When she narrowed her gaze at him, he relented. "The duke."

"Phillip told you?" Cassandra blinked in astonishment. "But—he—"

"I saw him at Simon's estate. He met with the Lord of Devil's Acre to discuss the outstanding debt." Reuben shook his head. "I know nothing of their conversation. We merely passed in the hall as I was leaving."

"And you did not strangle each other?" She arched a brow. "How suspicious."

"He found me later at a tavern," Reuben explained. "We came to an understanding, and he told me about the masquerade. Then he gave me his blessing, along with an invitation."

"His blessing." Cassandra mulled the words before a smile brightened her features. "While I understand his position dictates I require his permission, I would gladly give it all up to be able to do whatever I please at my own discretion. However, I am certainly relieved that whatever quarrel lay between you both has reached an end."

Reuben ran his hand along her spine, pressing her closer. "You would do as you please, regardless of his council?"

Cassandra nodded, her eyes darkening with a familiar hunger he knew too well.

"Would you take me as your lover?" he asked, brushing his lips against her jaw. "Boldly declaring your possession and independence? Even if it means losing your status—your finances."

"I—yes." Cassandra moaned when his grip tightened on her waist and he ground his hips against her.

"Marry me, Cassandra."

"You—" She stilled in his arms, her breathing rapid and uneven. When she drew back to search his face, she softened when she found no trace of humor. "Are you in earnest, Reuben?" she asked, breathless.

"Quite." His heart beat like a war drum inside his ribcage. "If you are willing to risk scandal for a lover, then I believe you are willing to risk it for an unsuitable husband."

Cassandra scowled. "Whoever said you would make an unsuitable husband?"

"I am of low birth. A servant. A scoundrel with a horrid past." He trailed his fingertips along her jaw in a featherlight caress.

"Those things are of no consequence." She rested her hand over his heart. "I know *you*, Reuben." Her scowl transformed into a radiant smile. "You are loyal. Considerate. Understanding. And most of all—passionate. I believe you would be the perfect husband."

Reuben held his breath, nearly bursting at the praise she bestowed upon him. He exhaled when she grasped his lapel and tugged him closer.

"Ask me again." Her words whispered across his mouth.

"Would you do me the honor of becoming my *wife*, Your

Grace?" he asked, his throat hoarse and head spinning. "I offer you all that I am. I love you and do not wish to be parted from you from this moment forward."

Cassandra drew a steady breath and pressed an achingly tender kiss to his lips. He accepted it without question, melting into the sensation. When she tilted her head, he deepened the kiss and surrendered completely. She tasted of cinnamon, cloves, and desire.

When she ended the kiss, he groaned in frustration at the loss of her touch.

"I will marry you, Reuben." She ran her thumb over his lower lip. "If you answer one question."

"Anything," he murmured. She could demand any task, and he would obey.

"Why would you take such a risk to protect me?" The question was soft, but not hesitant.

"Every day, I saw how he treated you. How he *hurt* you with every callous word and consistent neglect." Reuben's fury returned at the memories. "But when I saw him strike you—" His hands balled into fists, and he struggled to maintain his composure. "I heard him, Cassandra. I heard you struggle as he took you by force." His voice cracked. "I heard your sobs after he left."

Reuben stroked his hand down her back to ground himself. "I could no longer stand idly by and allow him to breathe after inflicting such pain on someone as beautiful and innocent as you." A tear ran down his cheek. "You deserved better, and I ensured it would *never* happen again."

"They said he died in his sleep."

"I—"

"No. Don't tell me. It does not matter. Not to me."

His hand stilled on her back. It had been simple, truly. A few extra doses of laudanum in his brandy. Two splashes of the liquid and a monster's life had been snuffed out. Reuben sighed. Unless she truly wanted to know the details, he would take that secret to his grave.

Cassandra stared at him, her tears mirroring his own. "I should be horrified by this knowledge, but I—I cannot tell you the measure of relief I felt when I found him dead."

"I know, darling." Reuben held her tighter. "I did what needed to be done. My only regret was that I could not save all those who came before you."

Cassandra shivered in his embrace. "Thank you, Reuben."

They stood in the dim conservatory, the distant strains of music filtering through the trees and bushes. Reuben allowed everything to fall away, his worry, the uncertainty. This moment was for them alone. A chance to find peace and begin anew.

"Reuben," Cassandra said, her voice muffled by his jacket. "Take me home."

Without further direction, Reuben took charge, replacing their masks. He took her arm and led her back to the masquerade. Curious gazes followed them as they wandered the perimeter of the room, but they remained to the shadowed edges of the group so as to not to make a spectacle of their departure. Cassandra waved to her friends watching from afar, who grinned in delight.

He left Cassandra to secure her wool cloak while he donned his coat and ventured out to locate her carriage. Within ten minutes, they were both tucked inside the warm confines of the carriage as it rattled toward Mayfair.

Cassandra rested her hand on his thigh, and he turned to meet her heated gaze. Without a word, her hand drifted higher.

Reuben sucked in a breath. "Perhaps we should wait until—"

"I have no intention of waiting another moment." Cassandra cupped him through the fabric of his trousers.

His cock, already hard, grew impossibly firm beneath her caress. He groaned at the insistent grip. Reuben leaned forward and kissed her. The tenderness from earlier vanished, replaced with a tempest of need.

Her hands fumbled with his trousers, attempting to free him, but he pushed her hand away. She moaned in disappointment.

Reuben shifted, pressing her back against the carriage cushion and gathering the fabric of her skirts, pushing them up. When he touched the silken skin of her bare inner thighs, Cassandra gasped and her hands gripped him tighter, one holding his jacket and the other taking hold of his hair.

The first brush of his fingers along the seam of her cunt sent a bolt of lust straight to his cock. She shivered beneath his touch.

"Fuck," he murmured against her cheek. He teased her opening before sliding two fingers deep inside her warm cunt. "Dripping for me again."

"Reuben," she whimpered, biting her lip. "Please."

"Do you want me to fuck you, darling?"

She ground her hips against his hand, taking him deeper. A gasp ripped from her throat.

"Say the words, Cassandra." He nipped at her lower lip. "Tell me what you *need*."

Both hands took hold of his hair. Her eyes blazed with heat. "I want—*need* you to fuck me, Reuben. Now." A feral growl unleashed from her as he removed his hand and licked her arousal from his fingers.

Her sweet taste lingered on his tongue as he freed himself from the confines of his trousers. With effort, he managed to pull her atop him. Her skirts rucked around her waist as she straddled his lap. When she sank down onto his cock, it took all his effort not to come.

Heaven. She felt like fucking heaven. Like redemption and salvation wrapped in a warm, guiding light. He rested his head against her shoulder, allowing himself a few breaths to steady the fire coursing through him.

Then Cassandra moved, and sparks ignited in the darkness. His hands on her waist, he thrust up, earning him a satisfied moan that echoed through the carriage.

They sank into unison, moving as one in tandem with the movement of the rocking carriage. Cassandra braced herself on his shoulders as he held her firmly on his cock.

Her head lolled back as he moved inside her. She ground her hips against his, her desire growing with every stroke. It was too much, but he held tight, strangling his rapidly building release as hers took to new heights.

Heat blossomed around them, the rustling of their clothes and gasping, panting moans filling the tight space. Surely, the driver could hear them, but Reuben could not bring himself to care. He needed this—needed her. Just as she needed him.

Passion burned through them both, and they surrendered to the demand willingly.

Reuben raked his teeth along her neck before capturing her mouth in a punishing kiss. He felt her tighten around him and knew she was close. He quickened the thrust of his hips, shifting the angle enough to draw a deep, keening moan from deep within her.

She shattered around him, her climax pulling him under and triggering his own. Her body drew it from him, clenching like a fist around his cock. He gasped at the sheer magnitude of the sensation coursing through him.

Cassandra collapsed against him, and he wrapped his arms around her, cradling her in his lap, completely sated and entwined in the aftermath of their passion.

The carriage slowly rolled to a stop, shaking them from their stupor.

"I believe we have arrived," Reuben murmured against her cheek.

Carefully, they disentangled themselves, managing to right their garments in time for the footman to open the door.

Reuben helped Cassandra from the carriage and offered his arm. She smiled and took it. As they ascended the stairs, a sense of peace settled over Reuben.

He'd found his purpose, his home. Cassandra. Whatever came next, he knew with absolute certainty that he had done the right thing.

When the footman opened the door, Reuben stood aside to

allow her to venture in from the cold. With a quizzical look at Reuben, the footman hurried forward and took their outer garments.

Mrs. Mercer stood at the end of the hall, her mouth agape. "Your Grace?" Her gaze fell to Reuben. "Mr. Evans. Well, this is quite a surprise."

"Would you mind giving us a moment alone?" Cassandra asked.

"Of course." Mrs. Mercer summoned the footman, and they left Cassandra and Reuben alone in the hall.

Turning back to her, Reuben paused mid-step. Cassandra stood watching him.

"Is something wrong?" he asked, coming to her side.

"Not at all." She caressed his cheek. "I just realized something."

"What?" He leaned into her touch.

"I never answered your question directly."

Realization dawned. "Ah, yes, well, you do not need to—"

"Yes, Reuben." Her eyes sparkled with delight. "I will marry you."

Effervescent joy filled him, and he caught her up in his arms. Her squeal of surprise shook the house. He lowered her to her feet and kissed her soundly. Then he swept her into his arms and carried her up the staircase to her bedchamber, where he made up for lost time by worshipping her in all the ways she deserved.

Chapter Eighteen

Six Months Later

THE CARRIAGE RATTLED down the lane leading to her new home, and Cassandra's breath caught in her throat. This was the moment of truth. After five months of searching, she and Phillip had secured the perfect country estate for her outside the city of London.

It was not so far removed she could not venture into town should she choose to do so, but it allowed her the chance to begin her new life with Reuben without being at the center of gossip. She rather liked the idea of having a small estate in the country rather than a house in town.

Phillip was set to move into the family home in Mayfair, forgoing his bachelor accommodations. He had found a woman he referenced frequently but still refused to reveal any details of this burgeoning romance. Although he did make frequent trips to Scotland, which also raised a lot of questions.

But since their heartfelt conversation, she allowed him the same grace that he bestowed upon her in her own amorous journey with Reuben. He seemed unsurprised by Reuben's proposal, and Cassandra knew he must have already come to peace with the possibility of such an arrangement.

Hyacinth, Victoria, and Eleanor were delighted to hear of the unexpected nuptials and her choice of residence. It would give them an opportunity to escape the confines of London should they require the reprieve. She would send an invitation for them to visit as soon as she settled into her new abode.

When the carriage rolled to a stop, Cassandra could barely contain her excitement. While she had toured the estate with her son several weeks ago, this would be her first arrival as lady of the house.

The door swung open and Cassandra stepped from the conveyance. The dark ivy clung to the stone manor. Tall rosebushes climbed to the lower windows, and a variety of flowers blossomed amid the lush greenery surrounding the cozy house.

It was nearly half the size of her son's home in London, but it boasted more charm and comfort than she ever could have hoped for in town. Her gaze drifted to the surrounding area, finding only open pasture and trees. Best of all, there were no wagging tongues to be found.

Cassandra took a deep breath of fresh country air. It was just as comfortable as their large country estate in Coventry, even though it was a fraction of the size. Much more manageable for her and Reuben without drawing undue attention.

Her heart fluttered at the thought of him. It had been two weeks since he'd departed to ensure the house was prepared adequately for her arrival. Completely upon his insistence.

"I wish to surprise you," he had said with a wink. And that was the last time she had seen him.

Anticipation unraveled inside her as she stared at the front of the house where the servants had assembled in a line, awaiting her arrival. Her new housekeeper, Mrs. Jennings, introduced herself and the rest of the staff, but the moment the front door opened, she fell silent.

A lone figure emerged from the front door. *Reuben.* Her soul took flight at the sight of him. So handsome in his dark-brown suit and deep-red waistcoat. He descended the steps with a smile, opening his arms when he reached the stone pathway where she stood waiting. The servants slowly retreated into the house.

"My darling," Reuben said warmly, "welcome home."

Cassandra fell into his embrace and basked in the spicy scent she associated only with him. "I missed you," she murmured against his chest.

"I missed you even more." He held her tightly for a moment before pulling back to meet her gaze. He leaned in for a tender kiss.

She melted into it, lost in the tenderness of the moment.

When he withdrew, he practically glowed with excitement. "I cannot wait to give you the private tour."

She eyed him suspiciously. "What have you done?"

"Nothing you won't thoroughly enjoy." He winked. "Don't you trust me?"

"I do," she said warily. "But I also know you better than anyone else."

"You wound me." He pressed his hand to his chest. "But I shall recover. Come, allow me to show you all of the delicious surprises I have in store for you."

"Reuben." Cassandra sighed in exasperation. "Your task was to ensure the house was established enough to be habitable."

"And I followed your instructions to the letter." He grinned. "With a few moderate additions—for your comfort, of course." Reuben offered his arm. "Shall we?"

Cassandra took his arm and followed him up the stairs.

Inside, she found it much the same as when she had seen it with Phillip. The last owners had sold all the furniture and ornamentation with the house. As she assessed the rooms, she realized there were touches of her own style, her own personal items scattered throughout the house. Art she had chosen. Pieces she had purchased that reflected her singular taste.

She reached out and cradled a peony blossom sitting in a lovely bouquet in the sitting room. It was perfect.

Room by room, Reuben led her on a tour of the house, until they reached the largest bedchamber. He paused outside the room.

"Close your eyes," he prompted with a mischievous grin.

"Why?" she asked, unconvinced of the wisdom of such an action.

"Because I asked nicely."

"Very well." Cassandra closed her eyes and waited.

The door creaked as he swung it open. Then he took her hand and led her forward. When he finally stopped, she licked her lips. The sunlight pink against the insides of her eyelids.

"Can I open them?" she asked.

"Yes." Reuben stood beside her, his hand on her arm.

Cassandra blinked, allowing her eyes to become accustomed to the light. Her gaze settled on the lovely golden oak desk sitting beside a window. The fern-green curtains were pulled back, sunlight glinting in the golden threads woven into the fabric. Her heart warmed as she took in the rest of the room.

All the pieces matched. The rich, gold wood tied the desk, chair, wardrobe, a small bookcase, matching nightstands, and the oversized four-poster bed dominating the center of the room. Golds, greens, creams, and the occasional splash of red filled her vision. It was magnificent and suited her to perfection.

The afternoon sun streamed through the windows, highlighting the plush carpet beneath her feet and the clean fireplace along the far wall. Cassandra walked the perimeter of the room, taking in the details and savoring the clean scent of fresh flowers and summer air.

A gentle breeze drifted in through the open window, ruffling a loose curl resting on her cheek.

Cassandra turned to find Reuben watching her in silence. "It is perfect."

He breathed out in relief and crossed to her side, taking her hand in his and pressing a kiss to her fingertips. "As are you, wife."

Cassandra heated at the simple expression. "Are you attempting to seduce me, husband?"

"Perhaps." His gaze darkened as he stroked the inside of her wrist, sending a bolt of need through her.

They had married in secret a month ago, securing a common license and finding a small parish outside London in which to formally bind them in holy matrimony. Almost no one knew of their elopement, and it was best if it came to light of its own accord.

To Cassandra, nothing mattered to her so much as spending the rest of her life with a man who truly valued her, who cared about her wellbeing and desires. A man who loved her beyond reason and logic.

"But—" Reuben withdrew enough to quell the ache building inside her. "Before I indulge in your lustful whims, I must inform you that your son will be joining us for dinner this evening."

Cassandra frowned. "I just saw him in London."

"I know. However, it was a formal request he made last week." Reuben shrugged. "I cannot deny him, as he is your son and a duke." He cleared his throat. "I will take my leave so you can rest after your journey. I have had a bath drawn for you in the next room. When you have finished, I will ensure a fresh pot of tea is delivered here and Sidlow sent to help you dress."

"I guess it can wait." Cassandra sighed dramatically before rising up on her toes and kissing him soundly. "After dinner, then."

His eyes flashed with hunger. "As my wife commands."

Reuben kissed her one last time before leaving her in the solitude of her chamber. No, *their* chamber. One of her demands was that they share a bed as they would share their lives. She was tired of hiding, tired of living by society's rules and standards. She desired to sleep with her husband—among indulging in other things.

The warm, scented bath revived her with a divine potency. Mrs. Jennings provided a fresh pot of tea and Sidlow helped her dress. Cassandra emerged from her chamber refreshed and ready to receive her dinner guest.

When she'd descended the stairs, she heard the distinct sound of men's voices coming from the parlor. Inside, she found Reuben and Phillip engaged in an animated discussion.

"Phillip." She greeted her son with a kiss to the cheek. "How lovely that you have joined us for dinner."

"I did not mean to intrude on your first night together as husband and wife in your new home." He sighed when she pressed a hand to her chest in mock surprise. "Yes, I knew of your elopement, Mother."

"And you said nothing?" she asked, surprised.

"I had already given my blessing." He softened. "You may do as you please."

"We are honored to have you as our first official guest, Your Grace," Reuben added.

"'Phillip,' please, as I told you before." Her son held out his hand. "We are family now."

Reuben shook it firmly, and the final uncertainty of their strained relationship fell away from her mind like the last leaf of the season. Her heart blossomed with joy at the sight of their newly forged bond.

"Has word spread through London of my elopement, then?" Cassandra asked.

"Not yet. But even if it does, it will not linger long, not with such fresh meat for them to feast upon." He gestured to himself. "I fear I have made the list of most eligible bachelors for the upcoming season."

"You have always been on that list, Phillip," Cassandra teased. "Why on earth would this season be any different?"

Phillip ducked his head almost bashfully, the tips of his ears turning red. "I—" He lifted his gaze and cleared his throat. "I may not be on the marriage mart for long, Mother."

"Oh?" Delight suffused her, even though she attempted to suppress her excitement so as not to make her son uncomfortable. "Anyone I know?"

"No, Mother." He shook his head. "But I promise, I will bring her to meet you as soon as I can manage it."

"Good." Pride filled her. "I cannot wait to meet the woman who stole my son's heart."

"You will like her." His eyes sparkled.

"I know I will." She took his hand and squeezed.

Reuben cleared his throat. "I believe dinner is prepared. Shall we?"

Phillip took her left arm and Reuben took her right. She glanced between them and grinned. This was her family. The loves of her life. She cherished them both and relished the fact that they were now of an accord.

Cassandra could think of nothing more fulfilling than this moment. Finally, there were no secrets. No lies. No fear. She could live—and she would do so to the fullest on her own terms.

⇉⇇

AFTER DINNER, PHILLIP joined Cassandra in the parlor to discuss estate matters. Reuben took the opportunity to retreat and prepare a delightful surprise for his wife for after their guest departed.

Their time together had taught him one thing for certain. Cassandra reveled in her passion. Now that she had unleashed it, there was nothing she was not willing to try when it came to pleasure.

Up until this point, he had indulged her every desire, but tonight, he craved something more… *familiar.* He changed into one of his old uniforms. The jacket fit a bit snugly, but he still managed to look presentable.

When he heard the front door close, he took a final glimpse of himself in the mirror. Phillip had left. Finally, they were alone. A confident smile reflected back at him.

"Reuben," Cassandra called out. "Where are—?" Her words evaporated when he stepped out onto the landing.

"How may I be of service, Your Grace?" he asked with a bow.

Cassandra slowly climbed the stairs, her eyes dark with unrestrained hunger. "What are you—?" She stopped on the landing a breath from him. "What farce is this?"

"No farce, madam." He rose, holding her gaze. "Has the duke left?"

"Yes, Phillip has returned to London." She studied him with suspicion. Her eyes widened. "That suit," she said, her breath catching. "You wore it the night you found me in the study—after the funeral."

Pride suffused him at her reaction. She remembered it as clearly as he did. He stepped closer. "You have a keen memory, madam."

"I—" Cassandra licked her lips, reaching for his tie. Her fingertips brushed his chest as she tightened her hold on the thin fabric. "I remember everything from that night."

"Is that so?" He stood firm as she ran her fingers along his lapels. Heat poured through him like molten steel, but he maintained his composure somehow.

Cassandra bit her lower lip and nodded, looking like a debutante a fraction of her age, and yet Reuben had never seen a woman as alluring as her. Aged like a fine wine, he wished to indulge until he drowned in her.

"You were not so coquettish that night," he observed with a smirk.

"I was in mourning." She tightened her grip on his tie. "How was I to know your true intentions?"

"What intentions?" he demurred. "I merely offered my services in whatever manner best befitted your desires in that moment."

"Tell me the truth." She raked a nail along his jaw. "If I would have been amenable, would you have seduced me that night?"

"You wish for my honest answer?"

"Of course." Her lashes fluttered, but he saw the flare of heat behind her eyes.

"I would have done whatever you asked of me, madam." His

cock swelled at the memory of her from that night—and the intimacy of their present exchange.

"Well, then." Cassandra released him. "Evans, I require your assistance."

"As you wish, madam." He followed her into the bedroom.

"Close the door."

Reuben closed and secured the lock. When he turned, he stood at attention, awaiting her instruction. For the last eight years, he had craved this, and now she indulged him, playing into his fantasy. A fantasy he knew she shared, if their history were any indication.

"Would you like for me to send for Sidlow to help you undress?" he asked, his voice hoarse but steady.

"That will not be necessary," Cassandra replied, methodically removing the pins holding her hair in place. Her heavy tresses fell against her shoulders in a thick waterfall of chestnut curls. She ran her hands through her hair and pulled the mass to one side, exposing the fastenings over her gown along her spine. "If you will be so kind," she directed, her gaze meeting his over her shoulder.

Maintaining his role, he reached for the fastenings. As he worked, he reminded himself of his part in this production. The servant aiding his mistress.

But it was more than that. It was a husband indulging his wife's fantasy. A wife allowing her husband to bring their deepest desires to life. This was a culmination of their passion. The moment it had all begun.

His fingertips brushed over her skin as he slowly unfastened her gown. Removing each garment, piece by piece, layer by layer. Savoring the sharp gasps and whimpered moans as he peeled the pieces from her body, exposing her one breath at a time. He unclipped her garters and slid her stockings down with care. Removed her shoes with a tender caress against her lovely ankles. And when the final piece revealed her glorious curves, leaving her bare before him, he groaned in appreciation.

"Wife," he muttered in reverence, breaking the spell between them.

"Is that what you wanted from the beginning?" she murmured, trailing her hand between her breasts. "To claim me as your own?"

Reuben caught her by the waist, unable to bear the tension a moment longer. "I have always desired you. Craved your attention—your love. But never did I ever believe I could claim you as my own." His gaze raked over her, his blood heating to a boiling point. "You are not a prize to be won, not a treasure to be claimed. But if I could be your equal—your partner—I count myself as the wealthiest man in the world."

Cassandra's breath caught; her eyes shone with tears. "You have made me the happiest of women."

"After all we have endured, we deserve it." He nuzzled her jaw with his nose, pressing a tender kiss to the corner of her mouth.

She turned, catching his lips in a kiss. "Mine," she growled, clinging to him. Her naked body pressed against him.

"Yours," he murmured in response, barely breaking the kiss.

In a tangle of limbs, they embraced the onslaught of passion. She tore at his clothes until he stood in the same state of undress. Her hands skimmed down his shoulders, over his torso and hips, resting on his bare backside. She squeezed his arse, earning a groan from him. His cock sprang to attention, pressing insistently against her stomach.

Reuben spun her around and wrapped his arm around her waist. His lips teased the soft shell of her ear, earning him a delighted moan from deep within her.

"Place your hands on the bed, darling," he whispered.

Cassandra obeyed, thrusting her arse toward him and arching her back. One glance revealed the glistening folds begging for his attention. He ran his hands over her hips. His thumb grazed the swollen center of her before he fit his cock to her sweet cunt.

"This"—he eased himself inside her in a fluid thrust—"is

mine."

Cassandra cried out as he pushed deep, her hands grasping the coverlet on the bed. "Yours." She gasped at the invasion. "Always."

Reuben could no longer hold back. He took her hips in his hands and pounded into her slick heat. She felt better than anything he remembered. Her body tightened around him, pulling him deeper, urging him to move faster.

The room echoed with the sweet aria of her frenzied cries and the erotic sounds of his flesh against hers. He basked in it all, allowing it to guide him—to bring them both exquisite pleasure. This was how it was meant to be between them. Pleasure—without pain. Desire—without hiding behind the fickle whims of society. There was only her and him and the beauty of their union.

When her cries evolved into erratic panting pleas, Reuben wrapped his arm around her waist and slid his hand between her thighs, teasing the bud at the apex of her sex. Cassandra swore and her cunt gripped him harder.

He quickened his pace, thrusting deep as he teased her with his fingers. His lips caressing her shoulder, his teeth gently teasing her skin. He fucked her harder, driving himself to the point of combustion.

"Reuben!" Cassandra shouted as her climax seized hold of her. Her body took her pleasure and in turn triggered his own.

He groaned her name as he came still buried deep inside of her.

Bound together, entwined and sated, they remained as their breathing slowed to a normal rhythm. Reuben leaned his head against her spine, placing a kiss in the center of her back before withdrawing.

As he helped her to her feet, Cassandra turned to face him. Her cheeks flushed a delicious rose hue, eyes bright and dazed by the effects of their passion. She grinned.

"If only you had been that attentive that night." She rose up on her toes and kissed him tenderly.

"Believe me, it took all of my restraint *not* to seduce you." He kissed the tip of her nose before backing away. "One moment."

Reuben retreated to the washbasin and retrieved a wet cloth. Once he'd cleaned her, he tucked her into bed. Then he tidied himself and joined her. Tucked beneath the blankets, he drew her close, burying his face against the curve of her neck and allowing her scent to lull him into a peaceful slumber.

"Reuben." Cassandra stirred him from his repose.

"Yes, darling?" He murmured in a daze.

"Thank you."

He rose up on his elbow and stared down at her. "For what?"

"For loving me." She cupped his cheek. "For protecting me."

"I will always do both, until the day I die." He kissed her palm. "You have my vow."

Effervescent joy spread across her face, lingering in her smile. "I never thought I would marry again."

"Is that so?"

"Mm-hmm." She nodded. "You made me a believer."

"In what?"

"Love."

Reuben's heart swelled to bursting. "That makes two of us."

Cassandra kissed him again, and they recklessly tumbled into pleasure once more. A delightful conclusion to a complicated arrangement.

Chapter Nineteen

When Cassandra received an invitation to Hyacinth's country estate for a week, she could hardly refuse. While she enjoyed her newfound bliss with Reuben, she had insisted she take some time to visit with her friends and enjoy their company. Reuben had agreed wholeheartedly and promised to come and retrieve her personally the following week.

Cassandra arrived at Lady Corby's country home prepared to face a barrage of inquiries. The housekeeper escorted her to the garden, where Hyacinth, Eleanor, and Victoria were taking a lovely afternoon tea. They stood upon her arrival, welcoming her with warmth and grace.

"Thank you for the invitation, Hyacinth." Cassandra took the open seat near the blooming wall of climbing roses.

"How was your journey?" she asked as she poured some tea for her guests.

"Uneventful." Cassandra chuckled. "But I much prefer that to the other possibilities."

"Like a highwayman!" Eleanor's eyes widened.

"Eleanor, you have been reading those confounded Gothic novels again." Victoria shook her head ruefully. "Forgive her. She takes the opportunity to romanticize everything now."

"Speaking of romance," Hyacinth murmured, handing Cassandra her tea. "How fares your new husband?"

Cassandra's face warmed at the mention of Reuben. "He is well."

"Marriage suits you," Hyacinth said with confidence. "You are positively aglow."

"*This* marriage suits me perfectly well," Cassandra clarified. "I admit, I had my reservations about entering into another marriage, especially in our situation, but I confess it has been transformative and—delightful."

The three ladies nodded in agreement just as the housekeeper arrived with a tray laden with a veritable assortment of culinary delights. Victoria took her time selecting one of each, as she explained she had given the recipes to the cook and wished to see how they tasted.

A lovely afternoon tea in the garden with close friends was exactly what Cassandra needed to bolster her spirits and rejuvenate her soul. They supported her quiet extraction from society and lauded her courage in following her heart against all odds.

Cassandra joined the other ladies on a walk through the magnificent gardens on the dowager viscountess's country estate. She marveled at the variety of flora and fauna. The late-summer flowers were just beginning to bloom, but already, her gardens boasted a vibrant array of variegated vegetation in a kaleidoscope of colors. She paused to admire a deep-magenta peony.

"Hyacinth, these flowers are by far the loveliest I have ever seen." Cassandra complimented her with sincerity and a touch of jealousy. "How on earth do you maintain such an immaculate garden?"

Hyacinth paused beside her, her face shaded beneath a wide-brimmed hat, but Cassandra saw the pink in her cheeks. "I have spent many days cultivating the garden, selecting the different breeds and variations. This year has been the most rewarding after all my time and effort."

"Your son gifted you this place as a dowager estate?" Cassandra glanced back at the house.

"Yes, this was my husband's favorite place, and my son knew how much I treasure the memories here." She sighed. "He much prefers his larger country estate in Dorset."

"You maintain this yourself?" Cassandra asked in awe.

"I cannot take *all* the credit." She brushed her fingertips over the peony blossom. "I have several servants who help me tend it."

"I would think it would take an army of servants to do so." Cassandra allowed her gaze to roam over the expansive garden.

In the distance, a figure rose up from a gnarled bed of thorns and deep-green foliage. Judging by the width of the shoulders and the height, it was a man. Cassandra squinted to get a better look at him, but he remained hidden in shadow, watching them from a distance.

"Who is that?" Cassandra asked, turning to Hyacinth.

Her friend turned a lovely shade of magenta to match the peonies. "I—well, that is the head gardener." Hyacinth cleared her throat. "Shall we return to the house? I have a lovely evening planned."

Hyacinth was *embarrassed*. Well, now, this was an interesting situation, indeed.

Cassandra glanced back at the gardener, whose form slowly grew as he approached them. Beside her, Hyacinth danced with impatience, fiddling with the hem of her gloves. She turned to Eleanor and Victoria in an attempt to draw them into conversation, but they were as interested in this new development as Cassandra was. It became increasingly apparent that Hyacinth did not wish to wait for the gardener to join them.

When he stepped into the sunlight, Cassandra stifled a gasp. She had assumed he was an older man with experience in horticulture. But he was gorgeous and young. Raven hair, a tad longer than fashionable, lent a striking mysterious quality. Soulful eyes the color of well-aged whisky. Strong, broad shoulders pulled the white linen shirt tight against his chest, tucked beneath suspenders. The man was devastatingly handsome even with the furrowed scowl on his face.

"Might I have a word, my lady?" he asked Hyacinth directly, completely ignoring the three women in stunned silence gaping at him.

"Can it not wait?" Hyacinth asked, her tone terse and irritated.

Cassandra blinked in surprise. She had never heard Hyacinth use such a tone with anyone, regardless of their social standing.

"No, it cannot." His jaw tensed, making the muscle twitch.

Cassandra took a tentative step back, feeling as though this conversation would be better suited without their presence. "Come along, ladies. We shall leave Hyacinth to her garden and seek out some shade beneath the terrace."

Gently nudging Eleanor and Victoria, Cassandra directed the other ladies to abandon the confrontational scene. Even though she longed to know the details of what transpired between Hyacinth and the strapping young gardener, Cassandra understood the often-strange dynamics between mistress and servant.

A glance over her shoulder showed both the gardener and Hyacinth locked in an animated argument. Both parties seemed irritated by the other. A battle of the wills. How interesting.

"Is it always this tense between the two of them?" Cassandra asked Eleanor and Victoria.

"Oh, yes." Eleanor nodded vehemently. "Her son hired him last summer as the head gardener to help tend the gardens and ensure it survived over winter. But it seemed they had a disagreement of sorts."

"Has she discussed it with either of you?" Cassandra watched as the gardener ran his hand through his hair in growing agitation.

"No," Victoria replied. "In fact, she quickly changes the subject the moment he appears or is mentioned in conversation."

"Indeed." Cassandra marked the moment Hyacinth spun away from the gardener.

A flicker of something crossed his face. Heat. Desire. In a shift of light, whatever it was vanished, leaving open distaste painted on his expression. She stifled a gasp and held her tongue.

The Dowager Viscountess Corby had an admirer, but Hyacinth did not seem to notice or care as he watched from a distance tangled in roses and gnarled vines. What a delightful turn of events.

ABOUT THE AUTHOR

Kirsten Blacketer writes the stories she's dying to read. She likes mystery and intrigue, handsome heroes, sassy heroines, and a chance to break the rules. She lives for sexual tension and loves kissing scenes. There's no way she can write in just one era, so don't be surprised if you see her jumping from medieval Scotland to prohibition on the Mississippi River to late Victorian London then onto contemporary Brooklyn. She follows wherever the muse leads her.

The KSB Guarantee: A Steamy Getaway and Always a HEA!

www.ingramcontent.com/pod-product-compliance
Lightning Source LLC
LaVergne TN
LVHW011932070526
838202LV00054B/4600